The Killing Code

The Killing Code

By

Craig Hurren

ISBN 978-1482349696

Dedication:

This novel is dedicated to my family.

Thank you for your love and support.

ACKNOWLEDGEMENTS

I sincerely thank my close friends, Dennis Jamison, U.S. Army helicopter pilot (CW4 retired) and CIA Operations Officer (retired), David R. (DMFF) Fouts (Former US Marine and private military contractor), and Karl Osborn (Computer guru) for their expert technical advice. Thank you to Colin Murray and Chris Holifield of Writers' Services UK for their professional editorial services. I also thank Randy Tinsley, Tim Young, Tom Dragoo, Bob Finch, my parents Geoffrey and Rita Hurren, and my beloved wife Robyn for their helpful input and assistance.

Chapter 1

D r. Helen Benson stood quietly but impatiently in the modern chic elevator, waiting to reach her floor in the luxurious Eleanor building. She had been at an international psychotropic pharmaceutical seminar in Washington for the past two days and was excited to reunite with her husband, Jim and her two daughters, Bethany and Crystal. Busy imagining the adoring faces of her darling little girls and the embrace of her loving husband as she opened the door and they came rushing to greet her, she hadn't paid much attention to the strange looking little man with piercing eyes standing behind her. Now though, she could feel those eyes on her, and her mind wandered to thoughts of him. He was in the elevator before she entered so she assumed he must have come from one of the parking levels below the ground floor but couldn't remember having seen him in the building before.

Helen and her family had been living in 'The Eleanor' since they bought their comfortable, modern, four bedroom condominium eighteen months earlier and despite the grand size of the building, and the fact that it contained ninety six apartments, she was familiar with many of the occupants. It wouldn't be unusual for a guest to be riding unaccompanied in the elevator, since the modern security system enabled occupants to allow entry to visitors via a camera-phone and remote access system but she couldn't help feeling slightly uneasy at his presence. Despite her tickling intuition, Helen admonished herself for being mildly paranoid and tried to put it out of her mind.

As the floor numbers flowed steadily and quietly past on the LED display beside the elevator doors, the anticipation of seeing her family was renewed. She longed for details of the last two days. She wanted to ask Bethany about her new school, and talk to

Crystal about her friends in kindergarten. Essentially, she just wanted her much needed dose of family time after the seemingly endless, dry hours of lectures, display booths, and scientific chatter that had been her time at the convention center in D.C.

Just as the display passed through floor ten and Helen was deep in thoughts of her family, she felt a slight prick in the skin of her neck, near the base of her skull. Before her mind could properly process what had happened, the small, sharp featured man's hand darted out toward the twelfth floor button and the elevator came to a smooth stop as Helen rubbed her neck with a puzzled look on her face. The man exited the car and as the doors began to close, Helen wondered if the mild pinch in her neck had come from him. With his hands deep in the pockets of his overcoat, he turned and glared straight into her eyes.

"Goodnight Dr. Benson - sleep well." he said, in what felt to Helen like a menacing tone, then he turned and paced briskly down the hall as the elevator doors met and he was lost from her view.

"What on earth was that?" Helen wondered aloud.

The pain was not at all intense and had quickly subsided to nothing more than a tingle but she felt confused by her thoughts on the origin of the pain and her interpretation of the man's intent. Could it really have been something he'd done to her or was it just an insect bite or perhaps a phantom pain from a pinched nerve? Her medical training and experience had taught her over many years that the human body and mind were capable of playing all sorts of tricks so perhaps this was one. There was no reason to suspect that a man in her safe, up-market residential building, particularly one who knew her by name, would do anything to hurt her so she wondered why suspicion had been her initial reaction? She also questioned how terse the man's voice had actually been. Her better nature was telling her that she must have misheard his tone – he had an accent so maybe he wasn't a native English speaker and his slightly inappropriate intonation was purely unintentional.

"There must be a logical explanation for the whole scenario." she thought. "Too much time away from home has got you imagining things Helen!" Her brow formed a frown, "Then again, why did he wait to select his floor until the elevator had almost reached it instead of when he first entered?"

Helen's logical mind once again gave way to anticipation and she decided to push such thoughts out and get on with the much more pleasant business of coming home to her family. As the elevator drew to a halt on the fourteenth floor she waited for the doors to open and walked purposefully toward the door of her family's condominium.

The welcome and familiar brass numbers, *1404* entered her field of vision and she pulled excitedly at the keys in her bag. In one quick movement, she reached for the lock and inserted her key. The bolt slid open with a familiar clunk so she pushed the heavy security door and breezed through the opening. As if on cue, her girls looked up simultaneously from their coloring books and with squeals of delight, ran toward their mother in flurry of excitement and giggles.

Bethany, the eldest, was first to reach her destination; half running and half jumping into her mother's arms. Helen hugged her tightly and began smothering her head with kisses as Crystal followed closely on her sister's heels, colliding lovingly into her mother's side and melting into the warm three-way embrace. Helen gripped Bethany with her left arm as her right hand dropped down to the middle of crystal's back and she bent to kiss her youngest daughter's sweet little face.

"How are my angels?" Helen gushed. "Have you been good girls for Daddy while I was away?"

"More like little monkeys!" Jim Benson interjected playfully. "I'm only kidding girls. They've been very helpful and well behaved; even made me breakfast one day... and once was more than enough!" he teased. "How was the conference honey?"

"Oh, I don't think you really want to know about the conference."

"Nope, you got that right!" shaking his head dramatically. "I'm just glad you're home safe."

Jim's eyes were locked on those of his wife as he strode toward his tightly huddled family. He and Helen had been married for over ten years and their love for each other had only grown deeper and more respectful during that time. They had been in college together when they met and though they courted for a year and a half before Jim proposed and they waited a further two years before they married, they had always known their futures would be inextricably entwined.

Jim was a successful nanotech engineer at a private company with connections to M.I.T. when Helen became pregnant with Bethany, and with her career in psychiatric pharmaceuticals taking off, they mutually agreed that he would be a stay at home dad. Jim was overjoyed with the decision as it would enable him to spend as much time as possible with the children while allowing him to focus more on his own design research than he could while he was in a formal job.

Jim reached his wife and two daughters, and the grand hug was complete. They held their embrace for a moment, only letting go to look into each other's eyes. As the excitement subsided, Jim asked his wife, "Are you hungry honey or did you eat on the plane?"

"Eat on the plane – really? I wanted to make it home alive, thank you!"

"Oh come on honey, it can't be all that bad, can it?"

"Well, it can and it was! One bite was all I could bear. I'm starving and I need a shower."

"OK, I've got the makings of a nice chef's salad waiting for you so go and get comfortable while I put it together."

Helen started toward their bedroom but found that she had developed a limp from the excess weight that was daughter number two. She had attached herself to her mother's left leg like a limpet and showed no signs of letting go.

"Come on now Crystal, let Mommy put her things away and have a shower then I'll be back out to see you soon." she said gently.

Crystal's grip released and she pouted dramatically as Helen towed her wheeled case behind her down the hall. Once in the bedroom, she decided that unpacking could wait and headed straight into the en suite bathroom for a well deserved shower. As the warm water pulsed on her head and neck, she felt a wave of relief and relaxation from being safely at home with her family. She loved her cutting edge work in psychiatric pharmaceuticals and neuro-hormones at Blue Sky Biotech but she had always tried to maintain as much balance in her life as possible so any conferences that went for longer than a day were an annoyance.

Helen finished her shower, dried herself and sat on the edge of the bed in her bathrobe. She suddenly felt overwhelmingly tired and despite her hunger and knowing that Jim was busily preparing a delicious meal for her, she felt strongly compelled to lie down.

"I'll just have a ten minute lie down..." she thought as she moved up the bed to lay her head on her pillow. "...and by the time Jim's got the salad ready, I'll be fine."

Despite her best intentions, Helen fell into a deep sleep and within a few minutes, Jim came in to check on her. He knew she would be exhausted but obviously she was much more so than he had expected so he decided it would be best to leave her to sleep. He went back into the dining room, took Helen's salad to the fridge then explained to the girls so they wouldn't disturb their mother while she rested.

Helen woke with a start just over an hour after she'd drifted off, and anxiously peered at the bedside clock.

"Damn!" she admonished herself. "The girls will be asleep already and Jim's salad will be wilted."

She was disappointed that she'd fallen asleep before spending as much time with her family as they all needed. She secured the knot in her bathrobe, turned the doorknob and went to apologize to her husband but entering the hallway, she noticed that everything was quiet - too quiet for this time of night. White noise emanated from the television in the living room down the hall, coming from a station that must have finished broadcasting for the night but that didn't make sense since it was still early in the evening.

Helen stepped slowly and deliberately so as not to disturb the girls in their rooms as she made her way in the darkness to the living room to talk to Jim. She could see the snow on the television screen and began to wonder if she had misread the clock on her bedside table. Standing at the back of the main sofa where Jim would often stretch out to watch TV, she thought he must have dozed off since there was nothing on this particular channel and he hadn't bothered to change it. She leaned forward and gently put her left hand on Jim's right shoulder; partly to wake him and partly to hold her weight as she reached with her free hand for the remote to turn off the TV. Strangely there was no response from Jim so before she turned off the TV, which would have extinguished the only light in the room, she gave him a little shake. He still didn't respond so she reached higher to stroke his hair and felt a strange, warm wetness covering his head. Helen stood to look at her hand and a sudden wave of adrenalin swept through her body. Her hand began to shake uncontrollably as she realized it was coated in thick, dark blood. She felt a scream welling up inside her but her throat clamped shut and refused to allow it to come forth. She immediately leaned over to shake Jim hard as her logical mind tried to fight the fear, shock, and disbelief. Her constricted voice box squeezed out his name as she shook him but he still didn't respond. Her mind was darting from thought to thought, unable to focus on any. Desperately searching for a pulse at Jim's carotid artery, she realized that he was gone and reeled back in horror. Despite Helen's intellect, she could not gather her thoughts to process the situation. Disbelief was giving way to shock and confusion as she turned to face the dining room, where a terrible new vision lay before her. Suddenly, viciously, and overwhelmingly, the scene now took over her thoughts and dictated her actions.

Her eyes took a brief moment to focus through her tears and her mind followed closely behind as stark realization hit her like a baseball bat. Her beautiful daughters were at the dining table sobbing quietly, their eyes brimming with fear. Bethany was alone on a chair beside her little sister, who was held tightly on the lap of a mad man. Helen immediately recognized the face of Bryan Adler and she knew with fatal realization, the tragedy that had befallen her family and the fate that awaited her.

Bryan Adler had been a patient of Helen's while she was working at a government facility in West Virginia, which housed some of the country's most dangerous criminally insane inmates. Bryan wasn't the average psychopath; he was an utter monster, bred and created by the purest of evil and the worst case she had ever seen. Her sadness for his victims was enough to shake her faith in anything, yet she also pitied him for his own suffering and that pity had been unsettling.

Before her first session with him, Helen had pored over Bryan's file for many hours examining his family history, home life, eventual foster care, and other relevant details, before finally moving on to his crimes. They were shocking, horrific events that had brought enormous notoriety to his case throughout the country. He had been dubbed, "The Orphan Maker" by the press; an appallingly dark moniker that Helen found repulsive in its diminution of his ghastly acts.

She knew Bryan Adler's motives and desires, and she knew the outcome was inevitable but she could understand neither how he could have escaped from the maximum security mental facility where he had been held all these years nor how he had found her home and gained access. He had been on long term injected sedation and a cocktail of anti-psychotic drugs for his entire incarceration so she couldn't understand how he was able to overcome not only the effects of the drugs but the security measures of possibly the most secure psychiatric institution in the country.

It didn't matter now anyway. He ordered Helen to sit in the empty chair opposite and she complied. She was all too familiar with his modus operandi and as he held the girls close to him, his signature drone began. Bethany had been gagged and her hands were bound in front of her since she was older and possibly capable of running from him. Crystal had the look of shock with which Helen was so familiar, from observing child victims of psychological trauma.

"Had they been forced to watch their father die?" she wondered fearfully. "Will they ever recover from this trauma?"

Her thoughts were completely detached from her own personal peril and she was only concerned that Bryan would leave her babies unharmed as he had always done with the children in his previous crimes. She was certain that this was an essential component of his psychosis so she steeled herself to follow his instructions without hesitation even though it meant her own death and a life without real parents for her daughters.

Helen knew Bryan could see the resignation in her eyes, just as she had always felt he could see her inner thoughts in their therapy sessions. A few minutes later, he stood slowly but purposefully, holding Crystal in his left arm, stepped to Helen's chair. He handed her a sharp knife and calmly returned to his seat.

"You know what must be done Dr. Benson."

"Please don't hurt my babies." was all Helen could muster.

She gazed lovingly into her daughters' eyes for a moment then looked down at the soft skin of her left forearm as tears clouded her vision.

"Mommy loves you my darlings. Take care of your little sister Bethany."

With that, Helen drew the knife diagonally across her forearm with the precision of a trained medical doctor and the blood came forth. It flowed faster than expected and she knew it wouldn't be long before she would go into shock. The coldness would come over her in a wave, then it would wane, then she would become sleepy and weak, eventually lapsing into unconsciousness and finally, death would come.

Helen looked up into the eyes of her children, who were now sobbing uncontrollably. She wanted so desperately to comfort them and shield them from this violence and pain but she was already feeling the waves of shock come over her body. Blood was quickly pooling on the carpet beneath her chair and as she became more and more drowsy, her daughters and Bryan Adler strangely began to fade from view. As she looked on in confusion, it became evident that there would soon be only vacant chairs and she couldn't understand what her eyes were telling her. With one final burst of strength, Helen tried to lunge toward the rapidly disappearing image of her girls but she and her chair toppled to the floor. Frantically searching for the sight of her children, her field of vision began darkening into an ever shrinking circle and she vaguely sensed strong hands tugging at her body, and a powerful pressure on her injured arm. She imagined she could hear the panicked voice of her husband Jim but how could that be.

The blood flow was too great and as she was beginning to drift into unconsciousness, she groaned softly then clearly whispered the name 'Bryan Adler'. The life flickering from her eyes, she thought she could see her husband's face come into focus above her, frantic and fearful, as she drifted away into the darkness.

Chapter 2

D etective Alan Beach sat at his desk in a remote corner of the Homicide Investigation Department of the Columbus, Ohio Division of Police. His slate grey eyes glanced up to survey the room as he ruminated on the wording of his latest report. His fellow detectives went about their business; some working at their desks, others talking or joking with one another here and there. It was a fairly typical day in the department where Alan had become used to being a loner. Not that being ignored by his colleagues particularly bothered him, as he didn't much care for them anyway but he did find it disappointing that he obviously hadn't escaped his past and the exclusion it had brought upon him.

An intelligent looking man in his late thirties, Beach carried a few extra pounds but certainly wasn't fat. With average height and medium build, he was always impeccably dressed in a well cut, dark suit and tie. His sandy hair was neatly trimmed at the back and sides but the top was slightly tousled. The hair, combined with vaguely chubby cheeks made him appear slightly younger than his age but his eyes betrayed an inner sadness.

He had transferred to Columbus three years previously from Boston, where he was a highly respected and successful homicide detective for ten years. Alan had been happy in Boston and had no desire to move - at least not until after 'the incident' and the ostracism that followed. His commanding officer in Boston had recommended the move from Massachusetts to Ohio as he feared that out of sheer frustration at the acts of his colleagues, his star detective would either leave the profession altogether or that one of Alan's calls for backup in emergency situations would be ignored and he might face mortal danger on the job. Alan knew that his boss had his best interests at heart and there was nothing he could do to assuage his colleagues' aggression toward him so he followed the advice. The Divisional Commander of Investigations at Columbus, an old friend of Alan's boss in Boston, was happy to have such a skilled investigator on her team and so the deal was struck.

Of course the scuttlebutt had arrived before Alan so he was unsurprised by the cool welcome he'd received from his new 'comrades'. One saving grace though, aside from his reduced cost of living, was that his lieutenant, while quite reserved and authoritative in his manner, obviously appreciated the addition to his team of someone with Alan's level of success in closing cases. Thomas Walker was a big, solid man with sparkling blue eyes, a thick neck, and a heavy jaw. His physical size and military haircut created an imposing appearance and on rare occasion, when he lost his temper and slammed one of his massive fists on a desk, there was no question as to who was in charge of his department.

Columbus had a surprisingly high crime rate and more than one hundred murders per year. Lieutenant Walker was tired of fielding questions from the media and dealing with attacks from the local government about the city's high murder rate and despite the fact that he had no direct control over crime rates, believed firmly that a high closure rate in his division would increase the deterrent for potential homicides, and reduce pressure on him. Beach was a strong asset and consistently outpaced the rest of the division in case closures, despite not having an assigned partner. Besides, Walker could identify with his new charge and he admired the younger man's character.

While it was standard operating procedure for detectives to be paired up, both for safety reasons and to increase effectiveness, an exception had to be made in Alan's case because no one would willingly work with him. Walker, being a pragmatic man, realized there was no point trying to force the issue as it would only be counterproductive so he let sleeping dogs lie, and Alan had flourished as a lone wolf so everyone was relatively happy.

As he observed the invisible line of demarcation between his colleagues and himself, Beach's mind briefly strayed to the day of his arrival at his new post in Columbus and he recalled with disgust, the greeting he had received back then. He remembered how the room had fallen silent upon his arrival and not a soul had greeted him until his new lieutenant showed him to his desk. Not that he'd expected a gushing font of warm handshakes but he had secretly hoped he might have escaped the treatment he was used to in Boston. He had settled into his chair and opened his drawer to find some stationery, only to discover a dead rat lying atop his pen shelf. The creature had congealed blood around its nose and something that resembled viscera trying to escape from its throat and anus, as if someone had stepped on it. While not particularly startled at the sight, he was saddened at this immediate indication that his past had followed him to his new life.

Alan had then nonchalantly wedged the end of his pencil under the rodent's incisor teeth, lifted it slowly from its resting place and toward his trash can then dropped it, pencil and all, watching vacantly as it thumped onto the bottom of the receptacle. He'd then calmly turned back to his drawer to withdraw a new pencil, and casually commenced writing his report. He preferred to hand write his reports in pencil before typing them into his computer terminal, finding the old method more familiar and helpful in clarifying details rather than fussing with computer programs and two finger typing.

"What's up Beach - rat got yer tongue?" Detective Richard Collier had rasped from across the room. Collier and the other detectives, watching bemused from several feet away, broke out in sneering laughter intended to highlight their disdain toward their new colleague and to try and get under his skin. As much as Alan would have liked to retort and make a fool of Collier, he knew it was pointless. As superior as his intellect was, no one would have been on his side or appreciated his wit so he'd seen no point in playing to an audience of one. He held his tongue and quietly continued his work. Collier, the obvious leader of the pack, had fired a warning shot over his bow and Beach hoped that by keeping his head down and not retaliating, he would make himself an uninteresting target and they would eventually move on. He was right; that first event and the obvious initial aggression had metamorphosed into a collective cold shoulder, with which he could live and work in peace.

Alan brought himself back to the task at hand and started making headway on his latest report until Lieutenant Walker strode into the room with his usual purposeful pace and called out, "Beach! Suspicious death at 'The Eleanor' building; apartment 1404. Uniforms are at the scene. Sounds like a suicide but look at the husband anyway." he said in his usual gruff tone.

Alan knew that Walker had to speak to him in this manner so that none of the other detectives would feel that he was playing favorites. His manner of speaking to the others wasn't much different so he never felt slighted and he knew that Walker tended to throw the more complex cases his way so he nodded in acknowledgement, pushed his report into his filing drawer and got up to leave.

"Yeah, you go and solve that suicide and leave the real murders to the big boys, Beach." jibed one of the other detectives.

"Shut up and get back to work ladies! It's like a Goddamn sewing circle in here!" shouted Walker at no one in particular as he strode back into his office.

Alan chuckled inwardly as he brushed past his estranged colleagues and out the door. He had wanted to be a detective since he was a boy and relished any new job, even if it was labeled only a suicide at this point. He knew that things were often not what they seemed and preferred the challenge of cases that weren't just, 'slam-dunks'. As he got into his car, he glanced straight at the, "No Smoking" symbol stuck to the dashboard, as there was in all city vehicles, pulled a cigarette from the pack in his pocket and lit it.

"Another advantage of having no partner." he muttered to himself as he drove out of the car park and turned toward The Eleanor. It was only a couple of miles away and the traffic was fairly thin so it wasn't long before he pulled into the, 'No Parking' zone directly in front of the building, slid his windscreen sign identifying his car as a police vehicle into place and walked toward the front doors. There were three marked squad cars and a Coroner's van parked at different angles around the front of the building and one of the uniformed officers was stationed at the entrance to vet people coming and going.

Alan respected the efficiency and professionalism of the uniforms, as they were called, and they seemed to realize this and generally treated him with due deference, despite the rumors they'd heard about his reason for coming to Columbus.

"Good evening Officer." Alan offered as he entered the building.

"Detective Beach." acknowledged the uniform. "It's straight through to the elevators and up to the fourteenth floor."

"Thank you. Any unusual movements since you've been here?"

"No, just owners and tenants going to and from."

"Have a good night officer, and do me a favor please?"

"What's that?"

"If you do notice anything unusual, please call me on my cell phone rather than waiting to report it later."

"Of course detective, and good luck on the case."

"Thank you." Alan called back as he made his way to the elevators just past the lobby.

The Eleanor's lobby security officer sat at his desk and surveyed Alan walking past, as if he were any other stranger in his territory. There were surveillance cameras positioned throughout the lobby and Alan guessed there would be a security room set up with monitors and digital recorders in such an up-market building.

"Security seems pretty professional." Alan noted, pushing the up button.

He entered the elevator and immediately spotted the security camera in the upper left rear corner. Upon reaching the fourteenth floor, he looked at the direction sign on the wall opposite the elevator to see where to find apartment, "1404". The door was open and Alan flashed his detective's shield to the uniformed officer as he entered the apartment. He hadn't met this particular uniform before so he introduced himself before walking in and glancing around the room to get some perspective of the scene. The large kitchen and dining area were off to the right while the living room was to the left of the entrance. The coroner was hunched over the body of the victim in the dining room and Alan could see it was lying in a particularly large pool of blood.

He was very used to examining murder scenes and certainly didn't have a weak stomach but was always surprised at just how much blood there could be when a victim completely bled out instead of dying from the damage of a bullet wound or some other trauma before they could completely exsanguinate. There were about ten pints of blood in her body while she was alive and Alan guessed that more than half of that had pooled and sunk into the carpet before her heart had stopped forcing it out of her body.

"Bit of a mess for you Detective Beach." the Medical Examiner called out.

"So I see Dr. Wescott. What's the damage?"

"Just the left forearm but both the ulnar and radial arteries were opened so wide, there would have been no stopping it; unless she had done it in a hospital emergency room. Someone really knew what they were doing!"

"Someone? You don't think it's a suicide?"

"That's for you to find out Detective Beach. She was a doctor and judging by the wound, and the position of the kitchen knife, it looks self-inflicted but it seems strange that it happened out in the open here, while the husband and kids were home."

"Where are they now?"

"The two young daughters are with a neighbor who sometimes baby-sits for the family and the husband is in the master bedroom but be warned, he was a mess when I got here. Don't know if he's calmed down much yet."

"Thanks, I'll go and see him while you finish up then I'd like to have a closer look at the body please."

"Your call Detective Beach."

Alan often wondered why this particular Medical Examiner chose to be polite but so formal as to continually use his full title instead of his first name. After all, they had known each other for over three years now and since they were usually on the same shift, had worked together many times. He had initially thought it was because of his past in Boston but it had become obvious that the doctor had great respect for Alan and his skills so he wasn't really sure what to make of his formal approach.

Alan pointed toward the hallway as he looked questioningly at Dr. Wescott.

"Yes, down the hall, last door at the end."

Alan walked down the hall, taking in the details of the layout of the large luxury apartment as he went. There were four other doorways in the hall, aside from the master bedroom at the end. He guessed one bedroom each for the daughters, one main bathroom and one study or computer room but didn't bother confirming yet. Entering the master bedroom, he saw the husband sitting on the end of the bed in shock, blood smeared heavily over his arms and clothing, his hands shaking and upturned in his lap. Standing in front of him was a uniformed officer with a notepad, asking questions quietly. Jim Benson looked up weakly each time the officer asked a question and seemed to try to answer but as he tried to form sentences, words would fail him and his speech would tail off into nothing. He had the vacant, expressionless look of a truly broken man - a man facing the most extreme, incomprehensible loss; a look that Alan knew too well.

"Thank you officer. I'll take it from here, if you don't mind." Alan said calmly.

"Yes sir." The Officer turned and moved close to Beach to whisper, "His name is Jim Benson. To be honest, he really hasn't said anything since he went into shock. Basically just mumbling and sobbing. When we first arrived, he was hysterical; just kept repeating that he couldn't stop the blood and asking how this could have happened."

"I understand officer. Has the crime scene unit and photographer finished with Mr. Benson?"

"Yes sir, all done."

"Again, thank you. Can I have the room please?"

"Of course."

Alan closed the door quietly behind the officer then sat gently on the bed next to Jim. He put his hand on the man's shoulder and spoke softly, "Do you know where you are Mr. Benson?"

Jim nodded slowly in acknowledgement.

"Do you understand that your wife has passed away?"

Again, he nodded.

"Mr. Benson; may I call you Jim?"

Another nod.

"Jim, my name is Alan Beach. I'm a detective from the Columbus Division of Police, Homicide Investigation. You can call me Alan. Do you understand?"

Slowly, as if struggling with a massive weight, Jim lifted his head to look at Alan and spoke, his voice raspy and dry, "I understand."

"That's good Jim. You don't have to speak to me or any other police officer without legal representation. Do you understand that?"

"I understand..." Jim replied weakly and opened his mouth to speak again but it took some seconds before any sound came forth. "...but why would I need a lawyer?"

"Don't worry Jim, it's just a formality but I am required by law to inform you of your rights. If you would like to have a lawyer present while we talk, I can arrange one for you unless you already have one you would like to call."

"We have a lawyer..." He paused. "...I have a lawyer but I don't need him to be here."

"OK but before we start, we have everything we need from your hands and clothing so I think it would be helpful if you wash your face and hands and change your shirt. Would you like to do that?"

Jim looked up at Alan and a small spark of cognition seemed to run through his eyes.

"Yes." was all he said as he stood slowly and began to unbutton his shirt.

Alan observed as he removed his shirt and undershirt then slowly began to wash the caked blood from his hands, arms and face. After a few minutes of washing and splashing water on his face, Jim walked from the bathroom to a chest of drawers to retrieve a T-shirt and pulled it on then sat down beside Alan again. He was obviously still in shock but the water had done its job and brought him back to a slightly more rational disposition.

"Have you ever been in love Detective Beach?"

"Please, call me Alan and yes, I have Jim."

Jim looked deeply into Alan's eyes. "Helen was the love of my life. She was my best friend, my lover and the mother of our children. I don't understand; how could she do this?" He lamented, his voice still croaking.

"I'm truly sorry for your loss Jim and I promise you that I will do everything I can to find out the truth." Alan said, knowing that the truth may well implicate the husband himself.

"The truth...the truth is that I don't know what to do any more Detective Beach. Everything used to be so clear to me. How do I tell my girls that their mother isn't coming home again? How do I go on without my Helen?"

"Your daughters don't know yet?"

"No, it was past their bedtime when she got home so once I realized Helen was asleep, I put them to bed and they were still asleep in their rooms when the police got here. I asked an officer to carry them to our neighbors' apartment. I couldn't let them see her… us, like that…and the blood, so much blood…I just knew I had to get them out."

"I understand Jim. Maybe you should wait a few days until you're more composed before you tell them. Do you have family nearby?"

"Helen's parents live just outside the city."

"Perhaps you should take the girls there for a few days and arrange for the scene to be cleaned before you come back."

"But what about Helen…her body?"

"We are required by law to perform an autopsy Jim. Her remains will be waiting for you when you return. I'll need your cell phone number and the number for Helen's parents' house. Now, do you think you can take me through what happened, step by step?"

"I'll try." He looked at the ceiling for a long moment then put his face in his hands and rubbed his eyes as though trying to wake himself from a nightmare. "We had been waiting for Helen to come home from her business trip. The girls were coloring at the table and I was reading the paper in the living room. When she came through the door, we were so happy to see her…" he started to well up again.

"Please Jim, just focus and stay with the facts so we can keep on track. What time was that?"

"I'm sorry; I'm trying. It was just after eight o'clock, I'd say eight fifteen. She said she was hungry and she needed a shower so I put a salad together for her while she came in here. When I'd finished the salad and she hadn't returned, I came to check on her. She didn't seem that tired when she got here but she must have been because she was asleep on the bed when I came in to our room, so I left her to rest and came out to tell the girls they could see her tomorrow. It was their bedtime anyway and I had only let them stay up to see her when she got home."

"How did she seem to you when she arrived home; what was her demeanor?"

"She was…she was just Helen. She was normal; happy to be home - jovial and affectionate as usual." he looked at Alan, uncertainty in his eyes.

"You're doing fine Jim, please continue."

"Then I sat on the sofa to watch some TV and I must have dozed off. The next thing I remember is hearing a loud thump. It startled me awake and I looked across to the dining room to see what it was. That's when I saw Helen on the floor. I thought she must have fallen or something so I called out to ask if she was OK but she didn't answer so I ran over to her. There was so much blood!" he began to sob but continued relating the events. "I looked for where the blood was coming from and tried to put pressure on the wound but it was so big! I ran to the kitchen, grabbed a towel and tried to stop the flow with a tourniquet but it was too late - she stopped breathing. I tried CPR but she had lost so much blood."

"Did she say anything or leave a note?"

"There was no note. She whispered a name just before she stopped breathing but I've never heard it before."

"What was the name Jim?"

"She said, 'Bryan Adler' but I don't recognize that name. It was only a whisper and I was in shock but my ear was very close to her face and I'm sure that's what she said."

"Is there any way that anyone else could have gotten into the apartment while you were asleep?"

"Not unless Helen let them in but visitors have to use the intercom system to get into the building and I would have heard it. Besides, I woke up as soon as I heard the thump and there was no one here." Jim said; his face contorted in confusion and frustration.

"OK, we will need to go over your statement again at the station to confirm everything but I think we can leave it at that for now. The Crime Scene Unit must be nearly finished so we'll leave shortly but I'm afraid we are going to have to take your daughters into protective custody until we can confirm it was suicide."

Jim's demeanor suddenly changed from meek and mourning to strong and protective. "What? No, you can't do that! They need their father or at least some familiar surroundings. I understand why you think you need to protect them but I can't let you do this to them."

"I'm sorry but the law requires it in such circumstances. It's really beyond my control."

"No, I can't let you do this. Put me in jail if you have to but leave the girls with our neighbors instead!" he demanded.

"Well, I suppose we could hold you at the station for questioning overnight. Are you certain the children are safe with the neighbors?"

"Yes, they love the girls and often baby-sit for us. They'll be fine there but not in some cold, sterile social services shelter!"

"OK, we'll do it your way but you will have to sign a consent form to indemnify the city."

"I don't care. I'll do whatever it takes to shield them from this." Jim eyes were red and swollen but set in determination.

"Alright then Jim, I'll have an officer organize the paperwork and we will have to inspect the neighbors' apartment but I think everything should be fine. As soon as suicide is confirmed, we can leave you to take the girls to Helen's parents' house. I'll give you a business card for a specialized cleaning company that can take care of the carpet and chair."

"Thank you Alan." Jim's face showed a vague glimmer of relief for the first time.

Alan took a quick look around the master bedroom and en suite bathroom then went out to inspect the rest of the apartment and examine the scene more closely. He knew that the body would have been jostled and moved during Jim Benson's attempts to revive his wife and the size of the blood pool made it difficult to detect movement and origin but the blood pattern on the seat of the chair showed that it began with her seated. She had obviously fallen to the floor as her strength waned but there was really very little else Alan could glean from what he saw, other than Jim's bloody footprints that verified his story of running to the kitchen and back for the towel and his bloody handprints on the telephone from when he'd called 911.

"I think I've got everything I can from this Dr. Wescott." Alan called over to the Medical Examiner, who was waiting in the kitchen. "If you're satisfied, you can take the body to the morgue."

"Thank you Detective Beach. I was just waiting for your say-so. The Crime Scene Unit has already left so we'll load the body and I'll start the autopsy when I get back to the office. Call me if you need anything."

"Thanks doctor, I'll do that."

Alan spoke briefly with the uniformed officer at the door to arrange an inspection of the neighbor's apartment and requested he take Jim Benson to be held for questioning at the police station and sign an indemnity form for the girls. He then headed back to the lobby of The Eleanor building to speak to the security staff. As he approached the security desk, he pulled his detective's shield from his belt to show it to the guard on duty.

"Detective Beach, Homicide." he announced.

"Homicide? I thought it was a suicide." queried the large man behind the counter. He had a stiff, humorless appearance like that of a serious former soldier.

"All unnatural deaths are treated as suspicious until we can clear them so it falls on us to investigate. May I see the security monitoring office please?"

"Follow me detective."

The big man seemed even bigger when he stood and led Alan to the door of The Eleanor's security monitoring room. He punched a code into the digital keypad beside the door and pressed his thumb against the biometric reader. The door opened with the loud clunk of a heavy duty magnetic lock.

"That's some security for a residential building." Alan remarked.

"People pay top dollar to live here detective; they expect the best protection for their money."

"Understandable."

They entered the room and Alan saw at least twelve monitors, each screen divided into four different picture feeds, a large bank of digital recording machines, an elaborate computer hardware rack and two seated guards watching the monitors.

"Gentlemen, this is Detective Beach from Homicide. He has a few questions for you and will want to see some footage, I assume."

"That's right, thank you." Alan confirmed, motioning to the monitoring system. "How many cameras are there?"

"One in each of the four residential elevators, one in the service elevator, four on each parking level, eight in the lobby, one each on the exterior at the front and rear of the building, three on each residential floor and four in the fitness and swimming pool areas." came the efficient response of the guard from the lobby, who seemed to be in charge.

"That's a lot of cameras. Before we look at footage, did Dr. Benson enter through the lobby or did she drive into the parking levels?"

"She arrived in a taxi at ten minutes past eight. I knew you would enquire so I already checked the log."

"Did she seem OK to you at the time?"

"Dr. Benson was her usual, polite and pleasant self. She always took the time to say hello to us."

"OK, can you show me the residential elevator footage from eight minutes past eight tonight please."

"Yes sir." replied one of the seated guards.

The monitor showed the interior of all four elevators simultaneously on the same screen. As the time code passed through into ten minutes past eight, they observed Dr. Benson enter one of the elevators where a small man in a hat and overcoat was already standing. They could not see the man's face or physical features because of his hat and coat but he stood diagonally to the right and behind the doctor. As the car travelled upward, they saw the man's hand dart out to the base of her skull then pull back and then his other hand thrust out toward the floor selector buttons.

"Stop it there!" Alan's raised voice commanded. "Can you get rid of the split-screen and make that one elevator full screen?"

"Of course. These cameras are not the usual cheap black and whites you see in some places."

The man pushed some buttons and the screen showed the one elevator more clearly now. He made the digital recording start again from just before the man's hand extended to the back of Helen's neck.

"Do you want slo-mo?"

"That would be great!"

The image played at about one third of its normal speed and Alan squinted, straining to see exactly what was happening on the small security monitor. As the man's hand reached her neck, he asked the guard to freeze the image. The man's gloved hand held a small, strange looking implement to Helen's neck for a split second before withdrawing. Alan's eyes narrowed into a frown and he tersely instructed the guards to give him a copy of the elevator footage five minutes before and after the event, so he could take it back to the crime lab and examine it properly on the large, high definition monitors. He also asked them to forward a copy of all the parking level and front entrance camera footage for the previous fifteen minutes to the station as soon as they could get it copied.

Alan's mind was racing now. According to Jim Benson, no one else could have gotten into their apartment so it had to be either spousicide or suicide but the image clearly showed a third party do something to the doctor before she got to her home. But if this man was to blame for her death, how could it be? What could someone possibly do to make another person commit suicide? His thoughts were now like a guided missile laser-locked on target. He grabbed the copy of the digital footage from the guard as soon as he'd burned the DVD for him and strode briskly toward his car. He was in no mood for traffic hold-ups so he turned on the flashing police lights situated behind the radiator grill and in the rear parcel shelf then began speeding through the lights and traffic to the station. This was out of character for the normally patient and methodical detective but he sensed he had to get on top of this as quickly as possible.

He skidded to a halt in the police parking garage and strode briskly to the stairs then quickly made his way to the Crime Lab.

"Larry, can you get this footage up on the big LED monitor straight away please!" he called to the technician as he walked through the sliding glass doors.

"Sure can Al. Is it a disc or a hard drive?"

Alan handed Larry the disc without speaking and he inserted it into a computer. He motioned for Alan to sit at the control panel and pointed to the controls.

"The joystick is to control forward and reverse motion as well as slo-mo and freeze-frame. This knob controls zoom. Be my guest."

Larry Phillips enjoyed working with Alan. He was polite, highly intelligent, thorough and intuitive but usually much calmer than he was now. Larry knew that it would take something out of the ordinary to cause his haste so he was happy to let him take the controls. As the image came up on the high definition, fifty five inch LED screen, Alan quickly familiarized himself with the controls. He moved the image forward until he reached the point where the man's hand went to the back of Helen's neck and froze the image.

"I still can't make this out Larry. Any ideas?"

They both went around the control panel to get closer to the monitor and peered intently at the image on the massive screen. It looked like a very small glue gun but the image was slightly blurred because of the speed with which the man's hand had moved.

"Sorry Alan but with the speed of movement, there doesn't seem to be a clear frame."

Alan suddenly lurched back from the monitor to grab the phone. He picked up the hand piece and quickly dialed the Medical Examiner.

"Dr. Wescott; it's Alan."

"Yes Alan, did you forget something?"

"No Doctor. Please don't take my tone the wrong way but this is urgent. Can you examine the back of Dr. Benson's neck right now and tell me what you see."

"Well, OK detective but..."

"Now please doctor!" Alan's voice came tersely.

"OK, I'm on it. I'll put you on speaker."

Dr. Wescott carefully rolled Helen's body on the examination table and drew the fluorescently lit magnifying glass toward her on its folding arm. He gently pulled her hair away from her neck and searched for anything out of the ordinary. As he came to the hairline approximately three quarters of an inch to the right of the centre of her spine, he called out.

"I've got something here - looks like a very small puncture wound!"

"Can you tell what it was made by?"

"Not really but I can tell you that it was smaller than a normal hypodermic needle, maybe even smaller than an insulin needle as far as I can tell. If you hadn't specified the location, I might not have picked it up at all. Does it tell you something detective?"

"It tells me three things doctor: This wasn't suicide, the husband is innocent, and I need to find out who Bryan Adler is. But first, we need to examine the rest of the security footage."

Chapter 3

Beach's frustration was palpable and filled the crime lab like a fog as he stared intently at the big screen. Larry was wary of interrupting his thoughts but decided it was time to break the deadlock.

"I'm sorry Alan but there really is nothing there. We've been through every frame of the security footage from the parking levels, the entry and exit, the elevators and the twelfth floor hallway that the Eleanor guards couriered over. This guy really knew what he was doing. Not once did he expose any recognizable feature to any camera."

"I know Larry. It's not your fault - I'm just frustrated!" Alan said in an uncharacteristic tone. "I'll leave you to your work. I apologize for my mood and for the wasted hours."

"That's OK but I don't think it was a waste of time. At least you know that this guy is a professional, which indicates he had a specific agenda."

Alan looked thoughtfully at his colleague.

"You know what Larry? You're right. I've been looking at this the wrong way and you've corrected my focus. I was so knotted up trying to find some physical identifier that I missed the subtlety. That is a wise observation and I commend you."

"Thanks Alan - glad I could help. What's your next step?"

"I've got to go with the only other lead I have for now and find Bryan Adler. If that doesn't lead to anything then I'll have to start interviewing friends, neighbors and colleagues. Thanks again. See you later."

"Good luck Alan." Larry called out as Beach breezed out the door.

Arriving at his desk, Alan woke his computer and began searching the police database for his quarry. There were two Bryan Adlers in the local database with minor traffic infringements but neither had a history of violence. One of them was a retired school teacher in his late seventies and the other was a former soldier who had recently been paralyzed by an IED while on a mission in the Middle East. He couldn't see any kind of connection between them and Helen Benson so he dismissed them both and widened his search. Accessing the national crime database, he came across some more interesting characters but one stood out in particular.

"Bryan Adler; convicted serial killer and diagnosed psychopath – now here's something I can work with." he murmured to himself.

He scribbled down the details of the psychiatric hospital where Adler was being held and picked up the phone to make an appointment. The facility was about one hundred and fifty miles away, near a small town in West Virginia. His appointment was set for ten o'clock the next morning so he decided to drive there that night and stay in a hotel to be fresh for his meeting with the serial killer. He then went to Lieutenant Walker's office to get the necessary permission to investigate across the state line. It was a request that would require a good deal of paperwork so Alan prepared himself for his boss's reaction. After knocking on the door, he opened it and walked over to Thomas Walker's desk. He fully expected an unpleasant conversation with some shouting thrown in so he decided he might as well just dive in and come straight to the point. As Alan finished his request, Walker looked up, his face tight in a grimace. Alan steeled himself for the tirade but it didn't come.

"This is a major pain in my ass Beach! But I trust your judgment so go ahead." his head tilted down toward the pile of paperwork in front of him as he sighed loudly. "I'll start on the documents and call the West Virginia State Police to get clearance. I assume you'll be armed?"

"You know me boss; safety first." Alan smiled widely.

"Don't be a smartass Beach. Just go! I'll have the approval by the time you hit the border. Call me with the name and fax number of your hotel so I can send you the form. And don't make any trouble over there!"

"No sir, I'll be in and out before you know it."

"Yeah, yeah… Well, what are you waiting for? Go!" Thompson waved dismissively at the door.

Alan always found his boss's gruff manner bemusing. He knew that underneath the tough exterior, Thompson was a great father to his children, a loving husband to his wife and a truly good man. He supposed the demeanor was designed to convey an air of authority but he wasn't fooling Alan.

"Thanks boss. See you in a couple of days."

Alan returned to his desk, shut down his computer terminal and grabbed a couple of things from his drawer. As he rounded the corner that led to the stairs, he saw Richard Collier ascending from the car park with a look of malicious intent. Beach didn't know what to expect but was in no mood for any of Collier's childish nonsense so he decided to preempt him with some nonsense of his own. "Walker is looking for you and he doesn't seem happy." he lied.

Collier creased his eyes in disbelief but was compelled to pick up his pace. He walked briskly past without a word and Alan started quickly down the stairs. Beach knew what he'd done was stupid and would come back to bite him later but it had the desired effect. He had made it to the car park unmolested and Collier's footsteps tailed off in the distance. He jumped into his car to drive home and pack an overnight bag.

Once home, Alan had a shower and changed his clothes. He sat on the end of the bed with a towel wrapped around his waist and took a moment to reflect on the investigation so far. As he collected his thoughts and put everything into logical order, his sad, slate grey eyes were drawn to the wall in front of him. Hanging there was a beautiful black and white photograph from his wedding to Kelly. The ornate, silver framed picture was tastefully composed and despite the formal circumstance, the couple looked relaxed, in love, and full of hope for the future. That was over ten years ago and they had two wonderful years of marriage before he lost the only woman he had ever loved to a car crash. Alan clearly recalled the unbearable pain of the event and how his initial disbelief and anger had eventually faded to emptiness and hopelessness. His loss was so profound it had very nearly consumed him. He couldn't see a path forward and didn't know how to go on without her. In the end, the only thing that kept him going was his work, into which he threw himself entirely, to drown out the pain.

Over time, his constant and total immersion in cases began to numb the pain to some extent and he was left in a kind of emotional no man's land. Over the years, friends and family had tried several times to set him up with other women but the wall he'd built around his heart prevented any chance of intimacy and he remained alone. The one positive outcome of this event in his life was that through his focus and dedication, he had developed into the most successful homicide detective in the city of Boston. His talent and potential as an investigator were obvious - so much so that he had been promoted to the rank of detective much younger than the norm. The tragic irony was that he would probably never have realized his full potential as a detective if Kelly hadn't died that terrible day, all those years ago.

Looking at that photograph always brought the memories and pain flooding back but doing so held a morbid attachment for him. Despite knowing the act was self destructive and part of the reason he couldn't move on, he just couldn't stop. Over the years, his mind had twisted events to apportion blame on himself for his wife's death and this ritual had become a form of self-flagellation. Even though Kelly was driving alone when the accident happened, Alan's mind had invented emotional tendrils to link him inextricably to the event. He would obsess over such unrealistic possibilities as: if he had been with her, he could have prevented it, or if he had bought her a safer car, she would have been better protected from the impact.

While Alan was at his lowest after Kelly's death, his boss had demanded he see a police psychologist. Alan resisted as long as he could until it became obvious the lieutenant wouldn't take, 'no' for an answer. Seeing a shrink was the last thing he wanted to do but in the end he gave in and visited Dr. Sarah Kellerman Psy.D., in the Police Administration Building. Their initial meeting was not overly productive because of Alan's unwillingness to open up but the doctor had anticipated his resistance and gradually, over the ensuing weeks they started to make some headway. She had educated him in the five stages of grief and the effect each stage had in the recovery process. They talked about his unhealthy thoughts of self blame and inability to let go and move forward with life.

"You know Alan, as strange as this may seem, the act of blaming yourself for something which you could not possibly have foreseen or influenced in any way, is actually your subconscious mind's way of coping with your conscious need for control." she explained carefully.

"Goodness! There's some well versed psycho-babble." Alan smiled.

"That psycho-babble as you call it, simply means that your conscious mind can't cope with the reality of your loss, and the fact that you had no control over the event. This caused you to feel that you have no real control over anything in life, so you developed this coping mechanism to deal with it. Your subconscious found unreasonable ways to blame yourself and rationalizes these illogical thoughts to your conscious mind. It's very similar to the phenomenon wherein children from broken homes blame themselves for their parents' divorce so they can make sense of it in their own minds. It is a common coping mechanism which you must eventually overcome to move forward. For now though, it remains in place to keep you sane."

"You psychologists have the most eloquently complex means of putting things in such a way as to be incomprehensible, hence the term psycho-babble."

She stared blankly at Beach and said nothing.

"I'm teasing now doctor – I understand what you mean and I will take it on board."

Their sessions had continued for a few months until Alan decided that his subconscious was not ready to let go and likely would not be ready for some time to come. At their final session, he thanked Dr. Kellerman for her kindness and they agreed that he should reach out to her in times of need.

He had learned from his visits with Sarah but the lessons faded into the distance when he gazed at that happy moment frozen in time on his wall. How he missed Kelly. How he longed for the happiness and love they'd shared. How could he have let this happen, he would torture himself time and time again. He consciously realized now, why he'd been so gentle questioning Jim Benson. He saw the pain in Jim's eyes; the same sickening, unrelenting blend of soul destroying emotions that he had felt when he lost Kelly. His intense empathy for Jim wouldn't allow him to cause further pain so he maintained his consoling demeanor despite the fact that the odds always favor the husband as a suspect when a wife dies in suspicious circumstances.

Having had his fill of self-blame, Alan stood himself up and pulled an old leather overnight bag from his closet. He stuffed the required clothing and toiletries into it and got dressed for the trip. With preparations complete, he went to the freezer to grab a frozen dinner and tossed it into the microwave. Waiting for the machine's timer to bleep, he thought about how he should eat better and exercise more often but could never seem to spare the time. As the oven played its musical notification, he retrieved his dinner and plopped it on the kitchen counter to eat. His mind wandered in an idle daydream to the frozen food factory as he imagined thousands of plates with little divided compartments rolling along the conveyer belt, machines dropping their premeasured portions of prepared stuff into their targeted spots then moving along to be packaged and sent off to the supermarket. He thought how this used to be quality time he would have spent talking to Kelly but now just needed to fill the void. Shaking himself out of it, he finished eating and dropped the plate into the trash can.

"Time to hit the road." he said to himself, scooping up his overnight bag.

Alan estimated the drive would take just under three hours. He figured there was bound to be a motel in town or near the high security psychiatric institution so he hadn't bothered to book ahead. The drive was uneventful and as fortune would have it, the facility was just off the main road he was traveling on the way into town. A few miles further to the edge of town, he spotted a cheap but comfortable looking motel, parked his car and went to check in. Alan rang the bell and the night clerk emerged from his lodgings behind the registration counter. He was a thin fellow in his late fifties, with unkempt hair and grey stubbly whiskers. Smiling to greet Alan, he revealed a number of missing teeth.

"Are ya traveling alone Mr... uh... Beach?" the clerk asked as he peered at Alan's driver's license.

"Yes, it's just me, and just one night please."

"Travelin' salesman, are ya?"

"No, just visiting someone."

"Well, we don't tolerate no funny business round here so I'll be keepin' an eye out."

"You do that sir."

Alan leant to pick up his bag and the man suddenly froze in a macabre, toothless grimace of shocked fear and Alan very nearly laughed at the bizarre image until he realized that his jacket had opened, exposing his Glock 9mm in its holster.

"Don't worry friend." Alan calmed him, pulling his badge from his belt to provide the startled man some relief. "I'm here on official police business. In fact, I'd appreciate your fax number so my lieutenant can send me some paperwork, if you wouldn't mind."

The man's face relaxed into a slightly less maniacally comical look as he leaned forward to examine Alan's badge. "Oh, OK then officer detective, sir." He fumbled, relieved but gently rubbing his chest over his heart.

The man gave Alan the hotel's fax number, his room key, and breakfast order form, still wide eyed and rubbing his chest. "Goodnight officer detective, sir."

"Just plain 'detective' is fine." Alan said smiling.

Alan went to his room and found a pizza delivery menu on the bedside table, picked up the phone to order and watched television to fill in some time. After eating he pulled his notebook out and fingered through the pages. His meeting was at ten o'clock but he decided to arrive a little early to give himself the chance to survey the building and security. Alan pondered what it would be like to have a conversation with this brutal murderer in the flesh and thought about the questions he would ask. Eventually, sleep came.

Chapter 4

Alan woke fresh and had breakfast. Having a bit of time to kill, he decided to take advantage and take a walk. He kept a brisk pace for half an hour, trying to fulfill his promise to himself to exercise more regularly. When the time came, he checked out of the motel, got in his car and drove away from town to his appointment.

Approaching the building, he pulled the car over on the side of the road and examined the institution's security measures through binoculars. There was an elaborate system of three different chain link fences standing over twelve feet high. All three had rolls of razor wire at their bottom and top, with the middle fence also bearing signs to warn of electrification and there were manned guard towers surrounding the expansive, four storied structure, sufficient to observe and prevent any attempt to escape. The wire mesh windows looked as though they had been recently updated with the latest locking mechanisms and were encased in steel bars. It seemed quite obvious to Alan from what he saw, that no one was getting out of this place without permission – and his evaluation didn't take into account any internal security measures they may have utilized.

Satisfied that Bryan Adler would not have been able to escape and return unnoticed without inside help or a very clever plan, Alan proceeded to the visitors' car park and on to the outer security check point. He pulled his badge from his belt to show the guard and surrendered his weapon then moved on to the secondary check point. The guard there checked for his name on the appointment roster and asked for any metal objects to be placed in a lockable tray. Alan held up his badge.

"This is metal but you can't have it."

"Understood Detective Beach but I will need to see it again when you leave to ensure you still have it with you." he said as he extended his hand toward Alan. "In the meantime, I'll need to have a closer look please."

"Wow, you guys really take this seriously!"

"This facility has successfully contained the country's most devious, depraved, and violent criminally insane inmates for over thirty years detective. No one wants that to change on their watch."

"I understand officer, thank you." Alan said, retrieving his detective's shield then he passed through the heavy rotating bars of the checkpoint.

His eyes moved searchingly over the front of the building as he walked the distance to the main doors finding nothing but the highest possible security standards. At the front door, there were four guards armed with automatic rifles. Two were positioned outside the doors and two inside. The exterior guards didn't ask for ID or even acknowledge Alan. Their purpose was purely to scan the grounds between the front door and the security check points. As Alan approached the doors, an interior guard swiped a card across a sensor and the heavy bullet-proof glass glided apart allowing entry. The guard motioned toward the step-through metal detection unit and Alan complied. The machine made a loud beep and one of the guards held a detection wand up. Alan pulled his shield out and handed it to the man but he continued his sweep anyway. Satisfied, the guard returned Alan's badge and instructed him to proceed to the waiting room outside the administration office. A couple of minutes later, a voice came from the door.

"Detective Beach, I'm David Tinsley, Head of Psychiatry at Sherbourne Institute for the Criminally Insane. Please follow me to my office."

The man was in his fifties, tall and sturdy with a goatee and glasses. He extended his hand to shake Alan's and with the formalities complete, they proceeded to Tinsley's office. The room reminded Alan of a dean's office in an old Ivy League school. It felt old and formal but richly historical with its timber walls and book cases, buttoned leather chairs with matching sofa and huge oak desk and chairs. The Chief Consultant Psychiatrist motioned to the sofa in the sitting area and sat himself down in one of the leather chairs. As Alan sat, he noticed a large file on the coffee table in front of the doctor.

"Would you like coffee or tea detective?"

"I'm fine thank you but please call me Alan."

"Alan it is then – indeed, let's dispense with formalities. You may call me David. I have Mr. Adler's complete file here but perhaps you would prefer to discuss the patient rather than wade through all these medical notes and terminology?"

"You read my mind David. I'm afraid they didn't teach, 'Medical' where I went to school."

"And where might that have been Alan? Your accent is faintly New England but I can't be sure."

"Well picked. I'm from Boston but I've managed to avoid the typical accent of the area."

"Ah yes, the wonderful city of Boston. I attended Harvard and have fond memories of my time there. But you've come from Columbus I believe?"

"That's right. I moved there a few years ago. It's a long story and not worth telling."

"Oh but all stories are worth telling Alan." Tinsley spoke with long held wisdom. "Still, for the sake of time, let's get to Mr. Adler shall we? How does he relate to your case?"

"I can't really discuss details of the case but there has been a suspicious death and Adler's name came up in the investigation. The victim was in your profession; Dr. Helen Benson."

David Tinsley's face sank. "Helen Benson the Neuro-Psychiatrist?"

"That's right, did you know her?"

"Everyone in this profession knows of Helen Benson. An extremely gifted woman and considered the leader in her field by many, including myself. This is a great and terrible loss! How did she die?" Tinsley's brow was tensed in a deep furrow and his eyes welled slightly.

"That's what I'm trying to find out. It appears as a suicide but there are suspicious circumstances which I can't go into at this point."

"Suicide - that's impossible detective!" he railed. "Dr. Benson would never have done such a thing to herself. Besides, she had two young daughters, a happy marriage and an incredibly bright future. How could anyone think such a thing?"

"I understand Doctor but she was found by her husband in their home with a massive, apparently self-inflicted wound to her forearm which caused exsanguination."

"My God... I can't believe this! I've had dinner in that very home with Helen, Jim and other friends and colleagues. When did this happen?"

"Last night - about eight fifteen."

"I don't understand. She was keynote speaker at the National Psychiatric Medicines Convention in Washington. She should have been there until today. I would be there myself but I sent some of our junior faculty for the experience."

"Her husband said she had already performed her formal duties in the first two days of the conference and missed her family so she asked a colleague to cover her remaining minor responsibilities and returned home last night."

"That poor man, he must be completely distraught!"

Alan winced slightly; recalling Jim's pain and how closely it mimicked his own.

"I apologize for my incredulity. This is very difficult to accept. Did you say she cut her own forearm?"

Alan composed himself, "That's right - does that mean something to you?"

"Yes - and it will certainly mean something to Bryan Adler!"

Tinsley went on to describe Adler's predilections and details of his long and brutal life as a serial killer. He explained how Helen had done a period of consultation and pharmacological research at Sherbourne, during which she had regular ongoing sessions with Adler for many months. He then used Helen's exhaustive notes and transcripts to detail the psychopath's history and pathology for Alan.

Bryan was born in the latter months of 1972 outside a rural Arkansas community to Curtis and Ruth Adler. It was a home birth and since his mother never ventured into town, no one outside the Adlers had ever known she was pregnant so there was no record of his birth. He was one of those statistics that just fell through the cracks of bureaucracy due to the sheer social and geographical isolation his parents had created. The Adlers had a small farm miles from the nearest town and his parents would allow no outside interaction so his upbringing had been extremely solitary, with only his parents and a few farm animals for company. He was never allowed to attend school; in fact, Bryan didn't even know what school was until later when he entered into foster care.

Curtis Adler was an extremely paranoid man and strict disciplinarian who hated any kind of interaction with anyone outside his direct family. They were self sufficiency farmers and the only time he went to town was to get seeds for their vegetable gardens, glass jars for pickling, heating oil, tools, and a few other items that they couldn't do without and couldn't make for themselves. It was a harsh way of life but the couple wanted it that way and Bryan was an unwelcome arrival. They believed that the world would end very soon and that they, by living the way they did and following the bible virtually to the letter, would be the only people saved from the wrath of God. In fact, they saw themselves as a kind of renaissance Adam and Eve in their own twisted minds.

Ruth was the illegitimate result of two first cousins in Tennessee, who were unable to control their lust and some reports had it that she had always been a bit 'touched'; even as a child. She was a social embarrassment to the cousins' families so they had sent her to be raised by her maternal grandparents in neighboring Arkansas. She was brought up in a very religious and strict household, where corporal punishment was the norm. By the time she was fifteen years old Ruth had met twenty year old Curtis at a church picnic and was smitten by his physical power and clear vision of what he believed righteous. Shortly after her sixteenth birthday, they were married in a small church ceremony with only one paid witness since her grandparents had both died mysteriously in their sleep a few weeks earlier and Curtis' parents had both died years before.

Curtis and Ruth took over her grandparents' property and set about converting it from a commercial crop growing operation to a self sufficiency farm to minimize their interaction with the outside world. They lived their harsh lifestyle far from the prying eyes of neighbors or townsfolk and about five years into their union, Ruth became pregnant with Bryan, which filled them both with dread at how God may judge them.

After Bryan was born, Curtis decided that Bryan must have been sent to them as a test by God so he quickly won Ruth over to his way of thinking and they raised him according to the strictest interpretation of biblical stories and proverbs. The overriding rule was: 'Spare the rod, spoil the child' and they enforced this rule and others with a sadistic savagery unimaginable to Helen Benson.

Of course there were no witnesses to Bryan's claims about these times, other than the hundreds of scars, which had been dated by medical experts as having been inflicted all throughout his childhood from a very early age. The knowledge that his parents had been so physically and mentally cruel to their son had filled Helen with anger toward Curtis and Ruth, and pity toward her patient. But as she progressed through his file to Bryan's psychotic deeds and the coldness with which he had recounted them to prosecutors when he was finally arrested; her ability to think rationally and clinically about her patient was challenged. Her clinical training and experience demanded that she act as a professional physician and treat him as psychiatric patient that needed her help but his lucidity, clarity of thought, and utter remorselessness toward his victims triggered her instincts and basic nature as a human being, causing her constant internal conflict when dealing with him. As a true professional and one of the leaders in her field, she kept her emotions fully in check during their sessions but she had an ominous feeling that he always knew her inner thoughts.

Bryan was a highly intelligent subject who, despite his complete lack of education until he was about fourteen years of age, was extremely devious, calculating, and meticulous in his every action. It was as though he could transcend normal thought and his pain threshold as well as his physical strength and capabilities far exceeded that of a normal man of his size and weight. His eyes were almost imperceptibly exotropic, which meant that they pointed slightly outward from each other so one could never be certain which eye to focus on when making eye contact or during a conversation. This was not only disconcerting but rather intimidating in his particular case. He had the condition from birth as far as anyone could tell and told of a designated weekly beating his father would give him on Saturdays because he saw the defect as a sign of the devil and another part of God's test.

When Bryan neared the fourteenth anniversary of his birth, he finally snapped during one particular unearned beating from Curtis. Bent over the workbench in the shed just off the house, the searing pain of his father's belt buckle burning into his back, he saw an old fencing hammer in front of his hand and instinct took over. He grabbed the hammer, turned violently and with strength born from years of built up anger and hatred, he struck out and landed a powerful blow to his father's head. Curtis reeled back severely dazed, lost his footing and fell to his knees while Bryan, his wiry frame strengthened from years of hard physical labor, his mind steeled by years of abuse, dropped the hammer to unleash an indescribable fury of violent, powerful punches on his father. He kept beating Curtis' unconscious head until his energy began to wane then he kneeled up and watched the foamy red blood gurgling from his father's mouth and nose. He stood, grabbed a rusty, old cut-throat razor from the bench and without hesitation, slit his father's throat, causing the carotid arteries to spew forth pulsing rivers of blood until the gurgling stopped and he knew that Curtis Adler was no more.

As he kneeled beside the body, the cut-throat razor resting on the floor about a foot above the head, Bryan's mother opened the door of the shed and entered. She absorbed what she saw before her and approached her husband's body, her face white with shock. Suddenly, she dropped down and grabbed the razor in her right hand. She thrust it outwards, toward Bryan with tears in her eyes and for a moment, he resigned himself to his fate. Then he watched in amazement as she drew the blade away from him and with one deep, even stroke, sliced her own arm diagonally from wrist to elbow, creating a long gaping wound in her arteries then calmly sat on the floor and stared into her son's eyes as the life drained out of her. Bryan didn't move a muscle. He just sat and watched, emotionless and clinical, until she expired before his eyes. After his mother slumped over dead, Bryan washed his hands and face, collected his few meager belongings and set off on foot down the long dirt driveway, onto the small country road to which it led and just kept walking until he eventually came upon a freight train with empty boxcars and began a hobo's life for the next few months. These details had been completely unknown to anyone but Bryan himself until he was eventually caught many years later and confessed all his crimes, including the one from which his psychotic murder scenario had originated.

Nobody went to the Adler farm, as had been the case for many years prior. It wasn't until the electricity company was installing new power poles in the area that a company representative discovered the skeletal remains of Ruth and Curtis Adler about three years after their deaths. The police, lacking any real evidence, aside from the rusty hammer, decided it must have been a murder suicide and since there was no evidence of any other inhabitants, the matter was concluded then and there.

Bryan lived and learned the clever ways of the hobo, with the help of a kind-hearted and experienced hand and he was a very quick learner. He developed heightened cunning, speed of thought, physical prowess and a growing desire to repeat what he had done to his parents. He lived this way for several months until one night, the police raided a small hobo encampment and Bryan was caught and taken into the care of Social Services as a minor. He was then passed around from foster home to foster home until it became obvious that he would have to stay in a group shelter, since no foster family would tolerate his cunning, anti-social behavior.

Once Helen had developed a strong sense of her patient, the actual face to face sessions began in earnest. Despite having no real choice in the matter, Bryan had willingly submitted to any and all forms of therapy that Helen felt appropriate for his treatment. This was another reason for her to suspect that he had ulterior motives in actively dealing with her instead of just resigning himself to his fate of internment for life without the possibility of release, as meted out by the court three years earlier.

In addition to the cocktails of potent anti-psychotics as well as some experimental drugs, his treatment included three sessions per week of psychoanalysis, including hypnotherapy. His treatment continued in this vein for over two years and at times, Helen actually thought she saw some glimmers of hope but these hopes were usually dashed by the time their next session came around.

Basically, Bryan's psyche was damaged beyond repair and try as she might, Helen knew she was essentially wasting her time with him but despite her gut feeling, she continued experimenting with the various combinations of drugs to glean as much scientific information as possible from her willing volunteer.

In one particularly chilling session, Bryan described one of his crimes in graphic detail. Helen had not wanted to go down this avenue in his therapy but to that point, nothing else had shown any promise and she found herself morbidly curious about the case and his recounting of it so let him continue.

Bryan's psychosis manifested itself in a bizarre modus operandi wherein he would seek out families with two parents and one young child. He would then observe them from a distance for several days, waiting and watching for what he needed to create the impetus to build his scenario; one simple act that demonstrated what was, in his opinion, a reason that the parents didn't deserve the love of their child. This could range from corporal punishment, to any form of neglect, causing the child to cry, or any other small matter he found objectionable in their parenting.

During his observations, he would also take his time to detail their daily routines, associations with outsiders, security measures and other individual behaviors until he was confident he had intimate knowledge of all aspects of their lives so that he could fulfill the scenario his psychosis demanded. Once he had established a reason to act, he would devise a detailed plan to ensure he was able to live out his fantasy unhindered.

He would gain access to the family's home by disguising himself as a delivery man using a stolen uniform and hold a box in front of him so that it seemed a believable scenario to anyone looking through a peephole or a window near the door. When either the husband or wife opened the door, he would calmly step forward to block the door from being shut, while removing the pistol he had concealed in a hole cut in the back of the box. As the box dropped from his other hand, he would hold his finger up to his lips in a menacing threat to keep quiet then force his victim backward into the house as he entered and locked the door behind him. If his victim began to make any noise, he would pistol whip them to prevent any disturbance but they would normally follow his instructions out of fear and shock.

At this point, he would force the wife to bind her husband to a chair using the plastic zip ties he had in his back pocket and gag him with a towel from their kitchen. He would then tie the wife to a chair facing her husband and silently savor the fear in their eyes for several moments before bringing their child in and extorting the mother to admit all their faults as parents, whether real or suggested by her tormentor, by holding the child on his lap and making the mother believe he would harm her child if she did not comply. Once the confession was complete to his satisfaction, he would gag the mother, and in an eerily controlled and methodical manner, beat the father senseless with his fists. When he was satisfied with his work and while the mother was whimpering in horror, he would draw a cut-throat razor from his pocket and calmly slit the father's throat at each carotid artery, then lean in to the mother's face to watch him bleed to death together.

The father of this now broken family no longer a threat, Bryan would then begin a slow, methodical psychological assault on the mother. He would repetitively ask her in a soft, toneless, emotionless manner, why she was such a bad mother; how she could be so neglectful, cruel, and uncaring toward her child, how could she think she deserved to have a trusting young child in her care. This mental torture would continue for as long as it took to psychologically break the mother. Knowing her tormentor's total control of the situation, having been forced to witness her husband's brutal death, listening for hours to his quiet, calm, controlled voice and observing his menacing glances at her child, she would eventually break and realize she had no choice but to comply with his demand that she take her own life. He would then cut the zip tie that bound her right hand and hold the cut throat razor out to her telling her it was time to release her child from the grip of its evil parents. Continuing to goad her hypnotically, to slit her own arm from the base of her hand, all the way up her forearm so there was no hope of stemming the blood flow, he would then watch bemused as the life drained from her eyes.

Bryan Adler would then put the child in its bedroom, pick up all his zip ties, his razor, and his delivery box, calmly leave through the front door, walk two or three blocks to where he had left his car and drive away into the night with a grim sense of satisfaction. He had no need for the police to suspect his crimes were murder/suicides. He didn't care, in any way whatsoever, what the police thought as he was so meticulous in his plans and actions that no incriminating evidence was ever found at his crime scenes so there was never any kind of link between him and his victims. The only thing the police knew was that there were suspicious deaths all over the country with the same details and modus operandi so they suspected there was a serial killer at work but they had nothing to give them any direction. The children, who were always left alive and physically well, were of no help because they were too young to be fully aware of the reality and unable to give a proper description other than the fact that the perpetrator was a man.

The eerie calm with which Bryan recounted his stories was the most disturbing experience Dr. Helen Benson had ever encountered. As he searched her eyes for any reaction, she tried desperately not to indulge his psychosis and kept her face and gaze as unwavering as possible but despite her best efforts, she felt that he could see right into her mind and know her exact thoughts. He obviously relished this part of the game the most. Reliving the events in his own mind was one thing but his satisfaction was highest when he could watch the responses of other people to his crimes. The obvious outrage and indignation of reporters, court officials, prosecutors and jurors had been gratifying, though a bit predictable and mundane in his mind but watching experienced medical professionals try to conceal their horror and personal reactions was the most titillating game for him. To observe glimmers in their eyes from the sheer strain of their ongoing mental battle, trying to remain clinical and unemotional, while dealing with their own personal psychological reactions, had become Bryan's new obsession since he no longer had the freedom to enact his true passion.

Beach sat enthralled by Tinsley's comprehensive review of Helen's notes until he finished. "Thank you for that detailed description – it's pretty grim stuff but quite helpful to my investigation. Now, I know this is a strange question but I have to ask. Is there any possible way that Adler could have been at the scene of Helen's death?" he asked.

Tinsley looked quizzically at Alan. "A strange question indeed but the answer is very simple. There is no possible way that Bryan could have been there. You've seen our exterior security measures as you came in but what you haven't seen is our interior systems, and I can assure you that these are even more elaborate than what you saw outside. No, that would be completely out of the question. Besides, even if he was there, why on earth would he have returned to captivity?"

"I agree but as I said, I had to ask."

"I'm sorry Alan, no disrespect intended. It's just such a ludicrous thought from my point of view."

"Understood. Well, I guess I'm as ready as I'll ever be to meet this guy so, shall we?"

"I'm afraid no one is ever truly ready to meet Bryan Adler but yes, we have prepared him for your visit. Be warned however, that his physical power is well beyond that of an average man his size and over the many years he's been here, he has developed significant resistance to all known tranquillizing agents. He is highly intelligent and devious, and may be particularly difficult since we have recently taken him off all medications to prepare him for a clinical trial being conducted with Blue Sky Biotech, for whom Helen worked as a senior consultant. The details of the therapy they are testing are so secret that not even I know its ingredients or mechanism – only that it is showing a great deal of promise. Under normal circumstances, I would not allow any patient to be subjected to clinical trials but I trusted Helen, and Bryan's illness is seemingly beyond treatment with any conventional therapy so I have allowed it. Besides, Helen's project is headed by Professor Linus Gelling so how could I refuse? The man is a virtual demigod in the medical field."

"Linus Gell... Is that spelt Gell-i-n-g?"

"That is correct Alan. Ask anyone in medicine and they will know of him."

"Thanks. Well, let's not keep Mr. Adler waiting."

"I know you must do what you must do. Bryan will be securely restrained but be prepared for the fact that he will be at his full mental potential without his meds. He is highly unpredictable and your visit could go either way, at his whim. Follow me to the restraint room."

They proceeded from Tinsley's office, down the hallway and on to the elevator with the doctor telling Alan some of the institution's history as they walked. Arriving on the third floor, Alan was immediately struck by the interior security measures Tinsley had mentioned. He hadn't seen anything like this before - not even when he had interviewed a murderer in a Federal Supermax prison. He knew for certain that there was no way Bryan or anyone else could have escaped from this place.

"It seems the public can rest assured with your security David."

"They certainly can. The criminally insane are often capable of thought processes and creativity that sane people are not so we must cover any and all possible means of evasion. It may seem like overkill to some but it works and no politician would dare question our ethics or federal funding when we are responsible for keeping these patients away from their families and friends."

"Indeed. So most of your funding is federal?"

"Yes, approximately seventy percent of it is. The remainder comes from a mix of state budget and private donations from corporations such as Blue Sky Biotech and others, for whom I approved specific research access to patient records and interviews. We also have a single, private patron who donates a significant amount each year. His son is held here for a killing spree in his high school. The donation is quite altruistic as he feels responsible for his son's actions so he thinks it fair that he pay for his incarceration and treatment."

"Now that is a guilt trip I'm glad I don't have a ticket for." Alan said, wide eyed.

"It nearly destroyed the poor man and his family. This is a way for him to try to assuage his guilt to some extent but his wound will never heal."

Dr. Tinsley stopped at a heavy security door, swiped his entry card across the sensor and placed his thumb over the biometric reader and the door yielded to his push. They continued down another hallway until they reached another large, heavy security door. The doctor repeated the previous process and they entered a darkened anteroom with some chairs positioned in front of a viewing window made of particularly thick one way glass.

"Two guards armed with tasers will be seated at those chairs observing while you're in the restraint room with Bryan. This is basically a redundant precaution but it is our protocol for such patients. He is securely restrained at his hands, feet and waist with heavy duty materials so he will not be able to reach you from his side of the table anyway."

"That's reassuring - thank you."

Alan began to approach the window and Bryan Adler came into view. He looked unremarkable at this distance, a little larger than the average man with neatly trimmed hair and a clean shaven face. His head was tilted slightly downward, looking at his hands. Just as Alan stopped at the glass, Bryan raised his head purposefully and seemed to glare directly into Alan's eyes. He knew this was not possible with the one way glass but it was quite disconcerting just the same. Then Alan noticed there was something peculiar about Adler's glare. He couldn't quite place it but it felt like he couldn't focus properly on the killer's eyes.

"There's something quite strange about his eyes. What is that?"

"Ah, you noticed even from here. That's very observant of you Alan. He has a condition known as 'Exotropia' wherein the eyes point outward from center. Bryan's case is so mild that it is almost imperceptible from some angles but when you look at him squarely, it creates a slight disorientation. Some people can't place the cause of their disorientation until they are told of it, because his ocular deviation is so slight. And I assure you that despite this condition, Bryan's vision is acute. Try to relax and maintain eye contact whenever possible. If you find that difficult, just choose an eye and focus on that. If you avoid eye contact, it will strengthen his dominance."

"His dominance? I'm the one asking the questions and he's the one in restraints." Alan said, his pride slightly wounded.

"Please don't be offended Alan but trust me when I tell you that Bryan will be dominant over anyone with whom he meets, not just you. It is his nature, and through his intellect and his disdain toward other people, he is fully capable of maintaining his position. He has nothing to lose so no one can take anything from him. He knows this full well."

"I see. Well, let's get this done."

"The guard will open the door and escort you to your chair then come back here to observe. Bryan will not speak to anyone with a guard in the room."

The burly guard swiped his card on the sensor, placed his thumb on the reader and motioned for Alan to precede him into the room. As they approached the table, Adler stared straight ahead as if ignoring their presence. Alan examined the restraints as he walked to his seat. They were wide and thick leather straps sewn onto a heavy duty rubberized base which covered dense cotton padding. The heavy buckles were padlocked and further secured with Velcro to ensure they couldn't come loose. His feet were secured to the base of a solid steel post mounted into the floor behind the chair, which was welded to the post. His waist was secured in the same manner further up the post and his hand straps were chained to a turnbuckle, bolted through the steel chair between his legs. Alan sat down in the certainty that no human being could escape those bonds. Once seated, he looked up, conscious to keep Adler's gaze as the doctor had instructed.

"Good morning detective." Adler started with a faint upward curl in the corner of his mouth. "Did you sleep well?" He asked in a strangely soothing southern drawl.

"I slept just fine, thank you."

Alan could now clearly see what Dr. Tinsley had meant when he explained that Adler's ocular condition could be disconcerting. When combined with the knowledge of his brutal, heartless crimes and his imposing personal presence, it caused difficulty in maintaining composure and confidence. But Alan was determined to do just that and his personal experiences in life and as a homicide detective allowed him more detachment than the average person could muster.

"I hope my eyes don't bother you. I enjoy the effect it has on the drones..." he suddenly cast his glare up to the viewing window and seemingly straight into the eyes of the guard who had escorted Alan into the room. The guard felt a chill as the hairs on the back of his neck raised. "…but I would expect a man of your caliber would be less susceptible to unreasonable fears."

"Your eyes don't concern me Mr. Adler. What does concern me, is a suspicious death in Columbus, Ohio last night."

"There's nothing suspicious about death detective. What comes after is a mystery but death comes to us all, there is nothing irregular about it."

"Let me clarify. A death in suspicious circumstances is what I meant."

"I know exactly what you meant; I just prefer accuracy over police vernacular."

"You're very well spoken for someone who didn't attend school for the first fourteen years of his life. Have it your way - the deceased in this case is Dr. Helen Benson, your former doctor here at Sherbourne."

"I'm well aware of Dr. Benson's passing, detective. I'm also well aware of the importance of a strong vocabulary and I feel slighted that you would think so poorly of me." Adler said, squaring his glare at Beach.

Alan ignored Adler's attempt to bait him on his level of education. "I don't see how that's possible. News of her death was only released to the press this morning and they would not have had time to go to print yet."

"The media is of no concern to me. I know of her death because I was there." Adler spoke calmly, his expression unchanged.

Somewhat taken aback, Alan managed to maintain his composure in the face of this revelation. His logical mind knew it was not possible and he needed to think on his feet in order to maintain his status in this conversation. He narrowed his eyes, taking on a superior expression to show he was unshaken.

"Well now Mr. Adler, I think you're trying to be too clever. You know it's not possible for you to have been there because you were safely tucked away in your bed at the time."

"Don't be facetious Mr. Beach; it doesn't suit you. If you must know, I was there in my dreams."

"Interesting; I assume you know how she died then?"

"Well, it was self inflicted exsanguination, of course."

Alan was now visibly rattled. How could Adler possibly have known these details? He wasn't sure where to go next and the cold blooded psychopath across the table could now see his discomfort. Adler audibly sucked air in through his teeth as his head tilted back, his face taking on a look of rapture for a moment before coming back to Alan.

"Aaah, that's what I was looking for, Mr. Beach. Thank you."

Suddenly Alan realized he'd been played. He knew from Dr. Tinsley that Adler gleaned his only true satisfaction through extracting shocked reactions from people he considered remotely close to his intellectual range. He realized too late that it would have been a case of logical conclusion for Adler to have guessed details that even Helen's former boss didn't know until Alan had told him. Adler had been informed that a detective from Columbus was to visit him and the only person he knew in Columbus was Helen Benson. He deduced that if Beach had come all this way to interview him when there was no possibility he could have been involved due to his incarceration, the circumstances of her death must fit those of his own modus operandi. He had made his earlier ethereal remark about suspicion and death purely to allow himself time to make his deductions.

Alan's regained composure. "That's a very clever guess Bryan. What trick will you perform next?"

"Now don't be a poor sport detective. Surely you must allow an imprisoned man his simple pleasures." Adler said wryly.

"Well, now you've proven your superiority and had your cheap thrill, can we continue?"

"As is your pleasure." Adler now smiled widely.

Alan decided on a more supplicant approach, "Well, quite simply, your name is the last thing Helen said before she died."

"It's nice to know her thoughts were with me even then.' Adler said through an evil grin as if imagining the scene in detail. "As much as I would like to think I could have had some influence on any event outside these walls, my obvious circumstances would not allow it. Dr. Benson was a very well balanced woman and I respected her resolve. I don't believe she would be capable of suicide in the true sense of the word. I do believe there must have been external influences involved."

"That's certainly the impression I get from her family and colleagues and yet the evidence shows the wound was self inflicted in exactly the same manner as your female victims. Is it possible that you have a copycat? I know that many serial killers receive fan mail. Have you received any such mail from a possible killer?"

"Lifeless trolls Mr. Beach. I don't entertain such vacuous scum. I am not some simple, "serial killer" as you put it. I had a mission; a clear mission to free abused children and I drew joy from watching their cruel, worthless parents suffer and die. I'm not some twisted beast who kills out of perverse motives."

Alan glared intently at Adler. He didn't want to indulge the psychopath's predilections any further and decided to leverage the man's ego in the hopes he might have something; anything useful to offer. "You're obviously a very intelligent man Bryan. Is there anything you can think of to help me with my investigation?"

"My goodness detective, it seems you are quite transparent. If you really think that pandering to my ego will get you what you want, you're even more desperate than I suspected. Still, out of respect for Dr. Benson, I'll tell you one thing. She wanted me to volunteer for a new clinical trial, which I refused to do until she gave me an idea of how the treatment works. She said she was bound by a strict confidentiality agreement but she must have really wanted me in the trial because she did tell me one thing. She said it would change the way I saw the world. Now doesn't that sound intriguing detective? I certainly found it intriguing so I thought, why not? I've got nothing to lose."

Beach pondered Helen's statement for a moment and decided there was no further information to be gained here. If he was to discover what the doctor meant, he would have to find out from Blue Sky Biotech. It was time to go but his disgust toward the psychopathic killer before him was overwhelming and he couldn't leave him thinking he'd won. He decided to score a point back before leaving this maniac to his keepers.

"You have a very tenuous grip Mr. Adler. You think you're special in some way but in reality, that tortured, abused little boy you so strenuously suppressed years ago to become the monster you are is still there. He is still at your core, no matter how much you have tried to bury him with education and devious intellect.

The atrocities you committed are just that. You don't spook the grown-ups and you're not a savior but a helpless child who silently cries himself to sleep at night and probably still wets the bed. You don't fool me Bryan."

Alan found himself carried away with his tirade and decided he'd said enough. He stood and turned to walk away as Bryan's face, for the first time in years, displayed the slightest loss of composure in the face of the truth.

"Your feeble attempt to undermine me is of no consequence Beach but you will regret it one day." he rasped.

"You're not the boogeyman Bryan - just a prisoner locked away from society for life. I hope you enjoy your own company."

Adler's arms strained imperceptibly at his restraints. He glared at Alan's back like a tiger stalking its prey as the door opened and he left the room.

"I really wish you hadn't done that detective." Tinsley admonished. "Despite what Bryan said to the contrary, you rattled him and he might cause problems later."

"I apologize doctor. He got under my skin and I wanted some revenge. I didn't intend to cause your staff any trouble."

"I understand. We'll leave it at that. Good guess on the bed-wetting, by the way. One of the guards will escort you to the front door. I'll stay and observe Bryan for a while. I'm sorry your visit was unproductive. Good luck with your case and if you see Jim Benson, please give him my deepest condolences."

"I'll do that. Thanks for your time and good luck with your patient."

Alan was frustrated with his interview with Adler but he felt a faint glimmer of hope. Dr. Tinsley had mentioned the experimental treatment they were going to test on Bryan Adler and Alan hoped that this might provide some kind of thread for him to follow. He needed to speak with Helen's colleagues at Blue Sky Biotech and see if he could pick up any leads there. He retrieved his gun and belongings from the check points, got in his car to drive home and focused his mind on how to approach the interviews with Helen's fellow scientists.

Chapter 5

"I'm telling you Senator Davies, if someone doesn't stop this guy, he'll completely monopolize the pharmaceutical and biotech sectors in the U.S! We've got to form an antitrust task force to investigate Devlin Industries and block this takeover before it's too late." Matt Lewis' face was tense with anxiety as he paced back and forth in front of the senator's desk.

"You need to calm down son - you'll give yourself a heart attack. I understand your concern but Alex Devlin is the most wealthy and powerful man in the country. We have to consider the possible repercussions of such a confrontational action." the aging Senator from New Jersey tried to sooth Lewis' angst.

The long time consumer rights advocate turned to gaze at the elder statesman and sighed heavily. His years of experience belied his relative youth. At only thirty six years of age, he had been highly successful in his field for almost fifteen years and this particular case had his hackles up.

"With respect senator, this situation calls for more than simple concern. Do you understand the level of influence this one man can have over the cost of healthcare if his latest acquisition goes ahead? He's already a multibillionaire, how much does one man need! Is there no end to his greed and lust for power?"

"I hear you son but we must proceed with caution. There are a lot of ducks we need to get in a row before we can make a move against Devlin. We also have to tread carefully to avoid tipping off his allies in Congress before we're fully prepared. If he gets wind of what we're doing before we're ready to fight, he could wipe us out and I have to think about my campaign for reelection."

"I get it. But please; can't I ask Congressman Taylor to at least get the wheels in motion? I've got a meeting with him tomorrow and I don't want to waste any more time."

"OK Matt, go ahead but make sure he clearly understands the need for discretion. That man is prone to loud and visible crusading. It's how he keeps getting reelected. If Taylor agrees, get him to call me so we can devise our strategy together. We need to weight the task force with allies if we want to win this battle."

"That's great Senator - thank you!" Lewis' eyes lit up and his furrowed brow relaxed.

"Call me when you've had your meeting so I can keep abreast of Taylor's movements on the matter."

"Will do. Thanks again." he called over his shoulder as he hastened out the door then left the building to catch a taxi back to his office.

It was a living, breathing shambles of papers, folders, documents and photos covering the desk, chairs, tables, walls and floor. He had been investigating Devlin Industries for the past three years, and his drive to stop Alex Devlin's rapidly creeping stranglehold on the healthcare industry bordered on obsession. Aside from the obvious potential for an all powerful monopoly in healthcare through the latest takeover Devlin was attempting, Lewis' very competent digging had turned up evidence of a network of companies which separately held significant interests in some of the country's major food manufacturers. When these companies' holdings were combined, their voting power was enough to hold significant sway over that vitally important sector as well.

Lewis had used all his wiles and experience to uncover the tenuous links of these virtually anonymous companies to Alex Devlin himself and he was determined to do something about it. The chaotic appearance of his office was an intentional effort to confuse any attempt to locate his evidence and only he knew exactly where to find the vital pieces that he hoped would eventually indict Devlin. He retrieved about forty documents from their various hiding places amongst the chaos and shoved them into the feeder tray of his photocopier. As the machine whirred away at its task, Lewis pulled an untraceable cell phone out of his pocket and dialed a number he had memorized long ago.

"It's me. I need to get a package to you for safe keeping. I'm getting very close to exposing Devlin and I need some insurance."

He listened intently and acknowledged the instructions from the man on the other end of the phone then hung up. The copier finished its work and Matt tucked the original documents into a manila envelope and sealed it. He took the photocopies and inserted them into a binding folder and put them into his briefcase then locked his office and briskly left the building.

Arriving at his destination, he looked nervously around the large bus station for the lockers he was told to find. Spotting them in the far corner of the terminal, Matt composed himself and waded through the sea of people that filled the building. He found the locker number as instructed, placed the manila folder full of originals inside, inserted some coins and turned the key to lock it. Shoving the key in his pocket, he then proceeded to the men's room around the corner, checked the stalls for occupants and entered the last stall to find the false ceiling tiles as described in his phone conversation. Standing on the toilet, he lifted the middle tile and placed the locker key inside, an inch to his left then dropped the tile back into place. He waited a moment in case anyone else had entered the room then flushed the toilet, washed his hands and left the terminal. Relieved in the knowledge that such vital evidence would soon be in very safe and capable hands, Matt left the building, flagged down a taxi and headed for home. He wanted to be fully prepared for his lunch meeting with the congressman the next day and also needed some well earned sleep before making the four hour drive to Washington.

Unknown to Matt, a pair of steely blue eyes followed and observed him from the upper floor of the bus terminal. These wise, knowing eyes which had seen so many things people should never have to, were set in a lean, chiseled face with a strong jaw line. He was handsome but for a deep, ugly scar running from his forehead to the middle of his right cheek. Standing six feet one inch, he was tall but not obviously so and had a lean but powerful frame developed through a life of elite military service and over two decades chasing perfection in a number of different martial arts.

Jake Riley, as he was known, watched to ensure that Matt Lewis hadn't been followed and no one suspicious entered the men's room after he left. Once fully satisfied that Matt's movements had gone unnoticed and no one had followed him, Riley pushed himself away from the railing and started down the stairs to the main terminal area.

Walking through the crowded room, his highly trained eyes searched for anything out of the ordinary until entering the men's room to retrieve the locker key from its hiding place. He then moved to the locker, opened it and folded the manila envelope into the inside pocket of his jacket. With one last visual sweep of the terminal, he stealthily disappeared into the crowd.

*****

At his modest but tasteful Washington apartment, Private First Class Damien Fraser of the United States Capitol Police sat on a chair in his bedroom, polishing his shoes. Following his daily regime, he had risen at five thirty in the morning and gone for a half hour run then returned to his home to do three sets of fifty pushups, three sets of twenty chin-ups and eat breakfast. After showering, he set out his crisply pressed shirt and suit then got out the shoe polish and brush. He was a former Marine who took pride in his professional appearance and enjoyed the reliability of a good routine. Damien had joined the US Capitol Police right after his military service ended and his experience as a Marine had allowed him to breeze through police training. He had served in several different areas of the Capitol Police since graduating and been promoted to Private First class in record time. Since being assigned to congressional protection, PFC Fraser had proven his worth protecting junior members for two years before being assigned to protect senior Congressman Stewart Taylor. He enjoyed his job and considered Taylor an honorable man who was firm but fair and in many ways reminded Damien of his favorite sergeant in the Marines.

Congressman Taylor had made a name for himself as a man of action in Washington. He was a very experienced representative who had successfully headed many committees and sub-committees investigating cases of corruption, fraud, antitrust and other serious matters. The vast majority of his constituents genuinely liked him and he consistently won reelection by a wide margin. His skills and capabilities were very well respected in most political circles and feared by anyone who had something to hide. Taylor's hand-picked staff members were the best in the business and through their skills, experience, mutual respect and trust, operated as a well-oiled machine. He had assembled the brightest researchers, investigators and legal minds available into a highly effective and cohesive unit. Any organization or individual who came under their scrutiny had very good reason to fear swift and decisive justice.

The congressman's long time friend and ally, Matt Lewis had put Devlin Industries onto his radar during a phone call a few days earlier and aside from the obvious potential antitrust case against the company, Matt had alluded to more sinister activities which he wanted to discuss in person. He had asked Taylor not to mention anything about the matters to his team until after they met and went over the mounting evidence together. Taylor honored Matt's request and was intrigued to see what his very competent and determined friend was getting his teeth into. Their meeting was set for twelve thirty in the afternoon and to maximize their time, the congressman had ordered lunch to be catered in his meeting room.

It was nine in the morning when he arrived at his office, his two US Capitol protection officers in tow. He had at first considered the precaution unnecessary and restrictive but had quickly changed his mind a few months later, when Officer Damien Fraser had prevented a deranged stalker from stabbing him. He had already warmed to Fraser before the event despite his initial feelings about the security detail but after the attack, his respect and appreciation of the former Marine rose to a whole new level.

"Good morning Rita." he called out to his personal secretary as he entered his outer office.

"Good morning congressman. Your coffee is on your desk along with the Post, the Times, and the Journal. There is nothing particularly remarkable in the newspapers so I've set the documents that require your signature up as your first order of business before your ten o'clock with the union people and the meeting room is prepared for your twelve thirty with Mr. Lewis. You've also got a conference call with the Mayor at eleven thirty."

"Thank you Rita - I don't know what I'd do without you."

"It's a good thing you don't need to think about that, there's no room for it in your schedule." Rita said with a wry grin.

The congressman smiled playfully, "I wish you could teach my wife some of your famous organizational skills."

"And I wish your wife would teach me some of her famous cooking skills. Please thank her again for the banana muffins; they were delicious."

"I'll do that. Hold my calls until after nine thirty Rita."

Damien Fraser opened the heavy oak door to the inner office, his eyes gave the room a once over and he nodded approval. Taylor walked into his office, sat at his desk and took a long draw of his coffee then looked down at the pile of unsigned documents. He picked up his pen to make a start as Fraser and his partner, George Geoffrey exchanged a few words before closing the door with Geoffrey remaining outside and Fraser taking up his post inside.

"Do please have a seat Damien." Congressman Taylor called across the large room. "You can't stand there all day."

"Thank you sir but I'm happy to stand for now."

"Suit yourself but it's going to be a long day."

"That's why they pay me the big bucks sir." Damien said dryly.

Amused by Fraser's humor but also genuinely concerned, Taylor replied, "From my point of view, they could triple your salary and it wouldn't come close to enough."

"Thank you sir but money isn't everything."

"Indeed not Damien. Indeed not."

With that, the congressman got on with his work and the day progressed as scheduled with Rita Hill's stern hand ensuring punctuality was strictly adhered to. As the time neared twelve fifteen, Damien Fraser excused himself to do a quick sweep of the congressman's meeting room. As he opened the office door and walked out, he absent mindedly scratched at the back of his neck and informed Geoffrey of the sweep.

Fraser exited the outer office and proceeded a short way down the hall to Taylor's meeting room. It was used by other members from time to time as needed but was designated as Taylor's due to his seniority and high volume of meetings. It was standard protocol to sweep the room before each meeting because of its shared nature. Damien held his pocket sized digital bug detector out and began his sweep. After checking all possible bugging sites, he went to the window and made sure the locking mechanisms were secure then left the room. There were two deadbolt locks on the door. One was for the use of other members and their staff and the other required a unique key that was only available to Congressman Taylor, his personal secretary, and the head of his security detail. Fraser pulled his key out and locked the door to ensure no one else entered between his sweep and the twelve thirty meeting. He then returned to Taylor's outer office where Matt Lewis was now seated, waiting for his meeting with Taylor. Fraser knew Lewis from his many previous meetings with the congressman and greeted him.

"Good afternoon Mr. Lewis. Right on time as usual, I see."

"Punctuality means respect."

"Excuse me while I see if Congressman Taylor is ready for you."

Fraser knocked on the door of the inner office, paused a moment then entered and informed Taylor of Lewis' arrival.

"Send him in please." he said without looking up.

"Yes sir and the meeting room is all clear when you're ready."

"Thank you Damien, we'll be out in a moment."

"Please go in Mr. Lewis." Fraser said, motioning to the office.

"Thanks. Rita; any chance I could have one of your excellent cappuccinos, please?"

"Of course Matt, I'll bring it to the meeting room with your lunch shortly."

"Great; thanks."

Lewis entered Taylor's office and greeted him warmly. Taylor busily finished up his notes from the previous meeting and stood to shake his old friend's hand.

"Great to see you Matt; it's been a while. You must have been very busy to stay away from Capitol Hill this long."

"Hi Stewart; great to see you too. Sorry it's been longer than usual but I've been really tied up with this Devlin Industries thing."

"I understand but let's not talk here. Lunch should be ready in a minute and the meeting room has already been swept so let's walk down, shall we?"

The two friends walked through the outer office with Damien Fraser leading the way and George Geoffrey following behind. As they reached the meeting room door, Fraser unlocked the congressman's dedicated deadbolt and opened the door for them to enter. Just as Lewis and Taylor sat down at the meeting table, Fraser's demeanor suddenly and dramatically changed.

"Gun!" he shouted as he drew his own weapon and shot both men dead in their chairs.

Officer Geoffrey's face dropped in disbelief as his mind struggled to process the surreal event he had witnessed. In a split second, his instincts, training, and experience took over and he drew his Glock 45, shouting at Fraser to drop his weapon. Fraser turned toward him and began to raise his gun when Geoffrey squeezed his trigger three times in quick succession and Fraser slumped to the floor, blood gurgling from his mouth. Damien looked up at his partner in complete confusion.

"Why?" he asked with his final breath.

Geoffrey was shocked and confused. His mind couldn't make sense of what just happened. Not only had his trusted partner just murdered his own protectee and a civilian friendly but he seemed surprised and confused that Geoffrey had then shot him. This made no sense whatsoever. He stood, gun in hand as his mind tried to assimilate the event. Rita came running from the congressman's office without fear for her own safety.

"What are you doing Officer Geoffrey? What happened?"

Arriving at the meeting room door, her eyes widened and her jaw dropped in disbelief. She looked at Geoffrey then down at Fraser and bent to shake the dead man.

"Officer Fraser? Damien?"

Rita realized in horror that Fraser was dead then looked up to see Matt Lewis and Congressman Taylor slumped in their chairs, each with a single bullet hole in their foreheads. A sound began to emanate from within her. At first, it started as a low guttural groan then picked up and grew into a despairing wail of disbelief as she walked, hunched over to Taylor's lifeless body. By this time, several uniformed US Capitol Police Officers had come running after hearing the shots, their guns drawn and trained on Officer Geoffrey.

"Drop it! Put your hands behind your head!" one of them ordered.

Geoffrey; still stunned by the event, robotically obeyed the instruction and his gun fell from his loosely hanging arm as he sunk to his knees. As though in a trance, his face was devoid of expression while he slowly laced his fingers behind his head. An officer quickly cuffed his hands behind his back then pushed him roughly against the wall. Another uniformed officer checked Fraser's body for signs of life while two more went into the meeting room, guns still at the ready. Once they realized the room was clear, one of them had to physically remove Rita from the body of her beloved boss. She was hysterical by now. Tears streamed from her eyes like rivulets, drawing dark lines of mascara down her cheeks and she wailed plaintively in denial of the reality before her.

At the end of the hallway, a small man with sharp features and gloved hands pulled a cell phone from the pocket of his overcoat and dialed a number.

"It's done." was all he said before turning to walk down the stairs.

Chapter 6

Alan arrived at the police station in Columbus to make some calls and arrange to interview Helen Benson's coworkers at Blue Sky Biotech. Entering the office of Homicide Investigations, a strange feeling struck him. The usual cacophony of voices and sounds that normally filled the room was gone. The only noise was that of ringing telephones going unanswered. He looked up and glanced around the office for any sign of life but there was no one there. Lieutenant Walker's office was vacant and even the coffee room was devoid of any people. He went back into the hallway and heard voices coming from the briefing room down the hall. Following the sound, he found Lieutenant Walker and the entire squad of detectives gathered around the large television staring intently, some speaking quietly to each other as they watched dumbfounded. Wary of entering the roomful of detectives who so often gave him grief, Alan stood in the doorway and focused on the television, trying to understand what was happening.

"Details are sketchy but we are able to confirm that Congressman Stewart Taylor and well known consumer rights advocate Matt Lewis have been murdered here at the Capitol Building in Washington." the reporter's voice wavered with emotion.

The station cut back to the news anchor who presented some background on Congressman Taylor's history and achievements as voices in the police briefing room began to grow in volume. Lieutenant Walker looked over at Alan and cocked his head in the direction of his office. Beach obeyed his silent gesture, went back to Walker's office before any of the other detectives noticed his presence and was already seated in front of his lieutenant's desk when he came in. Walker's eyes held the look of futility they would often get when society threw up such an affront to civility. While his many years on the force had hardened him to most acts people perpetrated against each other, he was not completely impervious and an event of such magnitude was capable of piercing his armor.

"They're keeping some information from the press." he said softly. "Don't go spreading this around but my buddy with the Capitol Police says one of Taylor's bodyguards went nuts and shot them both before his partner killed him."

"Unbelievable!" Alan responded with a shocked look.

"Yeah, former US Marine with a perfect service record too. Just doesn't make any sense."

"Are you OK boss?"

"Don't go getting all psychoanalytical on me Beach." his usual gruff demeanor returned. "Just because you visited a nut house, doesn't mean you can examine my head!"

Alan gave Walker a crooked smile, "I wouldn't dare lieutenant."

"See now there ya go being a smartass again. Quit screwing around and tell me about this Adler guy."

Alan explained the events at Sherbourne and told Walker that there was no way Adler could have gotten past their security. Walker listened intently then asked about the possibility of a copycat.

"Well, it's possible but I'm confident that if it was a copycat, it wasn't some kind of fan directly influenced by Adler. He's too arrogant to communicate with what he referred to as, 'lifeless trolls' and 'vacuous scum'. His ego is quite different to some of the famous serial killers and it seems he will only entertain people he considers intellectually worthy of his attention."

"Freak thinks he's a rocket scientist, huh?"

"He's surprisingly intelligent, as many psychopaths are but this one is particularly clever. He has unusually efficient powers of deduction and he used them to play me for a fool - purely to get his kicks. Anyway, I don't think Adler really enters the picture in this case. I need to work with what I've got: the man in the elevator, the mark on the back of the victim's neck, and the fact that there was no forced entry at the Benson home."

"So your next move is to talk to her employer?"

"Yes, I've come in to set up appointments with the relevant people at Blue Sky Biotech. They work on some serious cutting edge technology so I don't know how accessible they'll be. I might need to call on your influence at some point."

"Alright, just let me know. I can't see us getting a warrant at this point but I can always call in a favor from the State's Attorney to push it through, if it comes down to that."

"I appreciate it boss. I'd better get back to it - unless there's anything else?"

"Actually there is." Walker's face turned stern. "Collier's on the warpath. He came and found me yesterday just after you left the office. Said he heard I was looking for him - any idea where he'd get that notion from?"

Alan explained what he had said to Collier and why.

"I'm sorry boss but we were alone together in the stairwell. I was in a hurry and didn't have time to deal with his crap so I thought I would head him off at the pass. It was stupid and I shouldn't have done it."

"Damn right you shouldn't have done it! I got enough trouble trying to keep these dipshits off your back as it is. I know this thing has been tough on you Beach but don't go kicking the hornets' nest, will ya! Ah hell; I'll talk to Collier but you gotta be the grownup here. You know you can't change these guys but you can minimize the problem if you just keep your head down."

"I know boss, you're right. It won't happen again."

"Damn right it won't or you'll find my size twelve boots stuck in your ass! Now get outta here and keep me updated."

"I will… and thanks."

Alan went to his desk, found the number for Blue Sky and dialed. A sultry but businesslike voice answered.

"Blue Sky Biotech; making medicine of the future, today. How may I direct your call?"

"This is Detective Beach of Homicide Investigation, Columbus Division of Police. I would like to arrange meetings with Dr. Helen Benson's former colleagues please."

The voice hesitated for a moment then replied in a less formal tone, "Homicide Investigation? We're all distraught at Dr. Benson's death but we were told it was suicide."

"I understand ma'am but I can't discuss the case. We just need to tie up some loose ends."

"Alright Mr. Beach, I'll connect you with Mr. Thomas Finch, the head of our Legal Department."

"Thank you."

Alan waited patiently as the classical sounds of Mozart flowed through the receiver for the next two minutes until a voice came on the other end.

"Good morning detective, this is Tom Finch. How can I help you?"

"Good morning. I'm doing some follow up on Helen Benson's death and I need to interview her direct work colleagues. Can we arrange a visit for tomorrow?"

"That should be fine but I'm not sure what you hope to achieve detective. These are all highly specialized scientists and both their individual and team success depends heavily on each other. They are all well paid but their potential bonuses for milestone achievements are enormous so they would have absolutely no motive to harm each other; quite the contrary. Besides, didn't Helen take her own life?"

"I'm sure you understand I can't discuss an ongoing case but let's just say I need to tie up loose ends before we can close the matter. How many people did she work with directly and what are their names and positions please?"

"Helen worked under Professor Linus Gelling, who is the team leader and head of our research department. He is a highly respected neurologist and board certified neuro-surgeon, but also a prominent endocrinologist and professor of clinical pharmacology. Then there is Eric Rothstein, famous computer game designer and programmer; Dr. Ellis McDonald, Nobel Prize winning chemical engineer; and finally the world-leading developer of specialized delivery mechanisms, Dr. Brian Sanders, so a total of four other specialists. Dr. Benson herself was a renowned neuropsychiatrist, behavioral neurologist and clinical pharmacology research fellow focusing on psychiatric pharmaceuticals"

"That's very informative – thank you. So she was only involved with four other people in the whole company?"

"Well, of course there is the standard interaction with human resources and security staff but aside from that, Helen worked only with her research team. Their work is on the cutting edge of technology and therefore very sensitive and well guarded so it's very much a closed circle. Industrial espionage can be a major problem in our business."

"I see. Well then, just her team will be fine – unless she had any friends outside that group."

"As far as I know, Helen was pleasant and courteous to everyone she encountered but she was extremely dedicated to her work and aside from getting her lunch from the cafeteria, she was always in her secure laboratory. In fact, her keycard records show that quite clearly. I can make those available for you if you like?"

"I would appreciate that Mr. Finch. Will I be able to access Dr. Benson's laboratory?"

"Certainly. We have removed all sensitive materials so that will not be a problem but I will need you to sign a strict confidentiality agreement to cover us in case you inadvertently see anything you shouldn't in the labs."

"You flatter me Mr. Finch. I'm quite sure I wouldn't have a clue what I was looking at even if I did see something of that nature. Anyway, I will have to ask my lieutenant if I am permitted to sign such a document. Can you please email me a copy for him to examine?"

Finch took Alan's email address and the meeting was set to start at noon the next day to minimize disruption of the team's work. Alan began to jot down some details about the investigation in pencil so he could reference them when he wrote his final report. Fifteen minutes later, Richard Collier came into the office and made a beeline for Beach's desk. His face was red with anger and Alan steeled himself for the coming onslaught. Just as Collier reached the desk, Lieutenant Walker's voice bellowed from his office doorway.

"Collier! Get in here – now!"

Collier looked at his boss and hissed at the interruption. "I'll be there in a minute - just need to deal with something first."

"What part of 'now' don't you understand detective. Get your ass in here!"

Collier, seething with anger, directed his glare at Alan. "This ain't over Beach - not by a long shot."

He begrudgingly turned and went into Walker's office. Walker stood as he passed then shut the door heavily. Vigorous argument erupted momentarily until suddenly, one side died down. The voices were severely muffled by Walker's thick windows and well sealed door but Alan got the distinct impression that things were not going Richard Collier's way. A moment later, Collier emerged from the office with the look of a caged animal trying to find a way out. He caught Alan's gaze, gave him a quick snarl and briskly left the office. Alan watched bemused as he disappeared into the hall and turned back to see Walker standing right in front of his desk.

"Have you got the confidentiality agreement from Blue Sky yet?"

"Uh…um…just checking my email." Alan fumbled, slightly disoriented by what he'd witnessed. "Yes, it's just come in. Should I forward it to you?"

"Do that. I'll send it on to the State's Attorney for his OK before you sign it."

With that, he turned and went back into his office without a word about Collier. Alan knew full well, his lieutenant's personal and positional power but had no idea he could have such an effect on Collier. Richard was a long term veteran of the squad and before Walker was promoted to Lieutenant, the two men had been partners. He was known for being somewhat difficult to reign in and the outcome of this interaction had Alan wondering if Walker had something over him aside from the chain of command. Alan shook himself away from these thoughts to forward the agreement to his boss and continued on his notes. Running out of details to record, he retrieved the file he was working on before the Benson case came up and began to type the final report into his computer.

A few hours later, Alan was still tying up loose ends when Walker came out again and said, "The S.A. says you can go ahead and sign the agreement."

"OK but won't that restrict me from using anything I find at Blue Sky?"

"Theoretically, they could bankrupt you and possibly put you in a minimum security prison for a couple of years if you breach the agreement but I wouldn't worry too much." Walker smiled knowingly.

"No, I don't suppose that *you* would worry but I certainly do!"

"Payback's a bitch isn't it? That was for the times you've been a smartass." he laughed. "The S.A. is waiting to talk you through the details on line four."

Walker returned to his office still chuckling at the look on his subordinate's face. Alan shook his head then picked up the phone and pressed line four.

"Mr. State's Attorney? It's Alan Beach, sir."

"Hello Mr. Beach. I'm pressed for time so let me get straight to the point. I've reviewed the agreement and it is legally binding and very thorough. If you reveal any intellectual property such as technological or scientific information discovered during your visit, thus causing financial loss or potential loss to Blue Sky Biotech, you may be sued in civil court and they could also press for criminal charges to be brought against you.

"That doesn't sound good. How am I supposed to…"

"Please don't interrupt detective; I haven't got time. What I can tell you is that state and federal laws supersede any restrictions placed on you by this agreement. In other words, you are not obliged to maintain confidentiality if any information covered by the agreement directly relates to a felony or a threat to national security. Basically, you can't talk to anyone outside Blue Sky about any intellectual property you see or hear of during your visit, unless it can be proven that it directly relates to your case. As a police detective, you are an officer of the court so if you find anything of that nature, it immediately becomes property of the court. Got it?"

"Yes, I understand sir."

"Good luck detective."

With that, the State's Attorney hung up the phone and Alan was left to ponder the situation.

"Clear as mud?" Walker asked, leaning out his office door.

"Thereabouts."

"Like I said; nothing to worry about. Just go and check the place out then take it from there. We'll have your back if the shit hits the fan."

"I hope so!"

Blue Sky Biotech was about ten miles out of the city so he would need to leave at eleven fifteen the next morning to allow for traffic. Alan finished up his report and found himself thinking about food. He had skipped lunch to do his notes and finish the report for his previous case and now found himself quite hungry. Tired of TV dinners at home, he decided to treat himself to a decent meal. He knew a comfortable place uptown with great char-grilled steaks so he grabbed his things and headed out the door. It was a short drive to the bistro style restaurant where Alan pulled into the small car park to the side, got out and locked his car. The aroma of beef on the grill wafted from the building and for the first time in a long time, the detective found himself savoring the thought of a good meal instead of just filling his stomach. It had been several weeks since he'd eaten at this restaurant so walking into the pleasant, inviting interior and breathing in the mouth watering aromas made him wonder why he'd waited so long to return.

"Good evening sir. Do you have a reservation?" enquired the assistant manager.

Alan looked around and saw they were doing a good trade but there were still some empty tables.

"I'm sorry but it was a last minute decision."

"No problem sir. Are you dining alone or meeting someone? You can wait at the bar if you'd like."

"No thanks. Just a quiet table for one please."

"Right this way sir."

The pleasant young man led Alan to a small table in the corner beside the window overlooking the main street.

"Is this alright for you?"

"Perfect."

"Very well sir, your server will be with you shortly."

Alan nodded thanks and sat looking out the window while he waited. A moment later, a smooth and soothing voice spoke from beside him.

"Welcome back. Would you like a drink while you look at the menu?"

Alan turned to the voice and saw a woman perhaps five years younger than he, with a very attractive face and soft, flowing brown hair to her shoulders. Her hazel eyes sparkled despite the low light and her full red lips formed an entrancing smile. He found her pleasing looks and easy manner disarming and looked at her quizzically.

"I'm sorry but do I know you?"

"No but I've seen you in here a couple of times before so I assume you're a local. This is the first time you've sat in my section." she smiled warmly.

Alan felt a wave of shyness come over him. "I haven't been here for a while; you must have quite a memory for faces."

"Only the ones I like. Oh, I'm sorry! That must have sounded very forward. I just meant that you have a kind face but your eyes seem somehow sad. Besides, you don't see many well dressed, good looking men eating alone here. It's more of a couples place."

Now Alan was definitely disarmed. Never before had he just met a woman who spoke to him like this – especially not one so attractive. It was both disconcerting and charming at once, and he found himself floundering and lost for words.

"I'm flattered miss but… I'm sorry; what's your name?"

"I'm Holly. What's yours?"

"It's Alan… Alan Beach."

"Well, it's nice to meet you." She held her hand out to shake and Alan felt the softness of a woman's touch for the first real time since he lost his wife. "So, about that drink…"

"Uh yes, sorry. Do you have anything good on tap?"

"Leave it to me Alan… Alan Beach." she said playfully.

"Just plain old 'Alan' will do fine Holly."

"OK Alan. I'll bring you one of our best microbrews."

Holly handed Alan a menu, backed away one step smiling then turned and walked to the bar casting him a glance over her shoulder as she went. Alan was affected by her attractive appearance and delicate fragrance but mostly bewildered by her flirtatious behavior. His confidence with women had long ago faded and he couldn't even be sure of his interpretations, let alone understand why a woman like her would show interest in him. He began to look at the menu but couldn't help stealing glances at her as she moved around the room. On one occasion, Holly looked up from a table she was clearing to catch him staring at her and smiled knowingly as he jerked his gaze back to the menu. A few moments passed and he saw her approaching with his beer in a frosty mug.

"Here it is Alan; our finest house ale - enjoy. Are you ready to order?"

"Yes please. I'll have a Caesar Salad and an Alberta rib eye, medium, with a baked potato."

"Good choice; we've got the best steaks in town but I guess you already knew that."

"I can't argue with you there."

Alan watched her leave again, almost hypnotically, until she disappeared into the kitchen. He took a long draw from his icy cold mug and enjoyed the complex flavors of the artfully crafted beer. The recent proliferation of microbreweries in the area was a welcome change to the usual mass produced bottled and canned beers and Alan enjoyed sampling the variety when time would allow. Sipping his beer and watching traffic and pedestrians pass by the window, he began to relax and feel some contentment creeping in for the first time in years.

"One Caesar Salad and one Canadian rib eye, medium, with a baked potato." Holly's silken voice brought him back. "Would you like to try a different beer Alan?"

"Thanks. I'll trust your expertise again."

"Oh, I'm no expert but I do know what I like. Back in a minute."

Alan pressed his knife into the thick, meaty steak and it yielded to the blade almost like butter. Holly came back with a Pilsener style beer and set it down in front of him with that disarming smile before breezing off to tend to other customers. Alan couldn't remember such a flavorful and satisfying meal. He had enjoyed the food at this restaurant on his previous visits but realized that Holly's presence enhanced the experience to a new level. Scolding himself for not noticing her before, he finished the last bit of salad and drained his beer as she approached again.

"You've got time for a piece of pecan pie before we start closing up, if you'd like."

"Is it that late already?"

"It's not late but we're closing at nine tonight. The young guy that greeted you when you came in is the owner's son. It's his twenty first birthday party tonight at a friend's bar up the road so the boss is letting everyone go early to celebrate."

"Well that's good of him but no thanks on the pie." Alan said patting his belly.

"No problem detective."

Alan looked down and realized his detective's shield was still hanging from his belt.

"Sorry about that, I usually carry it in my pocket – must have forgotten to put it away."

"That's quite alright, makes me feel safe to have one of Columbus' finest around. So it's Detective Alan... Alan Beach then." she teased.

Alan just smiled back at her. She looked into his expressive grey eyes and raised her left brow slightly.

"Why don't you join us as my 'plus one'?"

"Me? But you don't even know me."

"Like I said before, I know what I like."

"What about the birthday boy?"

"He can get his own date." she joked. "Come on, it'll be fun."

Alan felt like he was being carried away on a carnival ride – and he didn't want it to stop. Before he could think, he had agreed to another beer while he waited for her to finish up and get ready. His head was swimming with thoughts. Sadness and guilt were supplanted by euphoria and excitement at the possibilities in front of him. This woman was so different; she had a very endearing sense of fun, she was bold yet demure, strong yet tender, and attractive yet modest. Alan had heard stories of instant attraction and whirlwind relationships but he'd never believed them to be true - Holly was beginning to change his mind. She returned in her street clothes, which showed off her firm but feminine form, and sat down opposite Alan. Her deep brown, hazel flecked eyes seemed to be sizing him up.

"You were married once but not anymore." she broke her silent study.

Alan was taken aback. He hadn't spoken of his wife since his final therapy session and didn't want to now but he felt so disarmed and magnetically drawn to this woman.

"She died a long time ago."

"I'm sorry. Do you miss her?"

"Every day. Does that sound emotionally stunted? I went to therapy afterwards and the psychiatrist said I needed to finish the grieving process and move on."

"Psychologist." She said matter-of-factly.

"Pardon?"

"Psychiatrists are medical doctors who treat sick people and may or may not do counseling. Psychologists may or may not be doctors who counsel healthy people with unhealthy thoughts or feelings. Since you can't be a detective if you have a mental illness, I'm assuming it was a psychologist."

Alan found that his jaw had dropped leaving his mouth slightly agape. He realized how this must have made him look and quickly closed it.

"Wow, you're full of surprises! Why do you know so much about psychiatrists and psychologists?"

"Because I am one... A psychologist, I mean."

"You're a psychologist?!" Alan looked incredulous. "Why do you work here?"

"Ah, the sixty four thousand dollar question. I'm currently completing my Ph.D, and working in this place allows me to gather data for my dissertation while providing an income to pay my rent."

"I'm sorry but you've caught me unaware. The only word that springs to mind is... wow!"

"That's OK; most people wouldn't have a clue either."

"I knew there was something different about you." Alan said.

"What do you mean?"

"Not in a bad way. I mean I've never met anyone like you before. You're very refreshing."

"I'll take that as a compliment. Speaking of refreshing, let's take a refreshing walk up to the party."

"On one condition... No psychoanalyzing please."

"I promise." she soothed.

The pair left the restaurant for the short walk up the road to the party. Alan was so enthralled with Holly's natural beauty and stimulating conversation as they walked, he didn't even think about his car. The party was in a large but comfortable English style pub, complete with dart boards, pool tables and brass ornaments. They took a seat together at the bar and talked the night away. Several of Holly's coworkers tried to interrupt them to play pool or darts but they were both so absorbed with each other's company they politely refused all invitations.

Gradually, some party-goers went home and others moved on to a nightclub until, by one in the morning, only one or two stragglers were left. Neither Alan nor Holly wanted the night to end but both had to work the next day so they agreed to meet for dinner at seven the following night; one of her two nights a week off work. Alan offered to take her home in a taxi but she said it was only two blocks to her condominium so he took her hand in his and they walked. At the front entrance of her building, they said goodnight and simultaneously leaned toward each other to kiss. Alan's mind flooded with thoughts as the excitement of the night's events cut through his normally composed demeanor and replaced his usual thoughts of work and sadness with feelings of hope and possibility. They looked deeply into each other's eyes and she gave him one last brief, tender kiss before turning to go inside.

Arriving at his car, Alan barely remembered the walk back. He hadn't felt this way in so many years and thought about pinching himself to be sure - but if this was a dream, he didn't want to wake. Holly was so absorbing, so captivating that Alan's one drink at the party had lasted all night and driving home posed no problem. He unlocked his apartment, took off his coat and turned on the television. Sleep would not come easily tonight so he decided to catch up on the day's news.

As the screen came to life, Alan changed to his favorite news station and watched one or two local news items before the anchor dramatically announced a major coup for the network. They had managed to get hold of some security footage from the hallway in the Capitol Building where Congressman Taylor and Matt Lewis were murdered. He watched enthralled as the scene was broadcast to the nation. The sudden change in Officer Damien Fraser's demeanor after the two victims entered the meeting room was very evident and the ensuing events played out like something from an episode of The Twilight Zone.

Despite the surreal nature of the event, Alan's years of experience forced his well trained eyes to watch for details as only a skilled detective could. As the uniformed officers arrived at the scene to handcuff George Geoffrey, the newscaster announced that the footage obviously cleared the second officer of wrongdoing but the veteran detective wasn't listening. His jaw suddenly dropped and the object of his shock was not the crime itself or the announcer's revelation but in the background of the security footage, beyond the crime scene. Alan almost didn't believe his own eyes but what they saw was undeniable. There, at the top of the stairs, was a small man in an overcoat and hat – the same overcoat and hat that Alan had spent hours in the crime lab trying to see past to identify the man beneath. The footage was not totally clear and the face was not visible but Alan knew in his gut that this was the same man who stood behind Helen Benson in the elevator the night she died. His instincts were tingling and his experience told him that no matter how difficult it might prove to be, he needed to examine that footage.

Chapter 7

"**B**oss, we've got to get hold of that footage." Alan said. Lieutenant Walker, still rubbing his eyes and yawning, was irritated at being woken from a sound sleep but also knew that Alan wouldn't call at this time without good reason.

"I hear you but what the hell! It's midnight and we gotta go through proper channels. As soon as I get to the office, I'll get our Divisional Commander to put in a call with the Deputy Chief of the US Capitol Police but considering what just happened, they've got bigger fish to fry. Let's face it; a suspicious circumstances case in Columbus takes a back seat to the assassination of a freaking US congressman! And this happened right in their own backyard so I doubt we'll be getting a response anytime soon."

"I realize that but that footage may show a connection between the assassination and Helen Benson's death. Surely they could have an assistant make a copy for us. I saw it on the news for God's sake – apparently it's not that difficult to… Damn - why didn't I think of that sooner?! I'll call the news station and get a copy from them. As long as the footage is digital, it won't lose any quality."

"Now that's the Beach I know. So get to it and let me get back to sleep!" The lieutenant hung up the phone and settled back into his pillow.

"What did Alan want honey?" his wife asked sleepily.

"Nothing babe; it's just Beach being Beach. Go back to sleep."

"Don't be like that Tom. Remember what it was like before he came along."

"Yeah, yeah, I know but don't tell him that."

"You really think he doesn't know how good he is? You should show him more appreciation."

"Aw geeze honey, I just wanna go back to sleep."

"Alright but we should have him around for dinner soon. Maybe we can invite my cousin Sally too. That poor man is so lonely; it's not natural for him to be on his own for so long."

Lieutenant Walker turned his eyes up in defeat and tried not to think about his wife's attempts at match-making.

"Yes dear." was all he could say as he pondered the awkwardness to come.

Alan examined his options. Washington was four hundred and twenty miles away so even with his police lights flashing the whole way, it would be at least a twelve hour round trip and he had to be sharp for his meeting at Blue Sky Biotech the next day. It was too late to fly and even if it wasn't, Lieutenant Walker would not be happy if he did, so he was left with one choice. His eyes turned to the ceiling as he sighed heavily and resigned himself to his task. Dialing the number into his phone, he knew full well what to expect from this call.

"This is Marissa Wilson." came the painfully chirpy voice at the other end.

"Marissa; it's Alan." he replied sheepishly.

"Wow, Detective Alan Beach calling me at midnight. This should be good! What can I do for you?" she spoke with the anticipation of a spider watching its prey coming close to her web.

Despite knowing what to expect, Alan groaned inwardly at the thought of what he was getting himself into. Marissa was a very ambitious television news reporter from Boston. She had been highly successful at breaking stories before any other reporter and it was due in no small part, to her fascination with Beach and the development of a symbiotic relationship over the years. This relationship became so beneficial to her career that she had transferred to Columbus when Alan did, despite having to go to a much smaller network affiliate. Aside from allowing the reporter to maintain her status as a scoop queen, the transfer came with a promotion to Segment Producer and part time News Presenter, which increased her authority and autonomy as well. The relationship had begun with small favors back and forth and became a full blown quid pro quo situation, which Alan tried to avoid whenever possible. Unfortunately, despite his disdain for her on a personal level, she had proven very useful on a number of cases so he had continued to give her information before other reporters when appropriate.

"I need a favor."

"Of course you do. Why else would you call me - and at this time of night too. Must be something really juicy."

Trying to downplay things so she didn't think she had the upper hand, Alan replied, "Not so juicy Marissa. In fact, I nearly didn't call but I think you can speed something up for me a bit. Your network released some footage from the assassination in the Capitol Building and I need to get a look at it."

"Now Alan; don't be coy. We're talking about the assassination of a senior United States congressman – if that's not juicy, I don't know what is."

"You would be right except I'm not interested in the congressman. There's something else in the footage that may relate to another case I'm working. I can't tell you about it yet but it may put a hole in someone's alibi. It's really not a big deal but you'd be saving me some time." Alan said, hopeful that he had downplayed the situation as much as possible.

"Hmmm… OK, since it's you, I'll get the footage sent over on our network link but I want first dibs on whatever you're up to – and if I find out this is more important than you're letting on, I'll be very disappointed Alan." she said in mock menace.

"Have I ever lied to you?"

"Does that include white lies?"

"Come on Marissa; we both get what we want out of this relationship so let's not pretend."

"Mostly true but I still want to continue what we started in the stairwell in Boston."

"That's not going to happen. Let's keep this professional."

Alan knew she would bring up the incident but it annoyed him anyway. Years earlier, not long after his wife died, Marissa's fascination for Beach led to her making a pass at him when they were meeting alone in the stairwell at Police Headquarters to exchange information on a case. He was in a vulnerable state at the time and it took a moment for reality to hit and to realize the folly involved in such a tryst. He had no romantic feelings for her at all but he missed his wife and the advance had been so unexpected that he came to his senses just in time to stop her hand from slipping into his pants. She was quite attractive in her own way but Alan knew her personality defects and her mercenary attitude would make for a very difficult relationship. Besides; he just wasn't ready at the time and since then, she had revealed more and more of her self-serving nature – she was definitely not his type.

"Oh come on; I don't see what the big deal is - it's just sex after all."

"It's not just sex and you know it. It's a conquest for you and I'm not going to let things get out of balance."

"OK, OK, have it your way spoilsport. I should get the feed at about seven in the morning. Do you want me to burn it to a disc?"

"Yes please, and send it to Larry at the crime lab."

"Alright but don't forget; you owe me."

Alan wanted to put her in her place and point out how much her career had benefited from the relationship but there was no point prolonging the conversation. "I owe you a small one."

"We'll see about that Detective Beach." she said. "Anyway, I'll have the disc sent to the crime lab by about noon tomorrow. I expect you to keep me in the loop. Goodnight."

Satisfied that he had saved himself a lot of time while hiding the true importance of the footage from Marissa, Alan showered and went to bed. He needed to rest and be fresh for the big day ahead but found his mind drifting back to Holly as schoolboy excitement flooded in to take over his thoughts until sleep came and changed them to dreams.

Alan woke and had breakfast then pulled out his notes to refresh his mind on Helen's team of coworkers. Not that he was any kind of authority but it seemed to him a strange mix of specialties. What kind of technology would require Helen's expertise, combined with that of an advanced computer programmer, a biochemical engineer, a mechanical engineer who specialized in drug delivery systems, and the revered and multi-disciplined Professor Linus Gelling? Alan could only hope that they were forthcoming enough for him to make some sense of the situation or he would be left with the security footage as his only lead. He had signed the confidentiality agreement and was an officer of the court but Tom Finch, the head of Blue Sky's legal department, was very protective toward their intellectual property and the detective did not expect an easy time.

Alan's satellite navigation spoke in a clear, instructive tone, "You have reached your destination."

He looked up at the very interesting example of modern architecture that was Blue Sky Biotech's headquarters. It was designed to complement the natural surrounds while presenting an air of technological advancement, and the architect had certainly earned his commission. Alan didn't much care for modern architectural style but this building was genuinely attractive. He parked in the visitors' car park and walked to the dark tinted glass front doors. Entering the building, he noticed a conspicuous absence of security personnel. There were a multitude of small black plastic bubbles concealing cameras in the ceiling throughout the lobby but no uniformed security staff to be seen. Approaching the reception desk, he presented his detective's shield and announced himself to the receptionist.

"Good morning Detective Beach. You're a few minutes early so please have a seat." She motioned to an inviting set of two opposing sofas with a glass coffee table between them. "Please make yourself comfortable. Would you like a coffee while you wait?"

"I like your style miss. A coffee would be great - thank you."

The friendly but professional woman looked to be in her late twenties and possessed an elegant, European beauty and warm smile. She touched an icon on the face of her computer screen. "Your coffee will be here in a moment detective. I'll notify Mr. Finch of your arrival."

Alan was impressed by the welcome he'd received and the obviously advanced technologies employed by the company. He sat on the sofa facing the front entrance and wondered how much these marvelous pieces of furniture must have cost. Their comfort and finish were far beyond anything he'd experienced before and a far cry from what the waiting room at the police station in Columbus had to offer. As promised, his coffee arrived promptly and he couldn't help admire the presentation. A very unusually sculpted cup sat atop an elongated saucer with a small dish built in, big enough for two small imported Italian cookies. Alongside was a matching cream and sugar set and beautifully designed teaspoon. He added some cream, put the cup to his mouth and was instantly captivated by the aroma and flavor of this exquisite blend. So taken with the coffee, he sampled a cookie and it too, far exceeded expectations. Alan was lost in the superb refreshments until a voice pulled him back from cloud nine.

"Good afternoon Detective Beach."

Alan looked at his watch. Indeed it was after noon; almost ten minutes had passed since he sat down, though it seemed like no time at all. "Mr. Finch?"

"That's right."

Alan stood to shake hands with the head of Blue Sky's legal department. Thomas Finch was very well dressed in a tailor-made suit and expensive Italian shoes, much as Alan had anticipated for a highly paid corporate lawyer but his manner was much more pleasant than expected. He seemed genuinely concerned and eager to assist Alan however he could.

"Once again detective, we are all deeply saddened by Dr. Benson's passing and will do whatever we can to assist you in your investigation. Before we proceed however, I'm sorry but I do need to reiterate your obligations under the confidentiality agreement which you signed and returned to me."

"The terms are fully understood Mr. Finch. My lips are sealed."

"I understand why your attitude may be somewhat flippant toward this legality but I hope you understand that in our business, a leaked secret could cost us millions or even billions of dollars in revenue."

"I think I understand but what exactly is it that you do here?"

"Predominantly, we conduct original research and development of novel medical treatments. Once patented, these therapies are usually offered for sale to major pharmaceutical or other healthcare companies but some of the technologies are retained for production in house as well."

"So what's the difference between a biotech company and a pharmaceutical company?"

"Well, the lines have become blurred in recent years but I'll give you the basic definitions. Shall we walk to the lab and I'll explain on the way?"

"Lead the way Mr. Finch."

Finch pressed his thumb against a biometric scanner and the heavy glass doors slid open revealing a hallway with Blue Sky's logo and mission statement emblazoned on the walls. They turned left and proceeded down the hall as Alan took in his surroundings and Finch's explanation.

"Originally, biotechnology involved purely the use of live organisms in development of new technologies and medicines, whereas pharmaceutical companies tended to deal exclusively with chemical medicines. It evolved over time, after many pharmaceutical giants began experimenting with biochemistry in addition to straight chemistry. Biochemical research became so important that some pharma companies set up exclusively biotechnological laboratories, separate from their normal research facilities and others even set up their own biotech companies as separate legal entities. At the same time, some scientists obtained financial backing from a variety of different sources to set up stand alone facilities and Blue Sky was one of those until we were acquired by Devlin Industries several years ago. I hope I'm not boring you detective."

"No, not at all - please continue."

"We now use several different technologies, including biological products, man-made molecular and physical structures, advanced computer technology and others, to achieve our goals. As I said before, we generally sell our patented products to large manufacturers because we are more focused on research than production and marketing but some of the technologies we develop are inappropriate for large pharmaceutical companies so we keep them in house."

"How do you decide which is which?"

"That is a complicated question but basically, if a pharma company has or is willing to set up the required facilities to manufacture a product that has mass market potential, we will sell it to them and also receive ongoing royalties until the patent runs out. On the other hand, if the product does not have mass market potential or requires highly specialized manufacturing processes, it is not generally cost effective for a major player to retool or build a new manufacturing facility. In those cases, we already have the capability to make the technologies because we developed them in the first place so we retain the technology and manufacture in small, highly controlled quantities."

"But if it's not cost effective for the big boys, how would it be for you?"

"Very simply: the selling price. If the product is important enough to secure the appropriate selling price we can afford to manufacture and market it. We also factor into the cost, the potential for refinement of the product and the development of additional products as we learn from the effects of the original. I hope that makes sense."

"I think so. You can learn more from using the product on a larger scale so you might be able to gain more from that knowledge."

"You catch on quickly detective. It's nice to know our police department chooses the right caliber of personnel."

"We do what we can Mr. Finch." Alan smiled.

"Here we are. This is the secure laboratory where Dr. Benson worked with the rest of the team." Finch said as he pressed the button on an intercom.

"Hello?" came a voice from the other end.

"It's Tom Finch with Detective Beach for your twelve o'clock meeting."

Alan looked at Finch, puzzled. "You don't have access to the lab?"

"Not without one of the team members or the president of the company. Their work is extremely sensitive so access is severely limited."

The door emitted a strange electronic buzz and Finch pushed it open. As they entered, the air smelled different and was slightly cooler than that in the hallway. Alan felt strangely invigorated as he looked around the laboratory in wide-eyed wonder. It was shaped like a honey comb with a strange reclining chair in the area at the centre, surrounded by a myriad of electronic equipment, wires, monitors, and other machines. Moving outward from the large central area, there were five separate laboratories with windows pointing in toward the center and the entrance made up the sixth side of the hexagon. To one side of each smaller lab there was a narrow walkway leading to a hallway that surrounded the whole complex. Despite the chaotic center of machines and cables, the whole lab looked well organized and sterile. Alan had never seen anything like it and thought how it seemed as though he was in the middle of a science fiction movie.

"Wow!"

"Yes, it is rather impressive." Finch concurred.

"Impressive is an understatement. It's almost an emotional experience."

Finch chuckled softly and explained, "That's the air. Not only is it oxygenated two percent higher than the normal atmosphere but it's highly micro-filtered and scrubbed, and the ions are negatively charged."

"Is there an English translation for what you just said?" Alan joked.

"The air in this laboratory is what you might call, 'super air'. It is kept this way for two reasons. Firstly, some of the biological and chemical compounds used in the technology are highly sensitive to pollutants and secondly, the negative ions and oxygen level helps the scientists' brains function at their highest potential."

"That's amazing! We could use this back at the station."

"I'm sure you could but I doubt your budget would allow it." Finch smiled.

"I'd like to see some of the brains I work with function at their highest potential."

Finch chuckled again and led Alan into the center of the room. As Alan looked at some of the electronic gadgetry surrounding the chair, an older man wearing a white lab coat and glasses approached. Alan thought he looked to be in his early fifties and had an expressive face that was both friendly and sad at the same time. Totally incongruous to this sterile environment, a beautiful burl wood pipe hung from his mouth. It was empty and clean so provided no smoke or nicotine but it was a habit the Professor was seemingly unable to give up completely.

"This is Professor Linus Gelling. Linus, this is Detective Beach."

Alan held his hand out and the professor took it and shook firmly but warmly.

"I wish we were meeting under happier circumstances detective...and call me Linus" Gelling's voice was warm and smooth, almost hypnotic, and had very faint traces of an indistinguishable accent.

"It's a pleasure to meet you Linus. My condolences on the loss of your colleague."

"Helen was much more than a colleague. I mentored her through some of her higher degrees and she became like a daughter to me. She was a very gifted scientist and an invaluable member of this team. Her husband and little girls must be devastated."

"Yes, Mr. Benson was inconsolable when I met him. I don't know how he will recover from her loss. He's taken the girls to Helen's parents' house to get away from the scene."

"That's understandable. We're ready to assist you in any way we can but I'm not sure what you expect to find here. Helen was not an unhappy person and she loved her work. Suicide doesn't make any logical sense."

"Please, call me Alan. Everyone I've spoken to about Helen says the same thing and that is part of the reason we are treating her death as suspicious. We need to examine all aspects of her life before we can close her case."

"I understand. Where would you like to start?"

"Well, the obvious first question is: what was she working on?"

Gelling looked up at Finch enquiringly.

"I'm sorry Alan but even with the confidentiality agreement, we can't reveal the nature of this project. Linus can explain Helen's role in the research but nothing about the product itself."

"That's OK. What was her area of expertise?"

Gelling started, "As I said, Helen was a very gifted scientist. She had several areas of expertise but her specialty in this project was the development of bioactive neuro-hormonal compounds."

"I'm sorry but you're going to need to put things into lay terms for me Linus."

"Of course Alan. Hormones are the body's messengers and neuro-hormones are messengers specific to the brain. Helen's breakthrough work was in designing synthetic neuro-hormones to have specific functions in the brain. I believe that's all I can say on the matter."

Finch nodded in agreement.

"I see, and what are these neuro-hormones supposed to treat?"

"On their own; nothing but combined with the other technologies we are developing, they will be used to treat a number of psychiatric disorders, such as severe depression, psychosis, violent behavior and others."

"What are the other technologies you're developing?"

Gelling again looked at Finch for approval before answering, "One technology is a specifically designed dendrimer." Seeing the confusion in Alan's eyes, he stopped to explain. "I'm sorry; picture a very elaborate snowflake under a microscope and multiply the intricacy of that snowflake by ten thousand times then make it three dimensional. Now you have a dendrimer. It is basically a man-made, molecular structure that is designed to carry things."

"I think I'll need to stop you there Linus." Finch interrupted.

"I'm sorry Tom but it's difficult to know where to begin and where to end. I haven't had to discuss details of our work with anyone other than the team and the company president before."

"That's quite alright professor. Please continue with caution."

"Another technology involved in this project is a custom made delivery system. I would call it a drug delivery system but it's not only delivering drugs. I don't think I can say any more on that. There is also a large amount of computer programming involved in the technology."

"I was going to ask you about that. I don't understand why you have a famous computer game designer on the team instead of some kind of engineer."

"A good question Alan but I'm afraid all I can say is that Eric Rothstein is an extremely gifted programmer and this project could not succeed without his talent and skill."

"I see. May I look around the facility and speak with the other team members?"

Tom Finch interrupted, "I'm afraid the other scientists are not available but Professor Gelling is the project leader so you've already been straight to the source, so to speak. Certainly, you may see Helen's laboratory but I'm afraid I can't let you see other areas without a search warrant. I'm sorry to change the mood Alan but I think we've been very cooperative and I don't see the need for you to see anywhere other than Helen's work area."

"Not only cooperative but hospitable as well." Alan tried to lighten the moment. "By the way, where do you get that incredible coffee I had in the lobby?"

"Oh, I'm glad you enjoyed it. I believe it comes from a subsidiary of Devlin Industries in the food sector. I can find out and get back to you."

"That would be great! So; Helen's lab?"

"If you're finished with Professor Gelling, I'll take you through."

"I am. Thank you very your explanations Linus. It was nice to meet you."

"And you Alan. I'm sorry I couldn't be of more help."

Alan politely acknowledged the professor's dilemma and followed Finch through the walkway beside Helen's lab, around the corner and into the room itself. It was normally protected by the sophisticated electronic security system but all sensitive materials had been removed and the door left ajar for Alan's visit. As he looked around, Alan could see that Blue Sky had been very thorough in their cleanup and just took a moment to get the feel of the room before leaving. It was a pleasant space with pictures of her family behind a hermetically sealed frame on the wall and despite its clinical nature, Alan couldn't see how it would be a depressing place to work. He thanked Tom Finch and said he was ready to go.

Back in the lobby, they were just about to say goodbye when Finch held up his finger and asked Alan to wait a moment. He disappeared through the glass doors and quickly reappeared with an elaborately packaged bag of the unique coffee.

"I'm sorry we can't spare more Alan but you should be able to find it in some boutique stores."

"There's no need to apologize – this is fantastic!" Alan gushed. "I'm spoiled for life after that first cup so I'll head straight out to the deli and see if they have it."

"Well, enjoy. Let me know if we can be of further assistance and please tell me how the case turns out in the end."

"I'll do that. Thanks again."

Alan had hoped for more from his visit but his limited access had shown nothing sinister going on at Blue Sky so he smiled, patted his pack of coffee gratefully, and left. Walking to his car, Beach began to feel frustrated at the lack of progress in his investigation. He knew that if there was nothing helpful in the security footage from Washington, the case would come to a standstill and not only he but Helen Benson's family would be forced to accept the uncertain outcome. He hated unsolved cases and worked tirelessly to overcome adversity and close them but he didn't know where to turn to next. As his car merged onto the main road back to Columbus, Alan tried to focus on the possibilities the footage may present.

As Alan's car exited the parking lot, Tom Finch answered a phone call from the most powerful man he had ever met. Alex Devlin normally only communicated with the President of Blue Sky on company matters, and occasionally with Linus Gelling but for some reason, he was now calling Finch direct. His boss' boss was now demanding to know why a police detective from Columbus was nosing around in his company. The experienced corporate lawyer looked around nervously, realizing that Devlin somehow knew the very moment Alan Beach had left the building.

Tom explained the details of Alan's visit and Devlin tersely warned Finch of the severe financial risks involved in industrial espionage. Tom was confident he had handled the situation appropriately and protected the company's interests but when he tried to express as much to Devlin, the man spoke over him; clearly threatening him with dismissal and legal action if he ever allowed anyone in the laboratory again without a duly authorized warrant. Finch apologized and began to assure him it wouldn't happen again but Devlin hung up before he could finish speaking. The cold, detached menace of Devlin's voice sunk in and Tom Finch knew that he could not afford to make an error in judgment like that again.

Devlin stood up from his desk and turned to look out the floor to ceiling windows of his massive office near Princeton New Jersey. His tall, lean figure looked imposing in his perfectly cut Savile Row suit, as he turned back to his cell phone and pressed the speed dial button for Kurt Rygaard. The strange little man had been Devlin's loyal right hand man for well over a decade. He was paid strictly in cash and lived under an assumed identity since staging his own death many years before in South Africa. There was absolutely no official connection between them so the billionaire could remain fully insulated from the former Secret Policeman's illicit actions.

"Kurt, find out everything you can about Detective Alan Beach from Columbus Police." he said glaring coldly through the glass.

"Of course Mr. Devlin." Rygaard replied in a thick South African accent.

*****

Alan soon arrived at the police station and climbed the stairs to the crime lab where Larry was busily examining some evidence for another detective's case. The technician looked up and smiled at his favorite detective when he came in.

"Good to see you Alan. I've got the CD loaded and waiting. You remember how to operate the joystick, right?"

'Hi Larry. Yes, I think I've got it. Do you have time to go through the footage with me? Two pairs of eyes are better than one and I'm hopeful you'll have another revelation for me."

"I hope it's not a case of one revelation per investigation. Let's have a look."

Alan clicked play on the control console and the big screen came to life. Marissa had received a full hour of footage from the Washington affiliate so Alan put the machine into fast-forward until they saw Officer Fraser go into the meeting room by himself. They watched carefully and timed how long he was in the room then observed as he exited and disappeared down the hall. In real time, it was just under three minutes before they saw Fraser return and unlock the door for Congressman Taylor and his visitor. Just before the men reached the meeting room, the small man in his overcoat and hat appeared at the top of the main stairwell beyond the meeting room and just stood there watching, his head tilted so the camera couldn't see his face. Taylor and Lewis entered the room and six seconds later, Fraser's body language changed completely as he shouted a single syllable, pulled out his sidearm and shot the victims. Officer George Geoffrey's reaction time was delayed a millisecond by the obvious shock of the event but he performed his duties well under the circumstances. Alan put the machine into slow motion and zoomed in on Fraser's face to clearly see the confusion and his questioning look before his mouth formed the single word, "Why?" Alan then reversed the footage to see if there was any hint of facial features from the small man but his disappointment was complete.

"Nothing!" Larry snapped in frustration. "Sorry Alan but it looks like you're back to square one again."

"Maybe not."

Alan tilted his head to one side and looked at Larry thoughtfully.

"He's wearing gloves like he was in the elevator footage, right?"

"Yeah?"

"That's the Capitol Building. Who could get access to such a secure building dressed like he was?"

"That might be a stretch Alan. After all, he would have had to go through a metal detector but if the thing didn't go off, they would have just let him through."

"Sure but wouldn't they want him to take his hat off for the security cameras at the front door?"

Alan smiled broadly at Larry, "Looks like the revelation is mine this time, my friend."

"Sounds like a possibility Al but how are you going to get the footage from the front door? It's not like they played that on the news."

"That may prove difficult but if anyone can make it happen, it's Lieutenant Walker and his connections. I've got to go Larry – thanks."

"Good luck!" Larry called out to him.

Beach bounded up the stairs to Homicide and went straight to Walker's office. He knocked and opened the door.

"Have you got a minute boss?"

"I got five. What's up?"

Alan updated him on his visit to Blue Sky and the security footage from Washington then explained his request for the security footage from the front entrance to the Capitol Building. "It seems to me that unless this guy is some kind of insider, he would have to have entered at the front, like anyone else. With Homeland Security requirements and the US Capitol Police as thorough as they are, you'd think they would make him remove his hat even if he didn't set off any alarms, wouldn't you?"

"Makes sense to me but don't pin all your hopes on one lead. One of the guards might have been slacking off and let him pass. Besides, even if you do get to see his face, there's no guarantee it will identify him. You still need to find other angles on this."

"I know boss but I don't see any other angles available to me at this point."

"You've been in worse spots before and come through. Just stick with it and you'll come up with something." Lieutenant Walker's face turned slightly red and he looked awkwardly but intently at Alan. After a seemingly indefinite pause, he said, "You know I appreciate you, right?"

Alan looked at the earnest sincerity in his boss' eyes and couldn't help himself -he broke into uncontrollable laughter.

"Goddamn, I knew it! Quit laughing Beach!"

Alan tried to compose himself, and suppressing his laughter as much as possible, he said, "You've got to stop listening to Mrs. Walker boss. I'm really sorry but that was unmistakably her talking through you. Bless her but you know I don't need you to show your appreciation. I know it's there; doesn't mean we have to talk about it." He laughed again.

"OK, OK; that's enough now smartass. You know how she is. Sometimes I could swear she wants to adopt you." Walker raised a crooked smile and continued, "Well, the joke's on you now. She wants to have you over for dinner...and she's gonna to fix you up with her cousin Susan." he blurted out and began a huge belly laugh.

Alan couldn't help laughing along with Walker. Tears streamed down their faces before Alan could speak. "Please tell Mrs. Walker that I would be delighted to join you both for dinner but I've met someone, so no cousin Susan please."

"You know she won't fall for that. She's many things but stupid ain't one of them. You're just gonna have to suck it up." Walker continued to chuckle.

"No really boss - I have."

Walker looked carefully at Alan as the laughter subsided. "You're not shitting me are you."

"I know it seems unlikely but it's true."

The big man broke into a cheerful smile. "Well that's great. You know you'll have to bring her along as evidence though. Mary won't let you off the hook without proof. I'm glad you finally decided to return to the land of the living."

"It's early days but so far, so good. In fact, we're having dinner tonight."

"What time tonight?"

"Seven o'clock - why?"

"Look at your watch dopey."

Alan looked to see it was just after six o'clock.

"You can't keep a woman waiting Beach. I know it's been a while but if you wanna keep her, you'd better get your shit together." he laughed again.

"Damn – I've got to go!" Alan called, already halfway out the door.

"Better shake a leg Casanova." Walker laughed.

Alan rushed home to get ready. Fortunately, his apartment was not far from the station and the Thai restaurant where they had agreed to meet was within walking distance from home. He showered and dressed in record time and walked briskly to the restaurant, arriving with five minutes to spare. He looked in through the glass doors and saw that Holly hadn't yet arrived so he waited outside for her.

It was a pleasant evening and Alan didn't want the complications of his case to cloud his thoughts and detract from the evening so he took a moment to look up at the first stars appearing in the sky and clear his mind for his time with Holly.

"Making a wish?" the smooth tone of Holly's voice broke his concentration.

Alan looked down to see her at his side, looking up as if trying to see what he was seeing. She was even more captivating than he remembered and before he could think, the words just came out, "My God, you're beautiful."

Alan felt a strange sense of panic. He had just said exactly what he was thinking with no filter and wondered if she would think him disingenuous.

"Well, you certainly know the way to a girl's heart." she cooed.

Relieved at her response, he leaned in and kissed her gently on the lips. "I'm sorry to be so forward. I was never very good with romantic etiquette and I must admit that I'm seriously out of practice."

"You seem to be handling things quite well from my point of view detective." She smiled warmly and took his arm. "Shall we go in?"

Alan opened the door for Holly and followed her in. One of the restaurant's staff members greeted them with her hands held together in front of her face in the traditional Thai greeting.

"Sawasdee kha and welcome to Lemon Grass. Do you have a reservation?"

"Yes, it's under Beach."

"Yes sir, please follow me."

The young lady led them to a pleasant corner table near a window, gave them a menu each and handed Alan the wine menu.

"Your server will be with you soon. Would you like a drink while you wait?"

"Would you like something now or would you prefer I order a bottle of wine?" Alan asked Holly.

"White wine would be nice."

Alan nodded to the waitress and she scuttled off with a smile, leaving him to look at the wine list.

"They have a nice New Zealand Sauvignon Blanc."

"That sounds good to me."

Alan put the wine list down and they chatted about Holly's day until their server arrived.

"Good evening, my name is Sally. Would you like to order wine with dinner?"

"Sally - that doesn't sound like a Thai name." Holly said playfully.

"It's my westernized name. I don't think you would be able to pronounce my real name." she said, smiling kindly.

"Fair enough Sally. We'll have the Sauvignon Blanc from Marlborough, New Zealand please." Alan replied cheerfully.

The pretty young lady commended their choice of wine then left them to look at their menus. They teased each other about their poor pronunciation of the names of some dishes as they tried to find something that sounded familiar.

"Why don't we be adventurous and try their set menu?" Holly suggested. "I don't know what most of it is but I doubt they'll serve us fried scorpions or anything like that."

Alan looked mildly shocked, "Fried scorpions?"

"Yes, they eat scorpions, insects, ants and other odd creatures in many parts of Thailand."

"I'm not sure I want to know how you know that."

"No big deal; I spent a month in Thailand studying Buddhist meditation techniques during a summer break from university. It was very enlightening."

"Sounds like an interesting trip. So you don't know the dishes here?"

"It was a few years ago and to be honest, I didn't really learn much Thai language. The food was fully catered by the meditation center so I'm afraid I'm not much help. Anyway, I'm sure this will be westernized Thai food. The real thing is way too spicy and exotic for most western palates."

"OK, let's give the set menu a try then."

Sally returned and took their orders, assuring them they would be happy with their choice and left them to enjoy their wine. They continued talking about Holly's visit to Thailand for a time until their dishes began to arrive. There were several dainty and delicious appetizers with interesting dipping sauces before the main dishes arrived and they talked happily as they sampled the various delicacies. Alan couldn't help thinking how easy and enjoyable their conversation was. There seemed to be none of the early relationship tensions that he remembered from his younger days and it was a joy to have someone so interesting and intelligent to speak with. They moved on to Holly's studies and some of the enlightening things she'd learned along the way, when suddenly she interrupted herself.

"You know, so far we've only talked about me tonight. I want to know more about you. Like, what did you do today, for example?"

Alan was so enjoying hearing about this entrancing woman that he hadn't even thought about his day or the case until now.

"OK, I'm working on a strange case at the moment. I can't really discuss details of an open investigation but since it's kind of in your area of expertise, I'd like to ask you a question."

"This sounds intriguing."

"Frustrating is more apt so I'm hoping you can help. Do you know much about neuro-hormones?"

"I know the basics but as I told you, I'm a psychologist, not a psychiatrist so I'm not a medical expert."

"Well, I have to figure out what kind of effect these things can have on the brain and how they might tie in with computer programming."

"That sounds a very odd combination. I know that neuro-hormones play a key role in brain function, thought processes, mood, heart rate, blood pressure – almost everything really. If this is important to your case though, you should talk to one of my old professors at Ohio State. If anyone can help you on that matter, it's Professor Guthrie."

"What's his specialty?"

"He's into all kinds of things but I know that he's done some ground-breaking research on neuro-hormones in psychiatric medicine so I'm sure he would be your best bet."

"That's great Holly. Do you have contact details for him?"

"I'm sure I've got something in my study notes at home. I can have a look when we get back to my place."

Alan looked at her wide-eyed. "We?" he repeated.

""Why not? I already told you; I know what I like, and I don't see why two consenting adults who obviously like each other, should have to tip-toe around dating protocols. I hope you feel the same way."

Alan stammered slightly, "I do, I do…it's just…well, it's been a very long time for me."

"It has for me too Alan. I've done nothing but study and work for several years now and I think we both deserve the chance to move on with our lives outside of work."

"I can honestly say that I have never met anyone quite like you before Holly. You are very special and I sometimes find it hard to understand how you can really be interested in me."

"Listen Alan...Alan Beach." she teased. "I could give you a long psychological explanation as to why you feel that way but I prefer the simple approach. We've both been alone for too long. It's having an effect on your self esteem and I hope you don't mind me breaking with the traditional boy chases girl scenario but I know that I don't want to be alone any more so can we just see where this goes and don't worry too much about the details?"

"I think I can do that." he said smiling as his hand reached across the table to hold hers.

They continued to enjoy their dinner and eventually, Holly asked tentatively about Alan's wife. He was hesitant at first but realized that her interest was genuine and caring so he opened up and told her the story and how it had affected him. He explained the compulsory therapy sessions and how Dr. Kellerman had helped him to see the folly in his self-destructive emotions but his misguided guilt wouldn't let him move on. Holly listened with the wisdom of a trained psychologist but without the normally intrinsic detachment. Her empathy and warmth toward Alan were genuine and comforting but he started to worry that the conversation was becoming more professional than romantic so he stopped himself.

"I don't mean any offence Holly but I'm worried that we might be creating a doctor/patient relationship here and that's not what I want."

"I understand why you might feel that way but I have a different opinion. Aside from physical attraction, an honest, caring relationship consists of trust, understanding, and tolerance. It should be give and take, and I think we should share our most intimate thoughts so we can really understand and trust each other. I'm not saying that as a psychologist but as someone who is genuinely interested in sharing with you."

"I see what you're saying but this is only our second date. I don't want to frighten you off with my emotional baggage."

"That's very sweet Alan but the pace doesn't frighten me if it doesn't bother you."

Alan's reticence was overwhelmed by Holly's heartfelt openness and honesty, and he surrendered. They talked until they had finished their meals and wine then Alan settled the bill and they began the walk to Holly's apartment. The couple strolled, arm in arm with such an easy familiarity that anyone observing would think they'd been together for months rather than a mere two days. At the front entrance of her building, Holly took her key out and opened the door then led Alan up the stairs to her first floor apartment. It was small but very cozy and inviting. Alan had forgotten what a woman's touch could do to a home and he was instantly at ease in his surroundings.

"Would you like a coffee?" Holly asked.

"Not really thanks."

"Have a seat on the sofa and I'll bring us some wine."

Alan sat on the comfortable old sofa and leaned into its soft cushions, glancing around the room at Holly's family photographs and other effects. He watched as she returned with a bottle and two glasses, which she set on the coffee table then sat down beside him. They looked into each other's eyes and neither could wait any longer; the wine went unpoured. They kissed gently at first then deeply as their passion grew and desire took over until Alan's cell phone suddenly interrupted. He retrieved it from his pocket, looking apologetically at Holly.

"I'm sorry but I have to get this." he said sheepishly as he opened the phone. "Your timing is impeccable Lieutenant. What's up?"

"Sorry to interrupt your date Beach but the Divisional Commander must have some serious juice with the Capitol Police. The footage from the entrance of the Capitol Building just came in on the wire. It's compressed so the quality ain't brilliant but the high definition DVD should arrive tomorrow. Just thought you should know."

"Um…I think I'll wait until tomorrow boss." Alan said as Holly got up and grabbed his free hand.

"I see; things are going well then…"

Alan cut Walker off as Holly pulled him playfully toward the bedroom, her smiling eyes full of mischief. Walker looked at his disconnected phone, smiled and said aloud, "It's about time Beach…it's about time."

Chapter 8

Larry Phillips stood tinkering with the gain adjustment on the back of one of his technical monitors, when the heavy glass door of the crime lab opened and he heard the sound of someone whistling a happy tune. This was rather an unfamiliar sound in the crime lab and Larry leaned back to identify the source. Even stranger than the sound itself, was the sight of who was creating it. Larry knew Beach to be a polite, considerate but somewhat somber man of high intelligence, with a sad and difficult past. Seeing Alan whistling a happy tune just didn't fit with him at all.

"Um…is that you Alan?" he called out as he emerged from behind the monitors.

"Hi Larry. How are you today?" Alan inquired cheerfully.

Larry's cocked his head slightly to one side and replied tentatively, "I'm fine thanks. How are you?"

"I'm good Larry; really good. Can I have a look at the footage from the Capitol Building please?"

Larry had to shake himself away from his confusion to answer. "Sure, it's loaded on the console. You know what to do."

"You're the man Larry, thanks."

Larry was flummoxed. He had always enjoyed working with Alan but even after solving some of his most difficult cases, the detective had never been close to this cheerful before. Larry stood a few feet from his colleague to observe his face for a moment as Alan handled the controls on the console while humming the same tune he was whistling when he came in. As realization suddenly began to flood in, Larry's face cracked into a broad smile.

"You got laid!" he blurted out before he could stop himself. "I mean… er…sorry Alan, I just meant…"

Alan chuckled at Larry's embarrassment as he cut him off. "No problem Larry. Not the most romantic turn of phrase I've heard but I can forgive it under the circumstances. Am I really that obvious?"

"I've known you a few years now and I've never heard you whistle or hum before. You're a really good guy but not what I would call a happy guy – not that anyone could blame you."

"I guess you're right; I haven't exactly been a bundle of joy. Sorry about that."

"Hey, no complaints here man; at least you're always nice to me and treat me as an equal. Most detectives seem to think I'm just some techno-geek put here to be at their beck and call. I'm pretty sure none of them would even know my name if it wasn't for my ID tag."

"I'm sorry to hear that Larry. I enjoy working with you and find your knowledge and skills indispensible." Alan soothed, easily empathizing with Larry's situation.

"Thanks - I appreciate it. Anyway, I'm really happy for you. So who is she? Oh sorry, I don't mean to pry." Larry fumbled.

"It's OK. She's a psychologist I met at a restaurant in town. We just hit it off. It's hard even for me to believe after all these years alone but there you have it."

"Well, I think it's great Al - just great!"

"Me too. Anyway, let's see if we can find the man in the hat, shall we?"

They both focused on the large LED display as Alan put the machine into fast-forward to save time. They couldn't be sure how long before the assassination the man had entered so they had to watch the footage from the beginning of the day and be patient but alert. Eventually, they spotted him. Only twenty minutes before the event, a small man in an overcoat, hat and gloves moved toward the security checkpoint. He removed some objects from his pocket to pass through the metal detector and retrieved them on the other side. Once clear of that check, an officer stood in front of him and spoke a few words then the small man opened his overcoat wide for the officer to inspect and a moment later, followed instructions to remove his hat.

"Bang! Now we've got you!" Larry burst out enthusiastically.

"Let's see how good the quality of this footage is." Alan said as he zoomed into the man's face.

Fortunately, the US Capitol Police had spared no expense in their security measures at the Capitol Building. The footage was shot in 1080p High Definition video through a Carl Zeiss lens. Even zooming in to four times normal, there was virtually no loss of quality and they had a very clear image of the man's face. His skin was unnaturally pale with sharp facial features and wire framed glasses that covered small, cold, soulless eyes, seemingly as dark as coal. Despite Alan's desperate desire to see the man's face, the mere sight of this characterless visage gave him a cold chill and his mood dropped.

"Can you print this and also send it to my phone please Larry."

Larry too, was a little subdued by the sight but he leaned over the control panel and clicked a couple of buttons. "It's on its way to your phone now and I'll have a high quality print for you in one minute."

"Thanks Larry. Is there any way you can run it through the FBI's facial recognition software?"

"I've got a contact in their tech department who might be able to help."

"Good; let's see if anyone knows this guy."

Alan walked out of the crime lab significantly less ebullient than he'd entered despite this small success. He wasn't exactly sure why the man's face had such a disquieting effect on him but his mood was diminished. Arriving at his desk, he sat and glared at the printed image, burning the face into his mind.

"Beach! Get in here!" came the familiar shout from Lieutenant Walker.

Alan went to Walker's office and sat down. Walker had been looking forward to good news about Alan's date with Holly but all he saw in his detective's face was a vacant look of preoccupation.

"Don't tell me you screwed it up!" he lamented.

"No, I got the picture here boss." Alan handed the printed image to Walker.

Without even glancing at the picture, Walker admonished, "Not that dopey – I'm talking about your date!"

Alan's face lit up a little as the warm memories came spilling back into his mind.

"Oh that." he smiled

"Yeah, that. What's the story? Did you break the drought?"

Alan's humor returned. "That's a bit personal, isn't it?" he teased.

"So call HR and make a complaint - after you tell me."

"OK, OK - does Mrs. Walker know about your penchant for gossip?"

"Beach." his voice feigned threat.

Alan told him about Holly and how naturally they seemed to fit and Walker stopped him before he went into any real detail. "Well, I'm just glad to hear you're back in the game so I don't have to see your depressing mug moping around here. Mary wants to do the dinner on Sunday night. That OK for you?"

"I'll have to see if Holly can get the night off and I'll let you know."

"OK, so let's have a look at this guy." Walker said, holding the picture up. He examined the image, emotionlessly for a moment before speaking.

"Creepy little feller, ain't he. At least he won't be hard to recognize. What are you going to do now?"

"Larry Phillips says he has a friend in the FBI Tech Department so he's going to see if he can run it through their facial recognition software. Other than that, there's not much else I can do with it. I do have another line of investigation to follow though. I'm heading out to Ohio State University campus soon to follow up."

"I told you you'd come up with something. Let me know how it goes."

"Will do; and I'll call Holly about Sunday."

Alan went to his desk and called the number Holly had given him for Professor Guthrie at the university.

The phone rang a few times before the professor answered, "Guthrie."

"Professor Guthrie, this is Detective Beach from the Columbus Police. I'm a friend of Holly Stuart and she suggested I call you."

"Ah, Holly – she was a wonderful student. How is she?"

"She's very well thanks but I'm not calling about her. I'm hoping for your expert advice on a matter related to a homicide investigation."

"That sounds intriguing but Holly would have told you that my specialty is not in criminal psychiatry."

"I'm aware of your specialty Professor and that's why I was hoping I could come and see you to speak in person. Do you have any time today?"

"Certainly; I'm marking papers all day so you can come whenever you like up until six o'clock."

"Perhaps I could buy you lunch. Is there somewhere decent to eat there?"

"Actually, the faculty cafeteria is quite good. We can meet there at noon if you like."

"That sounds fine professor. Oh – how will I know you?"

"Don't worry; I'm quite sure I will know you. After more than thirty years as a psychiatrist, I should have no problem picking a police detective out of a crowd of university faculty members."

"That makes sense. Thank you professor – I'll see you soon."

Alan hung up and then dialed Holly's number.

"Hi Alan. Were you able to see Professor Guthrie?"

"Hi Holly. I'm meeting him for lunch today but that's not why I'm calling. My lieutenant's wife has invited us to dinner at their home on Sunday night. I'm sorry but it's kind of like a 'meet the parents' thing. If you're not comfortable with it, I understand."

"Nonsense! I think it's very sweet that she is so concerned about you. I'm sure I can get someone to take my shift that night. Everyone loves Sunday overtime pay."

"Great! I'll let them know and I'll pick you up at six o'clock Sunday."

"So I have to wait until then to see you again?" Holly said, feigning indignation.

Alan was slightly caught off guard. "No...no - not at all. I was just talking about Sunday night."

Holly felt the mild panic and awkwardness in Alan's voice and said, "I'm just teasing Alan. You really should learn to stop being so serious."

"You got me there. What time do you finish tonight?"

"My shift ends at ten thirty. Do you want to have a drink afterwards?"

"Sounds good to me; I'll pick you up at the restaurant."

"See you then - and give my regards to Professor Guthrie."

"I will. See you tonight."

Alan made himself a coffee and sat at his desk looking at Blue Sky Biotech's web site. He knew it wouldn't reveal anything about the technology on which Professor Gelling and his team were working but he wanted to find out as much as he could about the company. Tom Finch had mentioned that they had been acquired by the giant conglomerate, Devlin Industries, some time ago so he also visited their website. There was a brief corporate profile, which while very professionally written and presented, seemed to explain virtually nothing about the company or its activities and holdings. It read more like a public relations shield than a corporate profile. There was nothing to be found about Alex Devlin himself on the site so Alan began searching his name on his web browser. There seemed to be an endless number of links to various different Alex Devlins around the world so he refined his search to display only Alex Devlin associated with Devlin Industries. There were several newspaper sites with articles and gossip about the powerful billionaire but none of them provided anything of interest to Alan so he continued picking through the links at random, hoping to find something relevant.

After more than an hour of frustration, he finally found something interesting. It was an obscure web site that seemed to insinuate, without actually pointing any fingers of accusation, that Devlin Industries was developing potentially unhealthy strangleholds on certain markets such as healthcare and food, among others. Ownership and contribution to the site was claimed by no one and its existence piqued Alan's curiosity. He called Larry's extension on his phone.

"Larry, do you know how to trace ownership of a web site?"

"I can try but the sources of some sites are very well hidden because the owners want to maintain anonymity for a variety of reasons."

"I bet whoever owns this site has good reason to do just that. Anyway, see what you can do please. I'll email the link to you now."

"I'm on it Al." Larry said enthusiastically and hung up.

Alan felt a slight pang of hunger and looked at his watch. It was perfect timing so he pulled on his jacket and went to his car to drive to the university campus for his meeting. At the entrance to the enormous campus he was confronted with a large, confusing array of options and had no idea where to go so he asked a security guard for directions.

"I've got a lunch meeting with Professor Guthrie. Can you help me with directions please?"

"Which Professor Guthrie are you meeting sir?"

"I didn't realize he wasn't the only one."

"It's a big campus sir; in fact it's the third largest university in the country. Anyway, you said, 'he' so that would have to be Professor Scott Guthrie. He works mainly in the Biomedical Research Tower."

"OK but I'm supposed to meet him at the faculty members' cafeteria."

The guard directed him to a visitors' car park near the cafeteria and to follow the signs on the walkway from there. On the walkway, Alan easily found the first sign and enjoyed the pleasant walk through campus grounds to the cafeteria. He entered the modern, inviting atmosphere of the building and the enticing smell of food filled his nostrils. As his hunger grew with the aromas, he felt a hand on his shoulder.

"Detective Beach, I presume."

Alan turned to see Professor Guthrie dressed in a tweed jacket with suede elbow patches and had to stop himself from commenting on his rather cliché appearance.

"Professor Guthrie?"

"That's right but call me Scott."

"And my name is Alan. Nice to meet you Scott - and thank you again for your time."

"My father told me never to turn down a free lunch; shall we order?" said Guthrie, gesturing toward the food service area.

Alan found the professor immediately good natured and likable. They went to the counter and Guthrie recommended a few of his favorite dishes to Alan.

"Any one of those sounds great to me. Why don't you order for both of us?"

"Two Butter Chickens with rice please." Guthrie said to the attendant.

The men waited for their food and chatted briefly about the campus until their meals arrived. After paying, Alan followed Guthrie with his tray to a table in the corner, away from other people. Beach thought how well liked Guthrie must have been as most people they passed offered him a warm smile or a friendly greeting.

As they sat, Alan commented, "You're making me wish I'd gone to university myself."

"Well, it's not for everyone but it certainly is a way of life for some and a means to a better one for others. By the way, how long have you been friends with Holly?"

"I guess I should have said we're more than just friends but we've known each other less than a week."

"Ah, young love; I remember it well. You are very fortunate man Alan. Holly is not only intelligent but she has a wonderful sense of humor and disposition. You would be wise to hold onto her."

"That is certainly my impression but I'm very new at this whole dating thing."

"I see. I'm sorry to pry but you don't seem young enough to be inexperienced in such matters."

"I know it seems strange and to be honest, before I met Holly, I wouldn't even have answered this question but now, everything seems different. I was married at a fairly young age to the only woman I had ever loved and she died several years ago. I never really got over it and I gave no thought to ever finding someone else. Holly is the first woman to crack through my shell since then."

"She is indeed a special woman."

"I certainly would not argue with you there. Now I'm sorry but do you mind if we turn to the matter at hand."

"Of course; how can I help?"

"This may sound like an odd question but Holly assures me that if anyone can help me, it's you." Alan retrieved his notebook and asked, "Can you think of anything that would require the combination of a particularly complex dendrimer, neuro-hormones, cutting edge computer programming and a specially designed delivery system?"

Guthrie looked intently at Alan without speaking.

"I'm sorry professor; did I not pronounce dendrimer correctly?"

Guthrie's head tilted slightly as he continued to study Alan's face and he took on a more serious demeanor. "Detective, do you mind showing me your credentials please?"

Alan was somewhat taken aback by the request but pulled his detective shield out and handed it to Guthrie. The professor examined it carefully and returned it.

"I'm sorry Scott; have I said something to upset you?"

"Not at all but this could be a highly sensitive matter." Guthrie's voice lowered significantly as he leaned forward to speak. "There is only one person who might be working to develop the kind of technology that would require the ingredients you have just listed. His name is Professor Linus Gelling."

"That's right; I met him in person but how do you know that."

"Linus Gelling is an incredibly gifted man. Not only is he well beyond most peoples' understanding of genius but he has been at the cutting edge of psychiatric pharmacology research for several decades. He is the undisputed leader in this field and a former mentor of mine."

Alan felt excitement build as he listened intently, hoping for a break in his case.

"It seems Holly was right to send me to you Scott. Please continue."

"Many years ago, long before chemical engineers discovered how to build dendrimers, Linus postulated a theory that if the right structure and delivery system could be developed, as yet undiscovered neuro-hormones could be used to influence brain function and human behavior."

"I'm sorry but I'm not sure I understand."

"Let me give you a quick, down and dirty lesson in basic brain function. If you imagine the organ is simply a mass of electrical conduits leading from one neuron, or nerve cell, to another and each signal or message that travels between neurons is influenced by a specific hormone, or chemical, then you can see that it is theoretically possible to influence these individual messages or responses."

"Sounds like science fiction to me Scott."

"I understand your misgivings but believe me; this is already science fact and has been for many years, albeit in a very rudimentary and inexact manner. I assume you haven't been hiding under a rock for the last couple of decades and would therefore be aware of the modern popularization of the term 'clinical depression'?"

"I could hardly miss it with all the commercials for various anti-depression drugs on television."

"Quite right. Well, many of the drugs you've seen advertised, and which are generally the treatments of choice for depression, are called SSRIs, or Selective Serotonin Reuptake Inhibitors."

"That's a mouthful!"

"To the layperson, yes but to a scientist, it makes perfect sense. Serotonin is a neuro-hormone which is partially responsible for regulating happiness and euphoria. If it becomes depleted or if the receptors which are designed to accept and react to Serotonin become damaged or over used, this can cause clinical depression. There are other neuro-hormones involved in this process but so far, Serotonin seems to be the predominant player in mood management. Hence, SSRIs are used to block the reuptake of Serotonin to make more of the compound available within the nerve synapse, or junction."

"I thought depression just meant that you're sad."

"Well, in lay terms it does but the fact is that long term sadness is now known as clinical depression and it is directly caused by neuro-hormonal imbalance or the inability of specific receptors in the brain to function correctly. When you consider that every message or signal that occurs in the brain is dictated or influenced by neuro-hormones, it becomes obvious that this phenomenon is also likely responsible for virtually all psychiatric illnesses."

"You said the science is rudimentary and inexact – it sounds pretty specific to me."

"Indeed the treatment is designed to affect specific receptors but when you see the television commercials, they mention a great number of potential adverse events. These unwanted effects are caused by the fact that SSRIs use a scattergun approach. In other words, they affect all of their target receptors when only certain ones require treatment. The result is that areas not requiring treatment are treated anyway and that can lead to unwanted effects."

"OK, I think I get it. So what you're saying is that Professor Gelling may have developed a much more specific approach to neuro-hormonal manipulation – is that it?"

"You are a quick study Alan - that is exactly what I mean. And be assured that if he and his team have made a significant breakthrough in that field, the potential profits could be enormous! I mean many billions of dollars."

Alan's mind raced to find a motive for Helen's death amongst the science and the potential profits the professor had just explained. Tom Finch had told him that each scientist in the Blue Sky research team was dependant on the others for their potential bonuses so he couldn't see how money would be a motive. Frustrated that nothing obvious was jumping out, he pulled himself back to the conversation to focus on one confounding point.

"You've explained a great deal for me Scott but one thing I'm missing is where the cutting edge computer programming comes into the picture."

The professor paused introspectively then turned his gaze back to Alan. "I can only suppose they are employing advanced computer technology to design intricate dendrimers to deliver whatever drugs they have developed to the specific sites they are targeting."

"I would agree with you except for one thing; the computer expert on their team is Eric Rothstein, the famous computer game designer and programmer. His expertise is in designing ultra lifelike animation so it really wouldn't fit with what you've explained to me."

Guthrie scratched his balding head and absent mindedly pushed some chicken around his plate. He seemed very deep in thought but slowly came back to say, "I need to ponder this for a while. There are some avenues I can look down. Can you give me a couple of days?"

"By all means; anything you can do to help would be greatly appreciated. One more question for now though; you said Gelling is altruistic. Can you expand on that a bit?"

"I've known Linus for many years and he is a true gentleman. He has no interest in personal wealth, no family, and lives only for his work. As long as I have known him, he has always strived to develop treatments to help his fellow man. From what I've heard, he doesn't even keep the patents to his discoveries for himself. In fact, as far as I'm aware, he donates them to charities. I've never met anyone as driven and selfless as him before."

"Sounds like quite a guy. I thank you very much for these insights and your time Scott. I certainly owe Holly a big thank you for sending me to you."

"It was my pleasure. I always enjoy an interesting hypothetical discussion. I also love this free Butter Chicken!"

"Not at all - and you're right; this is some of the best Butter Chicken I've ever had."

The two men continued chatting on lighter subjects as they finished their lunch then Alan thanked Guthrie again and left. Walking back to the car, his mind was still swimming with the possible ramifications of such a theory, when his phone rang. The display showed Larry Phillips' name and he pressed the button to accept the call.

"Hi Larry. Any luck with your FBI contact?"

"Well, I've got some bad news, some more bad news, and a significant revelation for you. What do you want first?"

"I guess we'd better start at the beginning."

"OK, the creepy little guy doesn't exist in the FBI database and my friend even searched the Interpol files too – sorry, no hits."

Alan groaned in disappointment. "OK, what next?"

"I tried to trace the owner of the web site you sent me. It led me down a very convoluted and well protected path until I finally got to the source page but as soon as it came up; the site crashed and simultaneously released a particularly nasty worm into my system which eventually shut the whole thing down. I don't know who set this thing up but their skills are way beyond mine. There are not many people around that could build such a fast-acting and effective booby trap as that. It's going to take all day to get my system back to full operational capabilities."

"I'm sorry to hear that Larry - I do appreciate your efforts though. You said there was a revelation?"

"Yes; the source page flared in the split second before it disappeared and left a temporary ghost shadow burned on the old CRT screen I was testing at the time so I boosted the gain and put the monitor into negative view, which allowed me to make out the ghost of the final screen. It wasn't clear but in the seconds before the shadow faded and I got a quick peek at an address in New Jersey. The crazy thing is that if I had been using one of the newer high definition monitors, I would never have been able to see it. Hold onto your hat, Al – you're never going to believe this. The address is leased to a consumer rights advocate called Matt Lewis."

Alan stopped in his tracks. "Wait a minute, you mean…"

"That's exactly who I mean. The same Matt Lewis who was murdered along with Congressman Taylor."

Chapter 9

Jake Riley sat at his work bench looking at a thirty inch LED monitor mounted at eye level behind the bench. He was reading scans of the documents Matt Lewis had left for him at the bus terminal, while cleaning one of his Heckler & Koch MP7A1 submachine guns. As his hands moved skillfully over the various parts and cleaning implements, his eyes didn't leave the screen.

"Advance image." he said quietly.

His voice activated computer responded, advancing to the next image on the screen as he finished lubricating the weapon and deftly reassembled it without looking down. He continued to read, committing as much information to memory as possible. Protocol dictated that in the event of Matt's demise, Jake would open the sealed envelope, review the information and determine an appropriate plan of action after taking all aspects into consideration. As he placed the finished submachine gun on the left side of the work bench, his encrypted cell phone vibrated angrily. Jake looked down at the screen to read the incoming text message. "1600 magenta" was all it said. He knew instantly, the meaning and gravity of the message as well as its relevance to the last few days of activity. His fingers moved over the keyboard and replied with the single word, "Accept" then deleted both messages, changed the phone's encryption code to the next prearranged setting and pushed the device into his pocket. Such extreme security measures had been an integral part of his life for so long that they were second nature, as were all aspects of his chosen existence. The source of the text message was completely trustworthy but even with the extreme security measures they employed, there was always a minor risk of discovery so the choice to be fully prepared was a simple one.

Jake calmly looked at his watch then picked up one of two identical Para Tactical semiautomatic handguns from the right side of the bench, quickly disassembled it for cleaning and continued to read the scanned documents. He cleaned, oiled and reassembled the gun then repeated the process with its twin, his eyes never leaving the monitor. Once all three weapons sat glistening to his left, Jake pushed himself away from the bench and his chair rolled smoothly toward a small desk with a computer terminal and monitor on top. He clicked the mouse and typed a few words on the keyboard, causing a secure screen to appear on the display. He quickly read the instructions for, "Security Protocol Magenta", noted the time and waited for the final seconds to tick away before clicking his mouse to connect with the sender of the text message at exactly 1600 hours.

As the page appeared, a row of strange coded digits rolled and fluttered at the top of the screen. Jake was highly computer literate but the security code system his contact used was only fully understood by a handful of elite computer scientists and hackers. It was specifically designed not only to stop anyone other than the two authorized parties from accessing the connection but to identify the source of any such attempt and cause the invader's own system to shut down in less than one second. Jake's contact had programmed this cyber-cipher system a few months earlier along with the color coded communication pathway protocol to ensure that even if their encrypted text messages were ever hacked, no one could reach this page without knowledge of the color coding system. As Jake watched the screen, his contact's message began to appear as it was typed in real-time.

"There was an attempted trace of Lewis' web site. Search originated from Columbus, Division of Police Crime Lab, Ohio. Automatic shut-down and worm triggered before information obtained. Why are Columbus Police trying to trace Matt's site?"

Jake thought briefly and typed his response.

"Will investigate and initiate contact protocol when I have answers."

"Acknowledged." was the reply.

Jake shut the secure page down and the computer automatically deleted all traces of the connection through its encrypted recycling system. He pushed himself back to the work bench, picked up the three guns and stood to place them in their holders in the weapons locker alongside other assorted rifles, side-arms, knives and tactical equipment then pushed the button on a small remote attached to his keychain and the entire locker folded into the wall, completely concealed from view.

He walked out of the room and pulled the heavy steel door closed behind him until a thick, high tensile alloy bolt magnetically shot past a strike plate and into its locking hole to secure the door. Now in the training area of his well camouflaged home base, he walked past various stations equipped with well used heavy punching bags, speed balls, Kung Fu dummies, weight racks and an assortment of training weapons and armor, then through the door and into the living area. It was an expansive, open plan area with a full chef's kitchen, dining suite, and luxurious lounge area with an enormous flat screen television, and state of the art entertainment system. Around the corner, was a walkway to the bedroom concealed by an arrangement of cleverly painted false walls, giving the impression of one single wall, completely covered by a large work of art. To anyone unfamiliar with the layout, watching someone enter the bedroom, it would seem as though they had disappeared into the wall itself. On the other side, the décor of the bedroom was rich yet elegantly minimalist and dimly lit with variable LED lighting. An over-sized bed was covered in the finest Egyptian cotton sheets, some large Turkish floor cushions lay about randomly and a few pieces of tastefully placed art adorned the walls. On the opposite side of the room there was a hidden walk-through wardrobe which led to a large, luxurious bathroom also decorated in minimalist style. The whole room was mirror polished concrete, with a beautifully tiled open shower area, a bath tub built into the floor with gold plated faucets and water spout, a hand basin molded into a single solid concrete vanity piece, with a large smoked glass mirror toiletry cabinet above, and an opulent matching toilet and bidet set in the corner. The left side wall of the bathroom concealed a doorway to the next room, which housed an exit to the outer hallway, a spiral staircase leading down to the ground floor, and a window facing the street, coated with a tinting film which allowed the occupant to see out while no one could see in. At the bottom of the staircase was a garage equipped with highly sophisticated security systems, protecting several highly customized vehicles and motorcycles.

This elaborate complex took up the entire first and second floors of the aging but well-built seven story apartment building in Jersey City. Jake had bought the building some years earlier then renovated the interior of the upper floors and customized the lower two floors to suit his needs. The five floors above him housed forty families, who paid a controlled rate of rent. The reason for this was partly for the benefit of the tenants but mainly to provide believable camouflage for Jake's base of operations. From the street it seemed a normal, secure apartment building in a respectable working class neighborhood, occupied by lower income families. To anyone looking through the security doors protecting the first or second floor hallways, they appeared identical to the other floors, with eight individual apartment doors. The difference being, that if one could look past the one-way peephole in each of the eight doors on floors one and two, one would see nothing. Whereas on the other floors each peephole would reveal a normal, blue collar family's living room. It was a very cleverly concealed home and base of operations which had served him well for the past few years.

Jake's past and the source of his considerable wealth were known only to a handful of people and his distinguished U.S. military service was highly classified. He joined the army at seventeen with his guardians' permission and applied for Advanced Military Training immediately after basic training. Successful completion was followed by Paratrooper training then he was endorsed to enter U.S. Ranger School where his innate discipline, mental and physical toughness, and positive attitude saw him thrive and excel. Though his age was a barrier at first, his patience, abilities, and obvious potential gained him favor with the Ranger Instructors and at graduation, he was awarded as a distinguished graduate and became one of the youngest men ever accepted as a modern U.S. Army Ranger, with a merit promotion to the rank of Sergeant E-5.

Following several successive, classified deployments, he was promoted to Staff Sergeant E-6 but began to feel the strict structure and constraints of the Ranger assignment may prevent him from realizing his full potential. He consulted with his NCO's and Officers, who recommended him for the Special Forces Assessment and Selection program. Special Forces training began shortly after his acceptance and as he advanced through the various phases, his intelligence, creativity, social astuteness, and durability shone through. His highly advanced martial arts skills and command of the French and Mandarin languages were well recognized throughout the grueling courses and about a year after commencing, Jake became a Special Forces Warrant Officer One, second in command of an Operational Detachment-A or ODA. Jake served two years in the Special Forces, mainly in South East Asia, before he was approached to join Delta Force where he underwent further Survival, Evasion, Resistance, and Escape or SERE training, as well as other advanced courses. During his time with The Unit, he was often seconded by the CIA's Special Operations Group because of his record and reputation.

After five years with Delta Force and many operations with the Special Activities Division of the CIA, Jake was seriously injured during a highly classified operation. He was shot three times in the right leg, which required full replacement surgery and left him with an almost imperceptible but permanent limp. At the same time, a large piece of shrapnel had lodged into the bone spanning above and below his right eye, leaving a deep, rippled scar which ran from two inches above his eyebrow down to the middle of his cheek. He had narrowly escaped blindness in his right eye but his other injuries meant that he could not maintain active duty status in The Unit. A few weeks after his injuries, Jake was informed that his older brother was killed in action while on highly classified Navy SEAL mission. The loss of his only remaining family member devastated Jake but his grief turned to resentment when he discovered details of the doomed mission. His loss of faith in the system overseen by elected officials rather than skilled military strategists, and faced with being forced into a training position or a desk job, made him opt for an honorable discharge from service. Due to the highly classified nature of his many missions and the inherent danger of being involved with such things, the CIA gave him a totally new identity for his new civilian life and Jake Riley was born.

Since leaving the service, Jake developed relationships with a number of people who uncovered and resisted abuse of power by civilian authorities and corrupt activities by powerful business moguls. Some of his contacts were former assets from his secondments to the CIA. They included a highly skilled small arms engineer, advanced electronics experts, and a particularly talented computer hacker known only as 'Equilibrium'. During one CIA mission, Jake had tried to uncover the identity of Equilibrium but was unable to do so. The hacker later sent Jake an encrypted email suggesting he use his skills for more altruistic endeavors once leaving the military and a clandestine partnership evolved with Equilibrium providing cases for Jake to work and intelligence for the operations they undertook. Jake never again tried to discover Equilibrium's true identity as he felt it would be safer for the enigmatic hacker to remain completely anonymous.

It was Equilibrium who introduced Matt Lewis to Jake and together they had foiled several corrupt ventures during their association. Though they rarely met face to face, Jake liked Matt and admired his resourcefulness and tenacity. The consumer rights advocate's death in Congressman Taylor's meeting room at the Capitol Building only strengthened Jake's resolve to continue their crusade against Alex Devlin and his ever expanding empire.

Jake packed a small bag and prepared for the trip to Teterboro Airport, where his Beechcraft King Air 350i Turboprop was hangared. Dressed casually, he left the building through the front door and hailed a taxi then phoned ahead to have his plane prepared and submit his flight plan. The taxi had him at the airport in just over twenty five minutes and as he walked toward his hangar, the aircraft mechanic met him at the main door.

"I'm almost finished fuelling her Jake. Do you know when you'll be back from Columbus?" he asked cheerfully.

"That depends how long it takes to close the deal Jimmy."

"Always wheeling and dealing; aren't you boss."

"It pays the bills." Jake smiled wryly, his deep facial scar wrinkling at the sides from the tension on his skin.

Jimmy had been contracting his services to Jake for several years and was an excellent mechanic. He contracted to several different private aircraft owners but had always favored Jake and was used to providing service at a moment's notice for the rather spontaneous investor. This was not only Jake's public cover to provide believable reasons for his erratic travel and strange hours but there was also an element of truth involved. Over the years, Jake had amassed a significant portfolio of commercial and residential properties throughout the USA and overseas, and was always on the lookout for new deals. His holdings were well hidden through a convoluted structure of investment companies and provided him with substantial financial returns to fund his other activities.

"Well, I hope it's a successful trip."

"Thanks Jimmy. See you soon."

Jake did his preflight check of the plane's exterior then boarded to complete the process and started the engines. He waved to Jimmy, began his taxi to the designated runway and soon took off to begin the brief flight. Cruising at 290 knots, he would arrive at Bolton Field in just over an hour and a half, where a rented car awaited him for the short drive to Columbus city center.

Alan had driven back to the station after his meeting with Professor Guthrie and walked into the Crime Lab to see Larry.

"Hi Larry. I wanted to ask you on the phone but I couldn't talk openly while I was with Professor Guthrie; can you look into the personal finances of Helen Benson's colleagues please. I haven't got time or sufficient evidence for a warrant so we need to keep this one between us. Can you get in under the radar and get me overviews and anomalies?"

"Sure thing Al - give me a couple of hours and I should have what you need."

"Much appreciated."

Alan left the lab to see Lieutenant Walker. He poked his head through the door to see Walker studying a crossword puzzle.

"Hi boss. I need to find out if there was a mark on the back of the shooter's neck from the Taylor assassination. Do you have any contacts at the Washington Coroner's office?"

Walker picked up the phone without speaking, dialed a number from his rolodex and held the receiver out toward Alan. He took the hand piece and put it to his ear.

"Dr. Alvarez." announced a voice at the other end.

Surprised, Alan responded, "Dr. Alvarez, this is Detective Beach from Columbus. Are you the Medical Examiner for the Taylor assassination victims?"

"Yes."

"Can you tell me if there was a very small puncture wound on the back of the perpetrator's neck please?'

"How did you know that? Wait a minute, what's going on here? Who is this?" the doctor enquired aggressively.

Alan fell silent. He wasn't sure it would be wise to spread the knowledge of this coinciding evidence so he simply hung up the phone.

"That was a bit rude." Walker said emotionlessly, his eyes never leaving the crossword.

"Sorry but I didn't want to spread the word and the doctor didn't seem to believe I was who I claimed so I thought that was the best way to handle it."

"No big deal; the guy's a prize jerk anyway. Why do you think I didn't want to talk to him myself." he said through a wry grin.

"Gee thanks. By the way, seven down is 'carphology'." Alan said casually.

"How the hell do you even know that?" asked Walker in disbelief.

"From an old case in Boston. A murder witness had the condition – 'delirious plucking of the bed sheets'."

Walker looked at him mystified.

"Smartass!" he called out as Alan turned and walked away with a satisfied grin.

It was time to get ready for dinner at Holly's restaurant, followed by drinks at a local bar. Alan wished she had more time off that they could spend alone together but he knew she had to support herself while she finished her Ph.D dissertation. The next best thing to being out to dinner together was eating at her restaurant so they could share time as much as possible. Since their first date, they had become very close very quickly and he still found the whole thing a little hard to believe at times. He hadn't felt so happy in many years and it all happened in such a whirlwind. He drove home to shower and change then caught a taxi to the grill. As he paid the driver, a pair of steel blue eyes watched him from behind the steering wheel of a rented car across the street.

Half an hour earlier, Jake had entered the police station disguised as a cleaner, with a false beard, baseball cap and coveralls. He went to the crime lab and found a note on the technician's desk, with bullet points reminding him of the main points of Alan's case so far.

Larry enjoyed trying to piece things together and his notes helped him to get things in perspective. He secretly wanted to be a detective but knew he couldn't pass the physical tests required to become a police officer so working in the crime lab was the next best thing. It allowed him to observe and assist on cases and he particularly enjoyed working with Alan because he valued Larry's input.

His note was headed with the name of the victim and several bullet points outlining pertinent developments, including the small man in the overcoat and some details of the Taylor assassination. Jake was unaware of the links between the two cases but all he had to do was access the computer database from the lab's terminal and enter 'Helen Benson' to find the investigating detective's name and ID photograph then follow him and look for opportunities to glean the desired information.

As Jake completed his search and was turning to leave the lab, he saw Larry staring at him, wide-eyed and with a mouthful of the sandwich he was holding in his hand. In the split second from when Jake turned around to when Larry tried to speak, Jake leapt forward and behind him, looping his right arm around Larry's neck to clamp his carotid arteries until the hapless technician fell unconscious. While ensuring his face was not visible to the security cameras, Jake leaned down to check Larry's pulse, and satisfied he was not seriously hurt, turned quickly to the door and disappeared from the building before Larry could regain consciousness. He then took up a position outside the station, waited for Alan to leave the building, and followed him to Holly's restaurant.

Observing Alan through the restaurant window, Jake noted the obvious relationship between the new lovers and snapped some pictures through his telephoto lens. He then pulled out his laptop, accessed the local wifi hotspot and began to do some research on Detective Alan Beach. He looked through public domains then hacked into the Boston Police website to retrieve more detailed information. He found that Alan was a decorated detective with a particularly high success rate in closing cases and wondered why such a man would relocate to a significantly smaller city. As he dug deeper, he found reference to an Internal Affairs investigation into Alan's partner, Shane Adams. The file was sealed and while Jake's hacking skills were reasonable, they weren't good enough to open the file without a significant time investment. He decided not to contact Equilibrium for assistance with the task in order to save time and instead, found court transcripts in the archives of a Boston newspaper, describing the trial and conviction of Adams.

It seemed that Adams had financial difficulties arising from his divorce and began to skim cash and drugs from crime scenes to supplement his income. Alan had caught his partner in the act, made him replace the loot and tried to counsel him. He even gave his partner money from his own savings to try to help him out of the hole. Adams promised Alan that it was the first time and he would never do it again but it wasn't long before his financial situation drove him to repeat the crime and this time, when Alan caught him, he reported him to Internal Affairs. Adams lost his job and his pension, and spent two years in prison under protective custody. Alan, himself was taken to task by Internal Affairs for not reporting the original crime but eventually decided he had acted in the best interest of the Boston Police Department and let the charges drop.

Jake thought how difficult it must have been for Alan to make such a decision and admired his ethics and courage. He knew now why Beach had transferred to Columbus, as he could imagine the blowback and retribution the detective would have experienced at the hands of his fellow officers. Even though the man had committed a crime - twice - Alan had broken a sacred bond and betrayed his partner. In the eyes of most police officers, there is no justification for such betrayal and they would have been merciless toward Beach in the aftermath. Jake himself had mixed feelings on the matter because of his own experiences in the grey, no man's land of covert and clandestine activities with the CIA. He had realized years ago that things are never truly black and white but his sense of justice demanded he respect Alan's principles and convictions.

Jake continued his surveillance until the couple left the restaurant and went together to Holly's apartment. He followed and watched as the lights went out and there was no point staying any longer. He reached for his encrypted cell phone to send a message to Equilibrium, asking for a secure communication session. One minute later, he received the reply, "2215 black" and signed into the secure web page to read the security protocol for 'black' and at precisely 2215, he clicked on the designated icon. The strange fluttering encryption digits popped up at the top of his screen and he typed.

"Source of trace located. Legitimate police enquiry involving a different case with unknown link to assassination. Staying the night to investigate possible connections tomorrow. Can you get me into Blue Sky Biotech main frame?"

"Affirmative." came the reply.

"Send link and password to my laptop."

"Acknowledged."

Jake drove to a small, unremarkable motel where he paid in cash, checked in and opened his laptop to find a trace link with user name and password for Blue Sky's main frame waiting for him. He wasn't sure exactly what to look for but he had seen the name, Professor Gelling on Larry's note so he started digging into all related files. It was a mammoth task but Jake was a very patient man with a great deal of experience in spotting relevant information. A few hours later, he found a highly encrypted folder called, "Project Hallucineers". The folder's security was too complex for the password attack software he used so he contacted Equilibrium again and passed the folder on. A moment later, the enigmatic hacker replied.

"Project Hallucineers folder protected by sophisticated multilayer encryption and rotating passwords. Will take several hours to crack."

"Acknowledged." Jake replied.

His years of specialized military experience had trained him to survive on very little rest but had also taught him to take full advantage of any opportunity to sleep. There was nothing else he could do toward the case so he showered and retired for the night.

Holly had been lying on her bed watching Alan quizzically as he looked intently through the curtains covering her bedroom window.

"Why are you sitting in the dark, looking out the window?"

"I've had a strange feeling that someone was following me tonight. I'm not sure if this case has got me on edge or if it's just my imagination but I could swear I'm being watched - call it instinct if you like."

"Your detective's brain is working overtime honey. Come to bed - I can take your mind off that." she said cheekily.

"I'm sure you can!"

Kurt Rygaard watched as Beach closed the curtains. It was obvious that his quarry was settled in for the night and since he'd already discovered everything he needed, the highly trained surveillance expert pulled the small binoculars away from his eyes and turned to leave his well hidden position.

Chapter 10

J ake awoke to a knock on his door at six o'clock. He had placed his breakfast order the previous night and it was now laid out neatly on a tray held by a teenage girl at his doorstep. She looked up at Jake's face and was perceptibly startled by his deep, ugly scar. Jake deftly reached out to catch the tray before she could drop it then he retreated into his room without a word as she stood gawking. He had grown quite familiar with the effect his appearance could have on some people and while somewhere deep inside, it pricked at his self esteem, his outer armor was far too thick to be pierced by the reaction of some pimply teeny-bopper at a motel.

Jake's many years of military service had ingrained the habit of eating a hearty breakfast whenever possible and despite the nondescript nature of the small motel, the bacon, eggs, sausage, and hash browns were quite delicious and he quickly cleaned his plate. He showered and dressed then checked his laptop to find an encrypted message from Equilibrium. It contained the Project Hallucineers folder that the hacker had decrypted and compressed to send to Jake via a secure server. He opened the main folder and found several subfolders containing various files.

As Jake read one file then another, and another, his normally dispassionate expression transformed to one of incredulity. The science described seemed unimaginable and if the file hadn't been so carefully secured, he would not have believed such technology possible. Through furrowed brow, Jake continued to scan various test results, scientific reviews, minutes of secret meetings, and other details of the complex technology and its development. Eventually he looked up from the screen, his astute mind processing the potential of such a discovery and he realized grimly, the modus operandi utilized for Matt Lewis' murder and the assassination of Congressman Taylor.

He also knew immediately the value of Project Hallucineers not only to Blue Sky Biotech and Devlin Industries but to the military and intelligence communities. Then and there, Jake understood it would be extremely difficult, if not impossible to prosecute Alex Devlin or his associates and resolved that if legal convictions were unachievable, he would have no choice but to employ his own formidable skills to exact justice upon the perpetrators. He didn't savor the idea of homicide, however justified it may be but when it came to the crunch, he would do what was necessary. The words of one of his Special Forces instructors echoed in his mind, "When faced with killing an enemy; rationalize, compartmentalize but do not empathize or sympathize." It may have sounded callous but for moral men, the reality and dilemma faced by front line military personnel had to be dealt with somehow and that was as good a motto as any.

Having read enough of the file to fully appreciate the ramifications, Jake put his laptop away and went to continue surveillance of Beach. He had mounted a small tracking device on the detective's car the previous night and found it was still parked at the restaurant where Holly worked so he assumed Alan was still at his girlfriend's apartment. The former soldier repacked his small bag, checked out of the hotel and drove back to the restaurant to wait. At eight o'clock, Alan rounded the corner to approach the car park, dressed in the same clothes he wore the previous night. Jake followed the detective to his own apartment and noted the address. Beach disappeared into his building just long enough to shower and change before reemerging to drive to the police station. Jake followed undetected, parked his car fifty yards down the road and turned off the engine.

Alan entered the crime lab, where Larry was sitting at his desk in the corner.

"Hi Larry. How are you?"

The technician looked up with an uncharacteristically impatient glare.

"I'm fine – I wish everyone would stop asking me how I am! I'm fine!"

Alan was mystified by his normally mild mannered and friendly colleague's response.

"Have I done something wrong?"

Larry shook his head and looked down at his desk then spoke in a conciliatory tone.

"I'm sorry Alan; I thought you must have heard what happened last evening. I guess I was wrong."

Alan face contorted with concern. "Last evening? What happened last evening?"

Hesitantly, Larry related the event and by the time he finished, his anger and embarrassment were obvious.

"Damn; I'm sorry to hear that Larry! Do they know who it was or the motivation behind the attack?"

"It happened so fast and he was obviously aware of the security cameras so there's really nothing to go on. I've gone over and over the incident in my mind and as angry as it makes me, I can see that it had nothing to do with me personally. The guy was after information and I just happened to interrupt him."

"OK but you're definitely unharmed?"

"Like I said, I'm fine. I'm just angry that I did absolutely nothing to stop him."

"You're being too hard on yourself Larry. From what you've described, it sounds like he was a pro and it was probably best that you didn't resist."

"I thought the same thing but it doesn't seem to make me feel any better."

"I understand. You need to give it some time. Maybe you should talk to the police psychologist. It helped me in Boston."

"I already did. He said much the same as you and gave me some mental exercises to take my mind off it. I was a lot worse than this before I saw him."

"Well, it's a start anyway. Can I see the security footage?"

"The Divisional Commander has restricted access to it during the investigation but I have a copy on disc."

Larry loaded the DVD and the image came up on the monitor. The two watched in silence as the well disguised intruder moved through the room, carefully concealing his face from the cameras. The man's movements and intelligent approach to his search made

Alan think that he was indeed a professional. They continued watching the scene until Larry's assailant checked the technician's pulse and left the room. Alan pondered the strange situation he'd just witnessed.

"Well, he obviously wasn't interested in hurting you. It seems pretty apparent that he was only interested in getting information and leaving undetected but your arrival made that impossible so he chose the simplest way out."

"That was my thinking." Larry said, slightly less tense.

"Have you been able to find out what he was looking for in the main frame?"

"That's the weird part – he was looking at Helen Benson's incident report."

Alan felt the hairs on the back of his neck stand up as he realized it was now much more likely his instinct about being followed was correct. He looked intently at the screen, gathering his thoughts then turned to Larry.

"This case just keeps getting stranger and stranger."

"You think?!" Larry retorted with uncharacteristic sarcasm.

"Sorry, I guess I'm preaching to the choir. Did you manage to look into the finances of Helen's colleagues?"

"I was just finishing when this happened. There's nothing out of the ordinary except how much these people get paid - I'm definitely in the wrong line of work! They are all on particularly munificent packages, including salary, performance bonuses, and stock options. The weird thing is that despite his huge salary, Professor Gelling has very little money in his bank accounts, his home is adequate but modest, and he drives a moderately priced car. Based on everything I can find, he seems to give all his money to obscure charities."

"It seems strange but that fits with what I've heard about the professor. Apparently he's quite a philanthropist but it would also seem that he likes to keep his generosity anonymous. Professor Guthrie told me that Gelling has no interest in money; I guess he was right. Nothing else out of the ordinary?"

"I suppose that depends on your definition of 'ordinary'. There is certainly nothing normal about Eric Rothstein's financial situation. The guy is worth millions from his computer game empire and yet he chooses to work for Blue Sky as well. I know I said they are very well paid but compared to what this guy makes from his own companies; it's a drop in the ocean."

"Maybe he's interested in the challenge and prestige of working with such a team. He has no real qualifications but he was hand-picked by Gelling so I can only assume it's a matter of pride."

"I suppose that makes sense. Anyway, his earnings are legitimate from what I can see but I'm no forensic accountant. One thing about Rothstein though, I've heard he's a high roller and a pretty successful gambler so a lot of his financial transactions would be untraceable."

"I don't think it matters that much; the guy obviously has no financial problems so there's no reason to think he's up to no good. Looks like another dead end."

"Sorry Al, I wish I could be of more help but nothing really stands out with any of them."

"Thanks for trying Larry – and I'm sorry for what happened to you."

"I'll get over it. I guess it was just bad timing."

Alan put his hand on Larry's shoulder and gave him a reassuring smile then left the room to see Lieutenant Walker in his office.

"I don't like that look on your face Beach. What do you need this time?"

"Sorry boss but I've got to go to Jersey City to investigate Matt Lewis' office. I need you to put the paperwork in."

"You really think his murder is connected to the Benson case?"

"There's no doubt in my mind. This case is probably the strangest I've ever seen and the more I look into it, the more it looks like a well funded and cleverly executed conspiracy. Matt Lewis is the only real lead I have but I'd also like to speak with Alex Devlin."

"Devlin?! That doesn't sound like a good idea - you know how much juice that guy's got?"

"His power and influence could pose serious problems but his company owns Blue Sky Biotech and their technology seems to be somehow connected to not only Helen's death but the assassination of a United States congressman, the murder of a well known consumer rights advocate, and the death of a US Capitol Police officer. Since I can find no motive within Helen's team, and her death now seems to be just one part of a bigger picture, I can only assume the string-pullers are higher up the food chain and are operating to an unknown agenda."

"OK I'll do the paperwork. Don't go kicking any hornets' nests though. If Devlin gets angry, there's no telling how hard his squadron of high priced lawyers and lobbyists could slap us. Besides, you'll be out of your jurisdiction so your badge won't mean much there. I guess you're going to eat into my budget and request a return flight too."

"Unless you want me to drive?"

"No way! If you drive, you won't be back for Sunday dinner and my wife would kill both of us!"

Alan smiled broadly. "Don't worry boss; we'll be there Sunday night to protect you from the missus."

"Always a smartass. Now get outta here – your plane ticket will be waiting at the airport. Stay out of trouble!"

Alan went to his car and drove home to pack a bag. Jake followed and watched as Alan reemerged from his building with an overnight bag, and quickly typed a text message on his encrypted cell phone. A few minutes later, he received a reply from Equilibrium.

"Detective Beach is booked on the 1330 flight to Newark. What is he up to?"

Jake contemplated the possibilities. Perhaps the Columbus Police crime lab technician had been able to discover the location of Matt Lewis' office before Equilibrium's computer worm did its job or maybe the detective was going to investigate Blue Sky Biotech's parent company, Devlin Industries just outside Princeton. Either way, he needed to get back to New Jersey so he started the car and calmly drove toward Bolton Field, calling ahead to have his King Air prepared for the trip and submit his flight plan. Knowing that police department budget constraints would demand Alan's flight have at least one stop before arrival at Newark, he was confident that at normal cruising speed, his turboprop Beechcraft would have him back at Teterboro Airport in plenty of time to get a taxi home then drive to Newark Airport to intercept Detective Beach and continue surveillance.

The short flight was uneventful and Jake landed at Teterboro ahead of schedule due to a decent tailwind. He checked his watch to see that Alan's plane had taken off from Columbus only half an hour earlier so he would easily make it to Newark Airport in time to park and await the detective's arrival. Jimmy's smiling face greeted him as he taxied into the private hangar and exited the craft.

"Make another million boss?"

"Slow and steady wins the race Jimmy. How's that new tool set I sent you?"

"Unbelievable! How did you know my old set needed replacing?"

"Just thought you were due for a bonus. I'm glad they could deliver it before I got back."

"I don't know what to say Jake. Thanks a million! I was going to start replacing them one at a time but Sarah and I are getting married in a few months and this means I can put the money away for our honeymoon."

"I wouldn't worry too much about paying for the honeymoon. Check your bank account; I put a wedding present in there for you."

Jimmy's jaw dropped in amazement.

"Sarah will want to kiss you on the lips when I tell her!"

"I think she'd better save that for you my friend."

Jake walked toward the taxi Jimmy had arranged for him. Jimmy watched him admiringly and called out, "I don't know how I got so lucky to work for you boss."

"Luck's got nothing to do with it Jimmy. Your work speaks for itself."

With that, the taxi drove off toward Jersey City and Jake's home base.

Half an hour later, at thirty thousand feet and about fifty miles east of Jake, Alan Beach looked up as the 'Fasten Seatbelts" sign came on with a bong and the Purser spoke over the intercom.

"Ladies and gentlemen; the captain has turned on the seatbelt lights for our descent into Newark International Airport. Please fasten your seatbelts and return your seats to the upright position, put away your tray tables and turn off all electronic devices. We'll be landing on schedule in fifteen minutes. Thank you."

Alan turned closed his laptop and complied with her other instructions. A flustered businessman beside him was still furiously working on his computer and obviously annoyed at the interruption. He turned to Alan, red-faced and demanding.

"Why the hell do we have to turn off our laptops? It's not like they really interfere with anything. Well I'm not turning mine off – what are they going to do about it!"

Alan smiled calmly at the man and opened his jacket to show his detective's shield. The tense businessman's face went from red to crimson as he slammed his laptop closed, fastened his seat belt and sat bolt upright until they landed.

After disembarking the aircraft, Alan strolled down the concourse to meet a New Jersey Police officer. He was a pleasant young fellow, who was to loan Alan a police issue Glock, since Walker hadn't had enough time to get the necessary approvals for Alan to fly armed. He checked Alan's identification, they signed the paperwork, and the young officer gave him the weapon and wished him luck. Alan then proceeded to one of the many competing booths to rent a car. He proceeded to the allocated car park, opened the plain white sedan and retrieved the map from the glove compartment. It was ten years since he'd been to New Jersey and it was his first time in Jersey City so he spent some time familiarizing himself with the city's layout and main roads. Alan had a gift for understanding and memorizing maps and liked to take advantage of that gift to ensure he only needed to look at the map again once he was already close to his destination. Satisfied, he folded the map so that only the vicinity of Matt Lewis' office was exposed and drove toward Jersey City.

As Alan's rented car exited the car park, Jake's thumb pressed on the starter button of his customized BMW R1200 R and the powerful but quiet twin cylinder boxer engine came to life. He had been a motorcycle enthusiast since he started riding dirt bikes in his early teens and his secure garage housed five different bikes. Jake chose the R 1200 R for the night's task because of its outstanding handling, constant reliable power and excellent braking. Experience had taught him that tailing a subject undetected was much more easily accomplished on such a machine than it was in a car. If there was the possibility of an active pursuit, the bike would be almost useless against a car but Jake expected no such behavior from the Columbus police detective so the bike was the best way to maintain the appropriate distance and avoid discovery.

They neared the area in which Matt's office was located and Jake fell back further, knowing where Alan was headed. He let the car disappear from view and cut through an alley to emerge at the other side of the row of single story store fronts where his former colleague's office was located. He concealed himself behind a parked car, turned the bike's engine off and pushed down the kickstand then sat watching as Alan slowly approached, looking for street numbers before pulling to a stop directly in front of Matt's office.

Alan looked at the frontage, wondering why a successful lobbyist would locate his office in such a place but as he approached the window, he could tell by the cheap furniture and chaos that Matt Lewis didn't much care about appearances. The detective deduced that Lewis likely chose the spot either for its possible proximity to his home or for the sake of anonymity and privacy. There were no markings or advertising on the windows; only the street number confirmed this was the right place and Alan was sure that most anyone looking through the window might assume the unit was derelict. He reached for the door handle and expected to have to try picking the lock but instead found that it pushed open beneath his hand. Looking at the soft wooden door jamb, it was obvious that someone had forced the door open. The bolt had gone right through the latch and the metal keep had fallen onto the floor several feet inside the office. Someone had definitely broken into the office of a murdered man and any misgivings Alan held about his conspiracy theory vanished with the discovery.

He slowly entered the office with his hand on his borrowed New Jersey Police issue Glock 9mm, and called out, "Police – is anyone here?"

As expected, there was no reply so he took his hand off his weapon's handle and proceeded toward the desk at the far end of the office. Alan had to carefully pick his way through the files, papers and detritus strewn about on the floor until he was close enough to see the top of the desk was just as chaotic. He could only assume that whoever had broken in wasn't concerned about disturbing the scene or being caught. Alan brought all his skills and experience to bear as he sifted through the mess and after two hours of searching he found only some news articles about Alex Devlin and some hand written notes about the mogul's movements. It would take days to properly examine all the contents of the office but Alan was confident from his search that there was nothing incriminating to be found and if there ever had been, it had already been removed. He sighed in resignation, knowing the only avenue left to him was to try to speak with possibly the most powerful man in America. Even if he could get an audience with the man, it was extremely unlikely the meeting would lead anywhere. Alan shook his head in disappointment as he thought about telling Jim Benson he couldn't bring his wife's killer to justice. He wasn't giving up yet but the outlook was grim.

Jake watched as Alan exited the office in obvious disappointment and couldn't help developing a good deal of respect for the detective's tenacity and resourcefulness. He considered the virtues of telling Beach what he knew and showing him the documents Lewis had given him for safe keeping but realized that such knowledge may bring danger to the man so he continued his quiet surveillance.

Alan got into his car and drove to his hotel in the Waterfront District downtown. As he drove, he dialed directory assistance and was put through to Devlin Industries' headquarters.

"Good evening, Devlin Industries. How may I direct your call?"

"I'd like to speak with Alex Devlin's secretary please."

"May I ask what it concerns?"

"I'm a police detective and I need to make an appointment to see Mr. Devlin."

There was a pause before the operator replied, "Please hold."

The phone rang eight times before a man's voice answered, "This is Peter Fenwick, Mr. Devlin's personal assistant. And you are detective…?"

"Beach. I would like to meet Mr. Devlin to ask some questions about an ongoing investigation."

"How does this pertain to Mr. Devlin?"

"I can't discuss details of the case but Mr. Devlin may have information that can assist in our enquiries."

"Mr. Devlin is a very busy man detective. Unless you can be more specific, you'll have to go through our legal counsel."

"There's no need for that. I'm sure that Mr. Devlin will want to dispel any possible doubts about the integrity of Blue Sky Biotech's security systems and a few minutes of his time will suffice."

"Hold the line please."

Alan waited as a string quartet played baroque music down the telephone line. A moment later, the music stopped and the P.A's voice returned.

"Are you certain the Head of Security can't handle the matter satisfactorily?"

"I don't mean to be indelicate but the issue may concern the Security Department's own protocols." Alan continued the lie to gain access.

"Alright; Mr. Devlin will see you tomorrow at eleven o'clock sharp for ten minutes only. Is that clear?"

Alan felt anger welling up at the impertinence of this officious man but controlled his anger to ensure he was allowed to see Devlin without going through legal channels.

"Yes, quite clear. Thank you."

"Are you staying in Princeton?"

"No, why do you ask?"

"I want to ensure that you arrive in time. Where are you staying?"

"I'm in the Waterfront District in Jersey City."

"Well you'll need to leave there by no later than nine o'clock to allow for traffic. I assume you have a map?"

Alan could no longer contain his contempt and said disdainfully, "Mr. Fenwick; I am a veteran police detective. I am quite capable of keeping an appointment."

"Indeed. I'll expect you at eleven tomorrow then."

As Alan approached the hotel, he was still seething at Fenwick's insolence and took a moment to compose himself before stopping at the hotel's valet stand. A cheerful young man in a smart uniform opened his car door to greet him. Alan grabbed his bag from the passenger seat and got out of the car.

"Good evening sir. Shall I park your car for you?"

"Yes please." Alan said, relieved to experience some civility.

"Are you staying at the hotel sir? Shall I take your bag for you?"

"I'm just checking in but I'll carry my own bag thank you."

"Can I have your name for the receipt please?"

"Beach."

The young man wrote on the parking receipt and tore the stub off and handed it to Alan.

"Enjoy your stay Detective Beach."

"Detective...How did you...?"

"I've been doing this for over five years, sir. I know a police detective when I see one. Welcome to Jersey City."

Alan smiled at the amiable valet. "It's that obvious, is it?"

"Actually, no but I saw your shield as you got out of the car, it pays to be observant." he said with a wink.

Alan had to chuckle, relieved to meet someone so clever and pleasant. The young man's angling for a good tip was amusing and completely inoffensive so he stripped a ten dollar bill from his billfold and handed it over.

"Thank you detective - completely unexpected though." he continued, broadening his smile.

Alan just laughed and shook his head as he climbed the stairs into the lobby and proceeded to the reception desk.

"Welcome sir. Are you checking in?"

"Yes, the name is Beach."

"Yes Mr. Beach; your room is prepaid. I just need a credit card imprint to cover any incidentals please."

Alan pulled out his card and handed it to the receptionist. She gave him his room key and asked, "Would you like someone to carry your bag sir?"

"No thanks, it's not heavy."

"Enjoy your stay then Mr. Beach."

Alan went to his room for a shower then got ready to go out and find somewhere to eat. He preferred to explore the local area over dining in hotels when he was out of town so now refreshed, he went back down to the lobby and continued outside. The cheerful young valet saw him coming and gave him a warm smile.

"Are you not dining in the hotel Detective Beach?"

"No, I like to get out and find a good local restaurant. Any suggestions?"

"Yes sir. There are quite a few eateries on Grove Street so I would suggest a taxi then just walk around until you find something you like."

"Great, thanks for your help."

"My pleasure – enjoy."

The valet hailed a taxi and opened the door for Alan and told the driver where to drop him off. It was a short trip and soon Alan was strolling along the street, looking at shop fronts and restaurants and trying to decide what he wanted to eat. He had walked about a mile thinking the exercise would pique his appetite when he suddenly felt a sharp pull on his right arm and a violent jolt against his left shoulder as he was physically dragged into a dark alley and forced behind a dumpster. His first instinct was to reach for his sidearm but as he did so, a powerful hand smashed down on his wrist shooting a jolt of white hot pain through his joint. He felt more strong hands on him as he was spun violently backward into the brick wall and his gun was taken from its holster.

"You won't be needing this." said a menacing voice then a swift blow to Alan's solar plexus completely knocked the wind out of him.

"Just finish him and let's get out of here." urged another voice as Alan tried desperately to refill his lungs.

Struggling for breath, he managed to whisper, "I'm a cop."

"Is that all you got Beach?" was the tormenting reply. "We know exactly who you are detective and that's why this alley is the last thing you're ever going to see but I'm going to have some fun before you're done."

Alan forced himself to straighten up just in time to see the man's huge fist cocked and ready to fly into his face. His arms were held tightly on either side so he shut his eyes and braced himself for impact but it didn't come. Instead, he heard a muffled cry of pain and a loud crack then opened his eyes to see the most frightening display of controlled violence he'd ever witnessed. A large man dressed in black motorcycle leathers had appeared from behind the first would-be assassin and in one alarmingly swift movement, wrenched the cocked arm backward and completely out of its socket. Almost simultaneously, his free arm shot around the assailant's face to smother his cry of pain then pulled back and around until his neck snapped violently. Alan's eyes just caught his rescuer dropping the body then turning his attention to the other two assailants with startling speed. He tried to watch as the leather-clad killing machine launched his attack before the other two men could even prepare to defend themselves but he could only hear whooshes of broken air as several blurred arm movements left one man dead where he stood, his nasal bone having been violently jammed through his skull and into his brain. As the second lifeless body dropped to the ground, the third man slumped against the wall from another unseen blow and before Alan could open his mouth to try to stop the carnage, his savior struck savagely into the hapless attacker's throat, crushing his larynx beyond salvation.

Alan stood wide-eyed, his mouth agape, and his brain trying to process the scene before him. He turned to look at the leather clad man and was filled with dread at the sight of his cold, emotionless face. He tried not to focus on the deep, ugly scar running from above his brow almost to his jaw, as he searched his strangely serene, steely blue eyes for any kind of emotion but they were completely devoid of sentiment. The experienced detective had never even heard of such a thing, let alone witnessing it himself. He tried to collect his thoughts but didn't need to. The man put a firm hand on Alan's shoulder and said simply,

"It's time to leave."

With that, he led Alan onto the street, flagged down a taxi then turned the beleaguered detective's body to face him and looked directly into his eyes.

"Those men were going to kill you. They were not going to reason with you or rob you; they were hired assassins. You must go back to your hotel and do not speak of this to anyone. Lives are at stake - do you understand?"

Alan was still in a daze of disbelief at the whole event and couldn't muster any words but nodded acknowledgement.

"Now get in the car. You've got an hour to collect your thoughts in your room then I'll call you on your cell. Clear?"

Again, Alan just nodded.

"You're in shock. Drink some orange juice or try to eat something. One hour detective."

With that, he told the taxi driver the name of Alan's hotel, closed the door and quickly disappeared down the street.

Chapter 11

A lan sat on the end of his bed still dazed from the attack and struggling to recall how he got back to his hotel room. Random thoughts raced through his mind in a confusing jumble until his mysterious rescuer's words suddenly echoed, urging him to get some orange juice from the mini bar. As he emptied the bottle, he strangely recalled watching Jim Benson splash cool water on his face which helped him to come out of his shock after his wife's gruesome death so Alan went to the bathroom to do the same. The cacophony of thoughts and images spinning through his mind subsided slightly with the water's touch and he decided a shower would be more beneficial so he stripped and dropped his clothes on the floor then turned on the cold tap.

The bracing water worked its magic and his mind gradually began to emerge from its fog. After several minutes he turned the tap off and dried himself, picked up his clothes then went to the bed and arranged pillows to prop him up. He sank into the pillows staring blankly into space, his mind gradually reclaiming images of the attack and slowly piecing them together into a coherent memory. The gravity of the situation struck him as he realized there were three dead bodies laying in an alley in downtown Jersey City and the man that killed them had done so to save him from that exact fate.

Alan's police mindset struggled with his rescuer's instructions as he fought back the powerful desire to call the local police and report the incident. He knew the bodies would soon be discovered, if they hadn't already, and he had broken the law by fleeing the scene. He also knew that he was continuing to break the law by not calling to report the incident but the whole event was such a shock, he couldn't think clearly enough to make a decision.

His rescuer's words kept replaying in his mind as he struggled to understand why the attackers would want to kill him and how the leather-clad man knew his name, his hotel and his cell number but that thought jolted him from his semi-stupor. It was almost an hour since the attack so he jumped to his feet and quickly dressed to be ready for the expected phone call.

Precisely one hour after the attack, Alan's phone rang and he looked at it tentatively before accepting the call.

"Beach; I hope you have recovered sufficiently to meet and debrief."

Alan hesitated before replying, "I think so."

"Good, go to the lobby and get a taxi to the Newport Center Mall. Stand outside the front entrance – I'll find you. Got it?"

"Yes, I understand."

The call terminated and Alan was left to ponder his dilemma. His background told him to call the police and have them converge on the meeting place but his instincts told him not to. Eventually, his logical mind decided that since he'd waited this long already, another half hour or so wouldn't make any difference and he needed to get some answers.

His dilemma temporarily resolved, Alan pulled on his jacket and realized in horror that his gun was missing and probably still at the crime scene, where it would surely implicate him in the deaths. He pushed the thought out of his mind to get on with the task at hand, turned the door handle and pulled the door open. Just as his body began to emerge into the hallway, he saw his rescuer facing him from the side of his doorway, holding Alan's own police issue Glock pointed straight at him. His mind was swimming again as he began to think that the man might now have decided to silence the only witness to his actions.

"Step back into your room detective."

Alan complied as the man followed him in and closed the door. He then turned the weapon around and offered it handle first to Alan. The seemingly endless series of shocks and surprises had taken their toll on the detective and he quickly snatched the gun, pointing it at his rescuer who cocked his head and smiled thinly.

"It's not loaded." said the man, pulling a handful of bullets from his pocket and offering them to Alan. "I know you're confused but you need to get your shit together and focus now."

Alan lowered his weapon, sat heavily on the end of the bed and looked up as the intimidating figure in front of him continued.

"Sorry for the ruse on the telephone but I couldn't be certain you wouldn't call the police. This way, if Devlin's goons are monitoring your calls, their attention will be diverted to the Newport Center Mall. It's is very important you don't talk about what happened to anyone. These are very dangerous, well funded and highly motivated people. The three from the alley are just the beginning and they weren't the first string team."

"I don't understand - I'm just a homicide detective from Columbus. What possible reason would they have for killing me? And how do you know all this – more to the point, who are you?" Alan's perplexity and frustration burst through in his voice.

"Call me Jake Riley. Let's just say I'm here to help. Matt Lewis was a friend so I've got some scores to settle."

"What do you mean when you say, I 'can call you Jake Riley'? Is that your name or not?"

"My real name is irrelevant and ancient history. Just call me Jake."

"So you changed your name? You use a false identity? How do I know you're not a bad guy yourself then?"

"Your police training has made you obsessed with details. My true identity and details of my service record are known to only three other people in the world. They created Jake Riley when I left the service several years ago."

Alan's jaw dropped. "So you're what... some kind of spy?"

"Not a spy - I did things for the agency; things that required my specific set of skills and training."

"So you're an assassin?!" the distaste was obvious in Alan's voice.

"It's not that simple. I have terminated targets when necessary but I was not usually sent to intentionally kill people."

"'Not usually' means that sometimes you were. You're an assassin!"

Jake reacted with a calm control that was very disconcerting to Alan, "I saved your life today; comprendo? Probably smarter to thank me instead of pointing your finger. I had to act quickly and decisively. If those men were still alive, they would come after you again and I might not be there to stop them next time."

Alan stared intently into Jake's eyes and the bare facts began to melt his indignation. It was true that the men spoke as though they were there to kill him and they hadn't even attempted to rob him so he could only conclude that Jake was telling him the truth. He was conflicted between gratitude and moral outrage but realized it was futile to argue the point.

"I know you want to report this through proper channels but let me to explain a few things before you make a decision either way. If you still want to make it official when I've finished, I won't stop you but you'll never see me again and you'll face the repercussions and your enemies alone."

"What do you mean, my 'enemies'? Who are these people and why are they my enemies?"

"Alex Devlin has a private army of mercenaries and he knows your investigations are leading you toward him - you're not safe. I've been watching you for two days and those thugs started following you right after you visited Matt Lewis' office so I went back to sweep for devices while you were safe in your room. I found three concealed cameras so they were obviously watching for anyone following up on Matt's death. His murder wouldn't warrant an official police investigation because it looks like he was collateral damage in the congressman's assassination. They knew that anyone following up on Matt would know there was a bigger picture and they can't afford that. The more crimes they commit, the more trails there are to follow and you already found another one with Helen Benson."

"How do you know about that?"

"As I said; I've been watching you. I found the links you noted in the active case file in your police department's main frame. It was pretty smart of you to discover the connection."

Alan's face turned red with rage as he blurted, "So it was you who attacked Larry in the crime lab!"

"Sometimes innocents get in the way. The only injury he sustained was to his pride and that'll heal soon enough."

"You are unbelievably callous! He's my friend and he wouldn't hurt a fly."

Jake's face became stern as he said impatiently, "Your thinking is illogical and emotional. You need to unfuck yourself right now, stop acting like a politically correct sissy, and start being pragmatic. Where I come from, hard decisions are made on a split second basis, and I couldn't allow myself to be discovered. Your man was in the right place at the wrong time and he's unhurt. Now pull yourself together and act like a police detective instead of a simpering fool – this is real life, not some sensitive, new age children's playground."

The redness in Alan's face deepened but now with embarrassment instead of anger as he suddenly realized Jake was right. He was being completely impractical and showing a distinct lack of appreciation for the man who saved his life and spared Larry's. The information Jake had given him sank in and he decided he was taking the wrong approach altogether. Some frustration and confusion remained but his glare softened as he looked at Jake's somewhat frightening but sincere and authoritative face.

"I...I'm sorry. I...well...you're right – I'm being ungrateful and foolish. I guess the shock of the last hour and a half has short circuited me a bit. I apologize and I thank you for saving my life. I'll listen to you and try not to interrupt."

Jake's visage transformed to a disarmingly warm smile as he spoke, "I'm glad your common sense is returning. I'd hate to have to change my opinion about you."

"You know enough about me to form an opinion?"

"I've done some homework. It took a lot of guts and integrity to report your former partner's crimes. The way you handled that situation, your case closure rate, your tenacity and intelligent investigation style all make you a standup guy in my opinion. I'm not blowing smoke up your ass but I respect you and I can work with men I respect."

Alan felt slightly violated at the thought of someone looking so deeply into his background but at the same time his heart lifted with Jake's praise.

"I don't know whether to thank you or arrest you for invasion of privacy." Alan smiled.

"Why don't we just get down to business instead – deal?"

"Deal."

"Roger that. We know you've upset Devlin's applecart by finding a connection between Helen Benson's death and the incident at the Capitol Building so we need to find out more about that link."

Alan said, "The only provable connections I've found are identical tiny puncture wounds on the backs of Helen Benson's and Damien Fraser's necks, and the same strange little man on security footage from both scenes. It's nowhere near enough evidence to convict the little guy, let alone connect anything to Alex Devlin but there is something else."

Alan's brow furrowed as he began to relate what Professor Guthrie had explained to him at their lunch meeting. Jake listened intently, his face devoid of emotion. After relating the details, Alan said, "I don't know how but maybe a new technology developed at Blue Sky Biotech could be responsible for such seemingly inexplicable events. The problem is that Blue Sky's secrets are extremely well secured and I don't have enough evidence to get a search warrant."

"Your instincts are right but the truth is far worse than you may have imagined - I'll bring you up to speed once we're in a safe place. Unlike you, I don't need a warrant and I obtained an encrypted file from Blue Sky's main frame confirming they've developed a startling new technology but it's far more dangerous than you might think. It's been in development for a few years and they already have successful human test results."

Alan's eyes widened as he processed the news then his expression turned to incredulity.

"I don't understand; how could you get past all their security systems? They've got cameras everywhere, high tech electronic doors, an unknown number of plain clothed guards, and who knows what else."

"I said, 'I obtained' the document; I didn't say I physically infiltrated the building. That would be a tough nut to crack – not impossible but difficult without the time to develop an intricate plan. No, this was an electronic infiltration."

"So you're a hacker too?"

"I know my way around computers but I ain't no expert. An associate of mine is truly gifted in that area and got the file for me. It would have taken some doing but all systems have weaknesses, no matter how well built and maintained."

"Who is this hacker and how do you know he can be trusted?"

"That's not your concern. There is a very solid bond of trust between us and in my field, identities are best kept secret. More importantly, we need to identify the best way to move forward. Have you been able to identify any motive for Dr. Benson's death?"

"I've been thinking about that ever since I suspected it wasn't a suicide. I checked out Blue Sky and Helen's research team but I can't see anything out of the ordinary there. Larry did financial checks on all of them and the only anomalies are the incredible wealth of Eric Rothstein, the computer programmer, and the almost obsessive philanthropy of the team leader, Professor Linus Gelling."

"So the programmer works at Blue Sky despite being rich?"

"Yes, he owns a large computer game company and is wildly successful. The only reason I can see for him to work for Blue Sky is to be at the cutting edge of computer science. Or maybe he thinks he can use the technology for his own benefit somehow."

"And Gelling; what about him?"

"Well, he gets paid a huge salary but lives quite modestly. He gives the vast majority of his money, including that made by his patented discoveries, to a variety of charities."

"Any particular charities?"

"I know what you're getting at but everything Larry could find showed Gelling as squeaky clean – apparently, he just likes giving to charity."

"I'm sure your friend is competent but I think I'll get my associate to look into the team's finances as well. If there's anything to be found, it will be."

"Well, that's your call but Larry is very good at his job so you're probably wasting your associate's time."

"That may be but a city employee can't compare to a world leading hacker - it's just a statement of fact."

"I understand. In the meantime, what about Devlin and the small man that was at both scenes? I ran him through all available facial recognition databases, including the FBI's and nothing."

"I'll give you a secure email address to send a copy of his image. There are other databases that are not known to most agencies."

"I feel like I'm in the middle of a spy movie."

"I assure you this is all very real and there are no stuntmen in this movie. We have to be careful now that you've been targeted - especially now that Devlin's teams will think you are more than capable of taking care of yourself."

"But I didn't do anything!"

"Of course you didn't but dead men tell no tales. Who do you think they are going to blame for the loss of three men that were sent after you? And now they'll strengthen the teams and probably arm them as well."

Alan tried to maintain composure but his face betrayed his fear.

"Don't worry; I have a safe place but you'll have to hole up for a while. Now, do you have any family they could use to get to you?"

"No, my parents died years ago and since my wife was killed, I've been alone."

"What about the lady you've been spending time with?"

"Holly - do you think she's in danger?!"

"I'm afraid she could well be if she's important to you."

"She is but nobody knows about her except my lieutenant."

"Well, I knew about her so maybe they do too. What about this lieutenant?"

"Thomas Walker and yes, he is also important to me."

Jake's eyes widened in surprise as he asked, "Thomas Walker – is he a big guy in his late forties with a big jaw, a thick neck, and a gruff personality?"

Alan was once again shocked by his new ally and his face showed it as he spoke.

"How did you know that?"

Jake's face contorted into a huge toothy smile, which caused heavy creases to appear in his scar, as he began a low rumbling chuckle that turned into a raging belly laugh. Alan was now in total confusion as he waited impatiently for the laughter to subside.

"That crusty ol' son of a gun!" Jake said fondly, still chuckling. "I can't believe your boss is one of my former US Ranger Instructors!"

"What? Lieutenant Walker was a Ranger?!"

"Not just a Ranger; a Ranger Instructor! That guy is one of the toughest and craftiest sons a' bitches I ever met in my life. He could easily have gone into the Special Forces or Delta but his wife wouldn't let him. She wanted him to become a civilian – I guess police work was the compromise. How is the ol' crocodile anyway?"

Alan tried to compose himself before answering, "He's just like you describe him – and his wife still wears the pants." he said, cracking a smile.

Jake again burst into laughter and it was a relief for Alan to see such an obviously dangerous man show a human side.

"Don't worry about Walker – he can take care of himself and his family but we'd better warn him. I told you not to discuss this with anyone - but for Walker, we can make an exception. Give me his number and I'll call him but don't bother trying to ask him who I really am because trust me, you couldn't torture it out of him."

Alan gave Jake the number and his face turned serious.

"What about Holly? What do we do about her?"

"Does she know the Walkers?"

"Not yet; we're supposed to eat dinner at their house together on Sunday night for the first time."

"OK, we need them to meet sooner than expected. If I know Mrs. Walker, she has a spare bedroom and Holly will have to use it until we get this shit storm squared away. You're going to have to get her to trust you without explaining anything to her. Just tell her you're investigating some organized crime gang and threats have been made. Walker will cover for you."

"Are you sure he can protect all of them?"

"If he doesn't think he can, he knows people who will help without question."

"OK, I'll call Holly."

Jake disappeared into the bathroom to call Walker as Alan dialed Holly's number and waited for her to answer. The phone rang several times before she finally answered in a tearful voice.

"What's wrong Holly?" Alan asked trying to sooth her.

"Professor Guthrie has committed suicide – I just saw it on a news bulletin." she sobbed.

Alan felt as though his chest was sinking into the pit of his stomach. His mouth opened but nothing would come out.

"Alan? Did you hear me?" Holly sniffled.

The detective desperately tried to pull himself together as the realization set in that Guthrie was likely silenced because of his investigations into Blue Sky's potential new discovery on Alan's behalf. Before he could collect himself to speak, Holly asked through her tears, "Did he seem alright when you met him? How could this have happened?"

Guilt and confusion pervading his mind, one thought cut through the collecting muddle – these people would let nothing stand in their way. They had found a way to kill with impunity and he had to make sure Holly was safe from these monsters. He spoke clearly and deliberately, "Holly, I need you to pack a bag right now. A large man with a thick neck called Lieutenant Thomas Walker will pick you up from your home soon. Do not open the door to anyone else – do you understand?"

"No, I don't understand Alan. What's going on? What do you know about Scott Guthrie's death? What aren't you telling me?" she said, panicked.

"I'm sorry Holly but I can't explain right now. Please just do as I say! Lieutenant Walker will be able to shed some light on it and I will fill you in as soon as I can. Just don't open your door to anyone other than Walker and do exactly as he says – please!"

Holly reluctantly agreed and when Alan hung up the phone, he could hear some laughter coming from the bathroom as Jake spoke with Walker. He jumped up from the bed and rushed to open the door. Jake immediately saw the panic on his face and told

Walker to hold. Alan quickly explained what had happened as Jake listened intently.

"If they got to Guthrie, they must know about Holly too! Please Jake; we have to keep her safe!" Alan blurted anxiously.

Without hesitation, Jake began speaking in rapid military terminology to Walker. He asked Alan for Holly's home address and relayed it to Alan's boss and his former Ranger Instructor in phonetic alphabet to be certain the message was clear and hung up the phone without saying goodbye.

"Are you sure Walker can keep her safe?" Alan asked insistently.

Jake came back in a reassuring tone, "If anyone can, it's Walker. How far is it from the station to Holly's apartment?"

"About ten minutes, I guess."

"Then we'll know in ten minutes."

"Should I call her back and stay on the line with her?"

"How do you think that would help? It would only make her more frightened and even if someone came for her, there's nothing we can do from here anyway. No, let her pack as you instructed and we wait to hear from Walker."

Alan paced briskly back and forth past the end of the bed as Jake sat in eerie calm watching him. A couple of minutes passed and Alan's cell phone broke the silence. Jake stood, knowing that this could only be bad news. If Walker had managed to get to Holly first, he would have called Jake's phone, not Alan's, so he now expected the worst. Alan fumbled briefly with his phone before he answered. His face contorted into an anguished grimace as he heard Holly's panicked voice down the line until Jake snatched the phone from Alan's hand.

"Listen to me very carefully Holly." Jake said in a calm, detached voice. "Is the door bolted? OK, in a moment or two they will gain access to your apartment – there's nothing you can do to stop that. Do you understand? I need you to breathe Holly – try to be calm so I can help you. Is there any other way out of the apartment? OK…are you calling from a land line? Good; do you have a cell phone? I want you to turn your cell phone off and conceal it in your underwear to minimize the possibility of detection – do you understand? Now, leave this handset off the hook but as close to the base as possible so I can hear everything that happens then go to the other side of the room and lie on the floor face down as though you have fallen. Do not move; do not tense your body even when they touch you or lift you – you must act as though you have fainted and are completely unconscious so that they're forced to carry you. Is that clear? OK, do it now."

Alan's face was a study in sheer panic as tears rolled involuntarily down his cheeks. The blood had drained from his face and every fiber of his being was screaming out at his own futility but his instincts told him there was nothing he could do so he remained silent. He felt as though he'd left his own body and all he could do was watch on in a stupor as the scene unfolded.

Jake held a finger in his free ear so he could focus solely on the sounds at the other end of the line. His eyes flicked this way and that as he strained to discern every noise in Holly's apartment. His gaze snapped to Alan then he suddenly took his finger from his ear and slapped Alan hard on the cheek then grabbed his own cell phone and held it out to the stunned detective. The slap brought Alan out of his stupor and he grabbed the phone as Jake covered the microphone on Alan's phone and said tersely, "Call Walker – now!"

Alan dialed the number and waited.

"Miss me already Riley?" came the jovial response.

"Lieutenant; it's Beach. They're at Holly's door now!"

Walker's demeanor changed immediately and he barked at Alan, "What is her cell number?"

Alan relayed the number to him and waited for a reply.

"I'm less than three minutes out and I'll have a GPS tracker on her cell phone in less than a minute. How many assailants?"

"I don't know." Alan said keeping himself together as well as he could. He looked at Jake and whispered, "How many?"

Jake held up three fingers.

"Three assailants." Alan relayed.

Walker came back solemnly, "Alan; I know this is hard but they are going to take her. I've got some serious badass brothers in arms on their way to me now. These guys are the best - we'll get her back. Do you understand? I can't risk going in alone so I have to let them take her but we will get her back! They won't hurt her because they want to use her as leverage to get to you. Trust me Beach."

Just then Jake hung up Alan's phone and looked into his eyes. "You have to trust us Alan. This is the only way."

Then he reached out to take his phone from the detective and began to speak to Walker. The language he used might as well have been Swahili as far as Alan was concerned. English words were scattered throughout but they were mixed in with all sorts of numbers and military jargon. He could only guess that this was the most efficient way for two former Rangers to communicate details of the situation.

The conversation continued for a moment then Jake hung up and said, "Alan, we have to leave now. There is nothing else we can do from here. I know it's hard to let go but you have to trust Walker."

"Not a chance!" Alan said vehemently. "I'm not moving until I know that she's safe! We can wait here just as easily as anywhere else but if we go now, I won't know if she's OK until we get there."

"OK, we wait." Jake conceded.

Chapter 12

Thomas Walker wound his unmarked police car through the city streets as quickly as he could without drawing undue attention. He had turned the flashing grill lights on but left the vehicle's siren off to maintain a degree of stealth. Fifteen minutes earlier, he had called Captain Fouts of the city's S.W.A.T. team and briefed him on the situation. He then told Fouts to avoid official channels and only involve two other very specific men. The S.W.A.T. captain knew immediately what Walker needed and with a sharp, "You got it!" he hung up and immediately called Sniper Specialist Albrecht and Breach Specialist Sergeant Kerr from his team.

As a captain in Columbus' elite S.W.A.T. team, Fouts technically outranked Tom Walker but the homicide lieutenant was one of his former instructors at U.S. Army Ranger School and they had a long and close association throughout their service. His respect for and trust in his mentor were absolute and as far as he was concerned, whatever Walker wanted, Walker got – proper channels be damned. The two other men were in the same position and Walker had given them all glowing recommendations to join the city's elite assault team when they finished their military tours some years previously. At the time, a major bank robbery had left two former S.W.A.T. team members dead and another permanently incapacitated so the Chief of Police was more than happy to quickly recruit such well trained and seasoned replacements.

Albrecht had been a sniper in the Rangers so his position in the team was obvious. Kerr was particularly skilled at close quarters combat so he became one of the lead breach team. Fouts himself had a reputation as an expert assault strategist with the Rangers and his capabilities facilitated his rapid rise to Captain in what was considered by many to be the top S.W.A.T. team in the country.

Each man, despite his official position, was fiercely loyal to Tom Walker and knew full well that he would never abuse their trust or enlist their services for a clandestine operation unless it was absolutely necessary. Fouts filled them in on the details as they drove to rendezvous with Walker in pursuit of the assailants who had kidnapped the civilian, Holly Stuart. They knew no further details other than the fact that the mission was a hostage rescue, it was off the books, and it was for Lieutenant Tom Walker - they required nothing further. Captain Fouts was in charge as usual so this was just another operation – except there would never be any paperwork submitted. Any possible witnesses would be advised that whatever they saw was simply a training exercise.

Walker had set up a conference call with the S.W.A.T. team members and gave them continuous directions as he followed the GPS tracking signal tuned to the SIM card in Holly's cellular phone from about a mile behind her. It was only moments before Fouts in his car, and Albrecht and Kerr together in their SUV, caught up to Walker and all three vehicles followed the signal from a safe distance. The assailants' vehicle soon merged onto Highway 71 heading north toward Cleveland but turned off the highway onto a small private road just past the top of Alum Creek Lake. The team stopped at the entrance to the small gravel road, got out of their cars, and Fouts immediately pulled up a detailed map and satellite images of the road on his laptop. The other men stood in silence as Fouts took in details of the road and the private properties dotted along its length. The signal from Holly's phone became stationary on a property not far from the creek and Fouts nodded in silence then they concealed Walker's car and all four men got into the SUV with Kerr at the wheel and the headlights turned off. The moon was bright but the night was still dark enough to offer good cover while allowing Kerr to safely guide the vehicle down the densely forested dirt road.

They proceeded slowly as Fouts zoomed in on a satellite image of the target property and began formulating a loose plan. He would need to see topography and obstacles with his own eyes before he could firm up the strategy and tactics but his razor sharp focus and years of experience quickly drew an outline of an assault and rescue plan. He gave a signal and Kerr turned off the engine to glide for thirty yards before he steered the SUV under the cover of some bushes about five hundred yards before the target property to avoid detection.

The men got out and while Fouts examined the property through his military grade image stabilized night vision binoculars, Albrecht and the others opened the vehicle's tailgate to retrieve their equipment. Walker and Kerr pulled out standard S.W.A.T. issue Armalite M4 assault rifles and donned bullet proof vests, while Albrecht drew out the long aluminum case which held his personal Remington XM2010 Enhanced Sniper Rifle, Advanced Armament Corp. sound suppressor, and Leupold Mark 4 6.5–20×50mm ER/T M5 Front Focal variable power telescopic sight. He set his equipment, checked his scope and double checked the entire system then stood waiting in silence.

Fouts joined them at the rear of the vehicle, set his laptop on the floor and grabbed an M4 and vest before laying out his plan. The battle proven Rangers clearly knew their roles in the operation, which was a minor variation of a standard Ranger assault pattern. Walker looked into each man's eyes then spoke, "The hostage is a VIP; let's keep this tight and surgical boys. Fouts has the lead."

The others nodded knowingly and Albrecht disappeared into the bushes with barely a rustle while the others waited for him to take up his position just over two hundred and fifty yards from the small disused timber dwelling near the middle of the two acre property. A brief squelch came into their high tech communication earpieces to signify that the sniper was in place then Walker, Fouts and Kerr began to make their way through the forested grounds toward the property's thirty yard driveway.

There were plenty of trees and bushes for cover and within ten minutes, the assault team had made its way to the edge of the property and took up positions fanning out fifteen yards apart from each other. Fouts again pulled out his binoculars to examine the situation. A few seconds later, he smiled knowingly and gave the others a series of hand signals. The assailants may have been former military but obviously were not elite forces, judging by their lack of discipline and focus. This was not an interrogation but prisoner security and yet, instead of securing the hostage then leaving her alone in the dwelling to take up defensible positions outside, one man remained inside with Holly, only one guarded the exterior, and the third sat idly in their big SUV with his feet on the dashboard. It was obvious that the assailants were blissfully unaware they'd been followed and were comfortable and lazy in their mission.

Fouts stayed at his outer viewing position to direct the operation while Walker and Kerr moved stealthily toward the cabin. Walker broke off and started toward the kidnappers' vehicle while Kerr continued toward the dwelling then both men sank to the ground and waited. Fouts issued a brief command to Albrecht and received a squelch in reply. The sniper skillfully maneuvered to a vantage point where he could see the victim through one of the cabin's windows then sent a second squelch to confirm his position. Fouts whispered into his microphone, "Albrecht has the lead." and the other two men squelched their devices in acknowledgement.

The full moon offered plenty of light for his high tech scope and Albrecht watched the interior guard carefully as he gauged the outer guard's pace of movement, ignoring the third assailant in the car. He watched in disgust as the interior guard began to grope the defenseless hostage's breasts but pushed his anger down to prioritize and keep the operation crisp. If he took the lecherous bastard out first, the sound of the window pane bursting would alert the outer guard and he could theoretically manage to hit the hostage with machine gun fire before he could be eliminated. He set his point of aim where the outer guard would come into his crosshairs in a few steps and waited patiently. The man's head entered the far right of Albrecht's scope and continued toward the center until the sniper's finger squeezed his trigger almost imperceptibly, causing a muffled, high pitched buzz to pierce the air. Walker and Kerr watched as the exterior guard's head partially exploded and both men immediately moved toward their targets. Kerr raced past the dead man to the thin wooden front door of the cabin and kicked it so violently that it flew off its hinges, crashing onto the floor. Simultaneous with the crash of the door, Walker's M4 rang out and the lazy guard in the SUV met his maker.

The interior guard was completely unprepared for Kerr's interruption of his lustful behavior but he had quick reflexes and ripped his knife from its scabbard toward Holly's neck. The man used Holly as a shield for his chest, knowing his assailant would be trained to aim for the center mass of his torso. Kerr followed the man's lurching head movement in his sights, and without hesitation or conscience, neatly placed a single round from his M4 into the center of the man's face, sending his head violently backward. As the kidnapper's nervous system quickly shut down, his arm and hand tensed, holding the knife rigidly in place and carrying it backward with the momentum of his fall until it sliced neatly into the meat of Holly's right shoulder and she let out a muffled cry of pain through the duct tape across her mouth. The cut was more than half an inch deep but severed no main arteries and Kerr's powerful hand was already applying pressure to her wound as Walker came rushing through the door a second later.

Walker called out, "Secure?" and Kerr replied in the affirmative. Fouts began to make his way toward the cabin but just as it became clear in his view, he felt a heavy thud on the back of his head. His vision flared bright white and his ears rang loudly as he fell forward, his face planting heavily into the leafy ground. He almost lost consciousness but soon rallied to turn and face his attacker. His eyes not yet clear, Fouts couldn't make out the assailant as he blindly searched for his M4 but it was laying about three feet out of reach. A menacing voice said, "That would be your final move." and the SWAT captain turned back to see the form of a small man wearing an overcoat and hat becoming clear as his vision returned.

As Kerr maintained pressure on Holly's wound, Walker cut the zip ties holding her hands and feet to a wooden chair then removed the duct tape and asked her if she was OK. Her panicked eyes darted from man to man and Walker realized she had no idea who he was or what just happened.

"I'm Tom Walker - Alan's boss from the Columbus Police. Everything will be OK now." he said soothingly.

Tears streamed down Holly's face, partly out of relief and partly from lasting fear and shock. She had studied the effects of traumatic stress at length during her training as a psychologist but her intellect was unable to overcome her natural responses and she shook uncontrollably with emotion.

Satisfied that Holly's injury was not serious and the cabin was clear, Walker felt a sense of urgency to allay his star detective's fear so he pulled his cell phone from his pocket to dial Alan's number. "Beach; it's done. Holly's safe and I'm taking her to a secure location. Stick with Jake and get this done. Understood?"

"Understood." Beach replied with firm resolve. "I don't know how to thank you…I will never forget this Tom."

Walker's thick arms engulfed Holly as he picked her up, cradled like a child, to carry her outside. He could see the lights of the SWAT team's SUV turning into the drive and as he strode toward them, he called for an all clear from Fouts but there was no reply. The vehicle stopped and Walker continued toward it apprehensively, with Kerr still holding pressure on Holly's wound. Suddenly the two men froze where they stood. Three big, heavily camouflaged men got out of the SUV and at the same time, a voice came from the darkness to the right flank of the Rangers. "Do you value your comrade's life?"

They turned to see Captain Fouts, blindfolded with his hands secured behind him. Beside him stood a small man with beady eyes and a cold, thin lipped grin holding a gun to Fouts' head. They were flanked by two more camouflaged men with automatic weapons trained on the Rangers.

Walker and Kerr immediately assessed the new threat but they could see the situation was futile. Even if they could draw their weapons before the men opened fire, Fouts would certainly die and Holly would most likely be hit in the crossfire. Walker's years of experience under fire suddenly broke through his anger and he knew what had to be done. He surreptitiously opened his transmitter so Albrecht could hear the conversation.

"It's over - drop your weapons and give me the bitch." the small man continued in a guttural South African accent.

Walker gave Kerr a defeated look and the two dropped their weapons on the ground. "She's injured - take me instead." the big lieutenant said.

"Where would be the fun in that - now, shut up and put her down!"

Holly sobbed with dread as Walker placed her gently on the ground. He leaned in and whispered, "Hold on Holly; we'll get you back."

"That's not going to happen you pompous shit! Get in the car bitch!" the small man snarled then turned to the three men from the SUV and ordered, "Get their guns and telephones then take all three of these toy soldiers into the cabin and make it look like they died in the shootout with those useless morons they killed earlier. Meet us back at the rendezvous in an hour."

While the small man in charge and the other two camouflaged men got into the SWAT SUV with Holly, the three remaining mercenaries silently searched Walker, Fouts and Kerr and handed their phones to their leader through the window. Walker watched in dismay as the vehicle disappeared down the drive. He was enraged at being so easily tricked and cursed under his breath in the realization that Alan and Jake would now have no idea that Holly wasn't safe with him at a secure location.

Albrecht had heard every word and silently moved into a new position. He glared coldly as the SUV made its way down the drive and onto the road where he would be unable to take out the tires through the cover of the thick forest. He forced himself to focus on his new task and turned his eye back to the high tech Leupold scope atop his personalized XM2010. He deftly removed the magazine loaded with lower powered hollow point rounds and replaced it with a clip of Winchester Magnum DM131 armor piercing bullets, capable of penetrating three quarters of an inch of armor plating at two hundred yards.

There would be no room for error on this shot. The distance was only two hundred and fifty yards, child's play for Albrecht, but the timing and the target required extreme precision. It wouldn't be enough to simply hit the man; the bullet must enter at exactly the right point, at exactly the right time, for his plan to work. He watched as Kerr followed Fouts through the cabin door as though they were in slow motion. Walker was on Kerr's heels and the three mercenaries followed immediately behind. The timing needed to be perfect and Albrecht's highly trained eyes monitored all parameters carefully until he saw them nearing perfect alignment. He needed to anticipate the next split second before releasing his single shot, knowing that just as the silencer emitted its high pitched buzz, the armor piercing round would more than double the speed of sound, creating a thunderous howl of shattered air. If he mistimed or missed his mark by the slightest margin, the remaining mercenaries would be alerted and his comrades would be dead.

Walker braced himself for what he hoped was coming. He poked Kerr in the right side of his back and despite his surprise, Kerr responded with cat-like reflexes, grabbing Fouts and jerking them both violently to the right as Walker jerked left, dragging the closest assailant to the ground with him. A split second later, came the roar of Albrecht's tungsten loaded round traveling at two thousand nine hundred feet per second, thundering through the air and the sickening thud Walker expected, arrived a millisecond before. The mercenary who was last in line flew forward into the man in front of him as the military ordnance, armor piercing round sped through him at more than twice the speed of sound. It ripped a massive gaping hole in his chest and continued, unfettered through the next man, then on through the far wall and into a tree where it finally came to rest. Walker had retrieved a knife from the third guard and plunged it into the man's gut, nicking his stomach then tearing downward through his intestines and bladder. His face contorted with pain and the realization that his comrades were dead and he was next.

Albrecht was already up and running at full speed toward the cabin, holding his rifle ready at his chest. Kerr grabbed a knife from one of the dead mercs and cut his captain's bindings then cleared the enemies' weapons. The first man the bullet went through had a tiny, neat hole in his back but his chest was virtually non-existent. Once the bullet had passed through him, it ripped through the second man, destroying his aorta and tearing out a great swath of flesh at the point of exit. Albrecht's aim had been perfect and the armor piercing round met or exceeded all performance specifications.

Walker's victim was groaning in pain as some blood flowed up his esophagus to mix with his saliva and bubble out the corner of his mouth. "You're not dead yet asshole!" Walker grunted.

He lifted the man's head and propped it up on his knee to drain the blood back to his stomach and clear his mouth. "Looks to me like you've got about half an hour to live - give or take. I might be able to get you to a hospital in time to save your life but if I do, you'll be pissing and shitting into a bag for the rest of your days and you'll certainly never work again. Of course, I could just leave you here to die slowly, or there's door number three, where you give me the rendezvous point and I give you a quick, clean soldier's death. Don't think too long, we ain't got time to waste."

The doomed man was an experienced former South African Special Forces 'Recce' and he knew Walker was right about his condition. The only question now was whether he'd tough it out for about an hour of sheer agony or betray his employer in exchange for mercy. Life as a cripple would never be an option for this soldier, and the big man with the thick neck above him knew that full well. He looked up at Walker and grunted, "I don't owe those pricks anything…"

Once Walker had the details of the rendezvous, he kept his word and put a round through the former Recce's brain to end his suffering and the former Rangers quickly collected all weapons, covered all traces of the event, and carried the six bodies to the assailants' vehicle. As they loaded bodies into the back and covered them with a blanket, Fouts looked at Walker and the big man said, "Off the books – completely. Get to the rendezvous as soon as you can – I think we're going to need you."

Fouts nodded solemnly and drove off into the night in the kidnappers' car with all evidence of the event. Walker didn't know where he would dispose of it and wasn't interested. He knew that Fouts would ensure no trace would ever be found. He also knew that despite their current status as policemen, this band of former Rangers would never speak a word of the night's events to anyone and nothing would ever tie the night's events to his former charges or himself.

Walker turned to Albrecht and said, "You took your sweet time Albrecht!" then his face slowly contorted to a wide grin as his huge bear paw slapped the sniper on the shoulder. "Good shooting son."

Kerr gave Albrecht a firm pat of thanks on his back.

"Just doing my job boss." the sniper said with typical Special Forces humility.

Walker gave him a knowing nod then turned toward the road. "Our mission is incomplete ladies. We need to get back to my car, head to their rendezvous, and end that slimy little bastard." Then he rubbed his chin thoughtfully and said, "Beach ain't the toughest guy in the world but I sure as hell don't want to have to tell him that we had his girl then lost her. Besides, my wife would kill me dead! Let's move out."

After running to Walker's car, the three former Rangers sat in silence as they sped back toward the city, where the kidnappers' had taken Holly. Walker didn't want to contemplate what would have happened if they hadn't extracted the rendezvous point from the last mercenary at the cabin. They no longer had Fouts' laptop to trace her signal and even if they did, her cell phone had probably been discovered by now.

Walker knew the locale of the rendezvous point and he was concerned that the new scenario would pose a significant new problem for him and his team. The location was in a warehouse district on the outskirts of town and he was worried about the possibility of witnesses and potential collateral damage. Despite the considerable threat to all their careers, he knew that he had no choice but to remain under the radar. If the situation became official, they would already be compromised, and they all knew it so they steeled themselves for what lie ahead.

Without Fouts to devise a plan and the aid of his night vision binoculars, they would have to rely completely on Albrecht's scope for an accurate assessment of the situation. Walker knew there was a training tower for the local fire department in the warehouse district so that was his first objective. If they couldn't get a clear view from there, he would have to improvise a close quarters attack. He broke the silence and described the area to his comrades and soon, they neared their objective.

Albrecht peered out the window at the six story training tower and instantly knew where to set up. Another moment and they were outside the chain mail fence designed to keep children and vandals out of the site. The men exited the vehicle and Walker got some wire cutters from his trunk. He cut a flap just big enough from them to climb through and they proceeded to the tower, weapons in hand. Albrecht bounded up the stairs, closely followed by the others but Walker slowed slightly as they neared the top, his advancing years catching up with him. When he reached the top, Kerr joked, "Back to the gym for you old-timer."

"Roger that! I'm getting too old for this shit." Walker puffed.

Albrecht's rifle was already in place and he was making final adjustments to his equipment as Walker began to catch his breath. The sniper took up a prone position on the outer deck of the platform and Walker directed him to what he believed to be the building where Holly was being held. The moon was still on their side and it wasn't long before Albrecht spotted the first of the two mercenaries in a well concealed position behind some empty oil barrels outside the warehouse. Assuming these men were well trained, he widened his search to include higher vantage points around the warehouse. In a few seconds, his experienced eyes found the second merc lying on top of an adjacent warehouse about thirty yards from his comrade's position. He had an AK47 trained on the front of the building where Holly was held. The strange little man was nowhere in sight but Albrecht spotted a small window at the far end of the unprotected wall. He informed Walker and Kerr of the situation and they began to formulate a plan.

The distance from the fire tower to the sniper on the roof was close to six hundred and fifty yards away, about half the maximum effective distance of the XM2010. The shot was no problem for a sniper of Albrecht's caliber but they had other concerns. It wasn't so much that the shot would immediately alert the man behind the oil drums. More importantly, they had not yet been able to locate the small man who was obviously in charge. He'd gotten the drop on Fouts at the cabin, so he was obviously highly skilled and cunning. Once the assault began, they needed to be certain they could contain the situation inside the warehouse. But they had no intelligence on the interior or exactly where Holly was restrained within the structure.

There was really no choice. Walker and Kerr would have to get close enough to see inside. That meant separating from Albrecht without any communication equipment. The base station for their high tech comms was in their SUV at the warehouse and the mercs had obviously shut it down. Their cell phones had been smashed by their captors at the cabin so they had to devise an alternative. The plan was that Walker and Kerr would get to the window to assess the interior situation. Albrecht would have to alternate his surveillance between the gunman on the roof, in case he spotted Walker or Kerr, and the side of the warehouse, to watch for Kerr's signal to take out the first target. If Kerr was unable to get a clean shot at the man behind the barrels, Albrecht would immediately direct his aim at him. The signal from Kerr would only come when Walker was satisfied he could secure Holly.

The former Ranger sniper inserted his hollow point magazine to avoid the ear shattering roar of the higher powered armor piercing rounds. He hoped that the lower velocity rounds and his high tech suppressor, combined with the distance from target, would muffle the sound of his shots sufficiently to maintain stealth. It was night and the warehouse district looked empty but there were bound to be security guards at other properties who would alert the authorities if they heard his shots. The team would have to move swiftly once the firing started and flee the scene as soon as Holly was secured.

The plan decided; Walker and Kerr disappeared down the stairs without another word. They made their way toward the target on foot, leaving Walker's car outside the fire tower fence for Albrecht. Ten minutes later, they reached the perimeter of the warehouse complex but there was no clear view of the front so they couldn't be sure that the man on the ground hadn't changed positions. The far side and the rear of the warehouse abutted other buildings so the front and near sides were their only access. Walker saw the window at the rear corner of the building and signaled Kerr to move out. Kerr couldn't reach his destination at the front corner without being exposed to the gunman on the roof so he followed closely behind Walker. Once at the window, he would make his way along the side of the building in the shadows. Based on the angle they observed from the tower, the man on the roof should be blind to his movement.

Since there were only two exterior guards, they could only properly cover the entrance. Walker knew they would be expecting their three comrades from the cabin as support but would not yet have reason to doubt they were coming. He was as satisfied as he could be in the circumstances, that their path would be clear. His main concern was the small man in charge and Holly's position in the building.

At the window, Kerr stopped briefly, waiting for Walker to report the situation. The big man peered through the dusty glass, carefully checking every corner but there was no sign of the small man. Holly was tied to a chair in the office just inside the front door, with a hood covering her head. Seeing no other signs of life in the building, Walker signaled Kerr to go ahead.

Kerr silently made his way along the side of the warehouse and crouched as he neared the corner. He pulled his M4 up to eye level, peering through its small scope, and slowly moved to achieve an angle of sight to the roof of the adjacent building. He could just see the muzzle tip of the rooftop gunman's AK47 and realized he would not be able to assess the location of the front door guard. Weighing the risk, he knew they were out of time so he pulled back from the corner, pointed his weapon at the wall and repeatedly clicked his weapon's laser sight on and off to signal Albrecht.

From the tower, Albrecht saw a small red dot flashing against the side of the building with his free eye, and moved his weapon slightly to view the source. He instantly confirmed it was Kerr and readjusted his point of aim back to the rooftop gunman. The familiar high pitched buzz issued from his suppressor, followed by a minor report from the lower velocity round. Without waiting for visual confirmation, Albrecht immediately adjusted his point of aim from the first target to the barrels but the man wasn't visible. Two tense seconds later, the mercenary's head rose above the barrel and less than a second later, it became part of the wall behind him.

Kerr heard the impact of the second shot and raced toward the barrels to confirm the kill as Walker sprinted to catch up. Albrecht quickly packed his rifle into its case, retrieved his spent cartridge cases, and hurried down the stairs to Walker's car. As he drove toward the warehouse, Walker and Kerr were already entering the building. Despite Walker's careful observations through the window, they maintained a cover formation as they made their way to the office door. Kerr held position outside the open door, his weapon pointing toward the center of the empty warehouse, as Walker quickly poked his head in and out of the office door, desperately searching for the little man. Holly was alone in the room but Walker wasn't ready to be fooled again. Despite what his eyes told him, he wasn't going to let his guard down this time.

He slowly approached Holly, his eyes darting to every corner of the room. It didn't make sense why the leader of the kidnappers would leave the scene and his captive unguarded. His mind raced frantically through the possibilities when he suddenly realized the source of the little man's confidence. Holly's restraints brought vivid memories flooding back into his head. He spoke aloud to Kerr, "He's gone. You'd better come and look at this."

Kerr reluctantly deserted his post to join Walker and he too, knew instantly why Holly was unguarded. Over her shoulders, around her waist, and over her legs, was an intricately woven web of strapping and wires which led under the chair. They crouched to see the wires led to a mercury control switch attached to a detonator, which pierced a chunk of C4 plastic explosive, encased in a tamper proof acrylic box. It wasn't the most sophisticated device they had ever seen but it was certainly enough to give pause, even to a bomb disposal expert.

The men looked at each other and Kerr said, "So much for a quick exit."

Holly tried to speak through the duct tape over her mouth and Walker suddenly remembered to remove her hood. She was obviously panicked but a wave of relief came over her face as she saw their familiar faces. Walker gently removed the tape from her mouth and she put on a brave face as he explained the predicament. It had been almost two hours since her initial abduction and she'd had time to regain her wits through the shock of the evening's events. Her fear was quickly being displaced by anger toward her captors, and Walker could see her strength of character and why Alan liked this woman so much.

With disarming calm, she asked, "What do we do now?"

Walker rubbed his chin for a moment before replying, "I'm sorry Holly but we can't call the Bomb Squad."

"Just because I'm a woman, doesn't mean I'm stupid. I'm pretty sure you didn't intend to take any prisoners. And I'm pretty sure you can't report any of this through official channels." she replied.

Walker looked at her admiringly. "You're a smart woman. Beach is a lucky man."

"Maybe, but he'd better have a damned good explanation for all this!"

"Trust me; it's a doozie! But believe me – none of it is his fault and his only concern is your safety."

"OK well, we've got a dinner at your place on Sunday night and I have no intention of breaking the date – how are you going to get me out of this mess?"

Walker couldn't help smiling at her glibness. "I don't suppose you've got a phone?"

"I thought you couldn't call the Bomb Squad?"

Kerr interrupted, "Don't need 'em ma'am."

"Why not? And I'm not your mother so don't call me that. My name is Holly."

"Yes ma'am…I mean no ma'am…sorry." Kerr fumbled. "It's a southern thing. Sorry but it's how I was raised."

"OK, if it's force of habit then so be it. Now can we get back to why you want a phone please?"

"Yes ma'am. Walker here has some experience in IED disposal but that was a long time ago so he's kinda worried about doing this. Captain Fouts is up to date. He was with us at the cabin. But we got no way to reach him."

"Well, why isn't he with you now?"

Walker interjected, "He had to take care of something else."

"You mean getting rid of the bodies from the cabin?" she asked calmly.

"Wow, you really are a cool customer, aren't ya."

"A realist. Now get your memory straightened out and get me out of this thing please."

Walker scratched nervously at his head. He knelt to examine the device and despite the years since his days as a Ranger Instructor, he could see this wasn't going to be easy.

"Whaddaya think?" Kerr asked.

"I gotta be honest; it doesn't look good."

Just then, Albrecht pulled up outside and Walker told Kerr to get his wire cutters and any other tools he could find from his trunk and check their SUV for anything useful. He looked around the office and saw an old first aid box. He opened it but there was nothing useful except an almost empty can of Freon. He knew that years ago; some first aid kits offered the gas to companies with a high risk of workplace burns. They would spray the burn to numb the pain until the patient could get to hospital. The practice was stopped because often the Freon would cause additional damage through frostbite.

He gave the can a shake and it was obvious he would get only a few seconds out of it but it was better than nothing. He could use it to chill the mercury switch in the hope it would make it slightly less sensitive while he dealt with the bomb. Kerr and Albrecht came in and handed him the clippers, along with a tiny blowtorch that Walker used to light his cigars – a passion that he tried desperately to keep from his rabidly anti-smoking wife. He looked apprehensively at the three implements, laid them out on the floor near the chair leg and knelt down again. He turned to lie on his back and stared up at the device for a few minutes then asked, "Albrecht; are we still dark?"

"I'm pretty sure no one heard anything. Haven't heard any sirens or chatter on your radio so I think we're OK."

The news was a minor relief which meant he had time to think. His mind was swimming, trying to recall all the details of his IED training and how to apply them to this device. He couldn't see which of the wires to cut since they were concealed by the switch but he knew he would have to choose. His thick fingers fumbled across the wires trying to get a feel for the device before he raised the cutters to the red wire then changed his mind to the blue then the green. Tension filled the room as Kerr and Albrecht watched on and Holly tilted her head to the ceiling with her eyes tightly shut. Beads of sweat formed on Walker's brow and just as he was about to squeeze the clippers closed on the yellow wire, a voice from the doorway broke his silence.

"What the hell's going on here?" Fouts demanded.

Kerr and Albrecht snapped their weapons up toward the door and Walker jumped at the disturbance. He had to jerk his hand away to avoid hitting the sensitive mercury switch. "Shit a brick!" he exclaimed, turning to see Fouts at the door. "What the hell took you so long?"

As Walker pulled himself out from under the chair, Fouts said, "I thought I was pretty damned quick under the circumstances. He looked at the clippers in Walker's hand and shook his head disdainfully. "Get outta there old man. I think you've been driving a desk too long." he joked.

"Gladly! It's all yours smartass."

Fouts introduced himself to Holly then crouched to have a look at the device. The detonator cap and C4 were visible through the acrylic cover so if he could get inside, he could simply pull the cap out and remove the explosive putty. C4 is remarkably stable and the only way it would detonate is if the switch triggered the cap while still close enough to the putty to initiate an explosion.

"Damn good thing I got here when I did or I'd have been scraping everyone off the walls with a putty knife. You can't cut the wires on this baby. Hand me that blow torch and the Freon."

Kerr gave Fouts what he wanted and the SWAT captain started whistling as he positioned himself under the chair. He sprayed the mercury switch and the outer edge of the detonator cap with Freon. The he clicked the little torch on and burned a neat slot in the acrylic cover, running from the left of the firing cap, along the side to the end. He then turned the corner to follow the end and turned again to continue down the right side back to the cap. His cut formed a flap of acrylic anchored at the detonator cap end. Then he sprayed the acrylic with Freon along the edge of the detonator end, pulled his Spyderco knife out and pried the acrylic flap open. He got his fingers under the flap and pulled down sharply until the frozen acrylic snapped off cleanly at the hinge. He reached into the box, pulled the detonator out of the C4 and folded it away from the explosive charge. Then he simply pulled the brick of puttied explosive from its mount, stood up and handed it to Walker. "Merry Christmas." he joked. "Now; everyone plug your ears."

With that he gave one of the chair legs a sharp kick and the detonator cap made a loud crack like a .38 round. Then he began to cut Holly's ties with his Spyderco and Kerr joined him. Walker just shook his head, tossed the stick of C4 in the air and caught it then said, "I told you I'm getting too old for this shit. Excuse my French Holly."

"No need." she said. "Four letter words are an excellent way to express many emotions."

Walker chuckled. "That's right – Beach said you're a shrink."

"Psychologist - and not quite yet but very soon."

"Remind me not to leave you alone with my wife on Sunday. Well, I guess I'd better find a phone and call Alan. He's gonna be pissed I let him down in round one but at least we came through in the end."

"I think we can just keep that our little secret. No point in getting him worked up. As you said; you came through in the end." She turned to the others and said, "And you boys – your money is no good where I work. Free beer whenever I'm working."

Fouts piped up saying, "Note to self...rescue at least one fair maiden a week."

Chapter 13

Alan had never been a motorcycle person. He had once ridden a police bike during his initial training many years before but despite its larger engine, the Harley couldn't compare to the brutal power of the customized BMW he now straddled behind Jake. His initial fear had faded as Jake's riding expertise became evident and he now found himself enjoying the brisk, smoothly weaving ride through Jersey City. With his head snug in a Schuberth C3 helmet, a firm grip on the passenger grab bar, and his euphoria at knowing Holly was now safe with Lieutenant Walker, Alan began to understand the thrill of riding with an expert, and exhilaration overcame him.

All too soon for Alan, Jake slowed the machine and pushed a concealed button in the big bike's dash. A garage door in the side of an old brick building began to roll open in front of them. Alan considered how odd it seemed that a man like Jake would live in an old, working class apartment building but his thoughts were soon interrupted by the sight of a large, shiny solid steel garage door inside the outer door they had just entered. As the outer door shut behind them, Jake removed his riding gloves and reached out to press his entire palm against a black glass panel. The panel lit with an eerie green glow and a deep hum emanated from the solid steel door as it slowly slid to one side revealing a huge, brightly lit garage with several exotic looking vehicles parked throughout.

"What the…" Alan said to himself in astonishment as the bike urged forward.

Jake parked the BMW beside some other bikes which Alan didn't recognize. His eyes darted around the room trying to take everything in when he was interrupted.

"You can get off now detective."

"Oh, right…yes, sorry." he fumbled as he pulled his right leg around behind him to dismount.

Jake joined him on the floor and removed his helmet then helped Alan with the unfamiliar buckle under his chin. Free of visual restriction, his eyes were wide as saucers as he surveyed the room and its contents.

"Is all this yours?"

"At least until I die." Jake said philosophically.

"This is unbelievable!"

"I suppose - if you're not used to it. I've been here for a few years now so I don't really think about it in terms other than security."

"So the whole building is yours?"

"Yes but I lease the upper floors out to tenants so it appears to be a normal apartment building."

"That's clever. I guess in your position, you have to think about cover all the time."

"That's been my way of life for many years so it's normal for me. Once this is all over, I would obviously appreciate your discretion about my location."

"Of course – I understand!" Alan nodded his head vehemently. "What I don't understand is how a former government employee can afford all of this."

"My parents died when I was young and left me a substantial inheritance. I've invested wisely and made it into a large fortune. Shall we?" Jake motioned toward a spiral staircase in the corner of the room.

Alan laughed, "It's like the 'Bat Cave'"

"If you say so."

Alan followed up the stairs into an empty landing and wondered what was next. He could see no door or exit and waited bemused for the next surprise. Jake pushed on part of the wall and a doorway appeared, leading into a large, luxurious bathroom. The pair walked through and Alan followed into the bedroom then on into the main living area.

"That's a pretty strange way for me to enter a man's home." Alan commented.

"It wasn't designed for guests." He motioned toward the kitchen and continued, "There's coffee and tea or cold drinks in the fridge - help yourself. I'm going to get out of these leathers."

Alan marveled at the interior of the complex as he walked to the kitchen. He reached for a cup from the top of the automatic espresso machine, placed it under the nozzle and pushed the button that indicated a full cup. The machine began humming and soon, rich espresso sputtered out to fill the cup. He opened the large double door refrigerator and topped his cup with milk then wandered over to the entertainment center. There was a complicated remote control unit on the table that Alan preferred not to touch so he turned away to explore further.

Walking away from the bedroom, he came to a door and turned the handle. The door gave way and his eyes widened as a large array of training equipment came into view, such as he'd never seen before. There was a small weight training area but most of the room was filled with a variety of different punching bags, speedballs, kung fu mannequins mounted on springs, and a strange wooden post with sticks poking out of it at various points and angles. His attention then turned to the rear wall where a plethora of martial arts weapons and training tools were mounted. Like a child magnetically drawn, he was soon holding a strange rattan stick by its handle. It had a guard between his hand and what seemed to be the business end of the device and it reminded him of an unopened umbrella with a rubber knob on the tip. His curiosity piqued, he was enthralled examining the device.

"Do you know Kendo?" Jake's voice boomed from the doorway.

Startled from his deep concentration, Alan dropped the weapon to the floor and turned to Jake, embarrassed by his own childlike curiosity.

"I guess not." smiled Jake. "It's a practice sword for the Japanese fighting style called 'Kendo'. It means 'way of the sword'."

"I'm sorry, I just…"

"No problem; there's nothing there you can break. Be careful with the pointy ones." Jake smiled wryly.

Alan tilted his head and gave a half grin at Jake's jibe, "You use all these things?"

"I train with all these 'things' as you call them but most of them are impractical in real life. They are simply a means to hone my skills."

"What are you; a black belt in Karate or something?"

"Karate is a good starting point but it has its limitations and the only belt I wear is specifically designed to hold up my pants."

"Oh, very droll. Can you explain for those of us in the cheap seats please?"

"It's hard not to be amused by the uninitiated. I've studied many different martial arts since I was quite young and travelled throughout the world to train in different styles. Colored belts are really only used in commercial schools to keep paying students motivated. True martial artists have no interest in them unless they are setting up a school and most exotic styles don't have belt systems anyway."

"Exotic styles?"

"I mean non-mainstream styles such as Indonesian Silat, Filipino Escrima, Chinese Chin Na, and others from East Asia. There are also many very good Eurpoean styles which seem to be neglected by commercial schools."

"And you do all of these 'styles'?"

"I've studied many styles but there are too many to be serious about all of them. You could say I'm highly proficient in four, proficient in four others and reasonably good at another half dozen or so."

"That sounds like a lifetime of study!"

"It is - but there are many similarities between styles. The human body is limited to certain movements and range so most styles only have minor variations between them. In real life situations, the number of truly effective techniques is not large so it's more a matter of perfecting those and keeping the rest as backup in case you run into someone with similar skills. It's a bit like war – it is best to keep a vast arsenal of weaponry but in most battles, artillery is used to soften the enemy from afar then tanks move in, followed by militia but if the enemy uses a similar strategy, it becomes a war of attrition so that's where innovation comes in to minimize losses and gain ground."

"Spoken like a soldier."

"Probably because I am a soldier. I won't go into detail but military service and martial arts have been my life."

"I still can't believe you know my lieutenant and that he was a Ranger."

"Believe it - he was not only one of my Ranger Instructors but also a trusted friend and mentor. He recommended me for Special Forces training after Ranger School and my career took off from there. I was surprised when he left the military but I understood his reasons. It's hard to have a real family life in the service and his job was particularly demanding."

"I understand – it just amazes me that I have never heard about it before."

"Most people who talk about being in elite military units are just wannabes who have never actually done it. True military specialists are not interested in bragging or telling tales – they don't need to. I would imagine your HR department has his service record but they're not going to tell anyone either so it makes sense to me that this is the first you've heard."

"I guess you're right. I'm just not sure how this will affect our relationship – especially since I now owe him for saving Holly."

"Believe me; he would never feel that you owe him for such a thing, and if you're smart, you won't let it change anything. Trust me - that's the last thing he wants. He has his reasons for not making his past public and I'm sure he would want you to respect his privacy."

"You're right – I guess it's just taking some time to get my head around it."

"Follow me; I've got something to take your mind off it."

Jake walked to a keypad on the wall beside a frame which concealed the heavy, reinforced door to his armory and computer room. He punched in a six digit code and the magnetic bolt clunked into its keep allowing him to push the door open. Alan followed him into the room, wide eyed again.

"Your lifestyle is going to give me a heart attack!"

"It may seem overwhelming but this situation requires a steep learning curve. You need to overcome your astonishment and keep up."

"I'm doing my best under the circumstances."

"You sound like a pussy. Sometimes your best isn't enough – just do it." Jake said then turned and spoke to no one, "Open file – Lewis documents."

Slightly insulted, Alan looked around as if expecting someone to appear from a secret doorway, when a large computer monitor above the workbench came to life and displayed a detailed document.

"OK, so now I'm in a science fiction novel."

"It's just voice activated computer. I find it useful to keep my hands free. Read the document detective."

As Alan read, his mouth opened in amazement. When he finished the page Jake instructed the computer to open the next document and the next until Alan had seen all the most relevant files.

He rubbed his eyes and scratched his head then turned to Jake, "This is way out of my league! I've never heard of such conspiracy in movies, let alone real life! Is it all true?"

"Devlin has developed the largest and most powerful corporate juggernaut I've ever heard of. Who knows what he intends to do with it."

"I don't understand how he's been able to do this! It goes against all anti-competitive laws – how did he get everything passed by the government?"

"Looks like antitrust limitations kicked in a few years ago and he couldn't expand further without being caught. I guess he's using Blue Sky's invention to circumvent the legal hurdles. He now controls over forty five percent of all food production, forty percent of all healthcare services and pharmaceuticals, over fifty percent of all oil and gas production and over sixty percent of all weapons manufacturing and development in the USA. We don't even know the extent of his holdings in Europe and Asia yet. His power in this country is well beyond that of the Executive Office and Congress combined."

"How could the CIA or NSA or whatever let this happen?"

"It's neither agency's responsibility to monitor such things; responsibility lies with industry regulators and legislative bodies. Criminal activities on a federal level are the sole responsibility of the FBI but there has been nothing to tip them off about any such activity. Devlin has used his vast resources to cover every sign of anti-competitive activity through complex corporate holdings that would take a very gifted forensic accountant to uncover. Matt Lewis has been working on this for years and with the help of my computer hacker associate, this is what he uncovered.

It's my guess that Congressman Taylor's assassination was a convenient bonus but Lewis was the actual target. These files are not enough to indict or convict him but Devlin didn't like someone getting as close to the truth as Lewis did. His meeting with Taylor was to expose this information and hope that Taylor was powerful enough to conduct a full investigation. That's obviously not going to happen now."

"Wow, this is a lot to take in! What are we going to do?"

"I can't speak for you but I won't rest until Devlin pays for what he's done and his labyrinth of power is destroyed."

"Count me in – although I don't really know how much use I can be against private armies and power unlike I've ever seen."

"Edmund Burke said 'All that is necessary for the triumph of evil is that good men do nothing'. I hold that statement sacred and I chose to live my life by it many years ago. We may not have the influence, reach or resources Devlin has but we can certainly wage war. Your position with the police can open some doors and now that Walker knows the story, he'll give you freedom to move. The most important weapons we have are surprise and stealth but before we do anything else, I had to secure our vulnerabilities. That's why I asked if there was anyone you cared about. We need to make sure the only way they can get to us is head on and with Walker and Holly covered; they have no way to flank us."

"I don't mean to sound ungrateful or repetitive but are you sure that Holly is completely safe now. I mean the kind of influence and resources we're dealing with – the whole thing just seems impossible."

"Private armies have one major fault; their allegiance is purely financial and throughout history, the best soldiers are always those that fight for a true cause - not for money. What I'm saying is that if Devlin does send more people against Holly or Walker, they'll be going up against superior fire power, and their loyalties will be tested and found wanting. Walker will take the necessary precautions and I'm certain he's taken Holly and his family somewhere that has no connection to any of them. He's already enlisted the help of former comrades in arms and these are serious soldiers, not hired mercenaries. I have complete faith in him so put that out of your mind and let's get on with our task."

Still overwhelmed, Alan replied, "You obviously understand this kind of thing better than I do, and it certainly sounds like you're on top of the strategy but we're still only two men – and I'm no soldier!"

"Actually, to them we are only one man. As far as they know, you're the one who dealt with your three assassins and they don't even know I exist. Equilibrium can provide all the intelligence we need and I'll provide the tactics and firepower."

Jake clicked a remote control and his secret armory emerged from its hiding place. Alan's jaw dropped and he whispered something unintelligible to himself. He recognized a few of the handguns, a shotgun, and one machine gun but the rest of the arsenal was alien to him.

"My God – it looks like you're preparing for World War III!"

"It pays to be well prepared. It may seem like overkill to a civilian but each weapon here has specific applications and their deployment will depend on the tactics required for a given situation."

"Well, you're the expert. I'll do what I can but I'm no killer – I have to follow the law."

"You won't be doing any killing. Your job is to stay safe right here and liaise with Equilibrium. You'll direct investigations with your detective skills while I carry out any missions required. But first I have to show you something very disturbing."

"And the good times just keep rolling." Alan sighed heavily. "Now what?"

"I mentioned it in your hotel room just before Holly was abducted but I wanted to wait until Holly was safe and you were sheltered here before showing you because this really is quite unsettling. While I was following you in Columbus, Equilibrium hacked into Blue Sky's mainframe and retrieved a highly encrypted folder called, 'Project Hallucineers"

"That's an odd name; what does it mean?"

"It's a made up word combining 'hallucination' and 'engineers' and it's a very accurate description of what Gelling's team at Blue Sky have discovered."

"I don't understand – what are you saying?"

"I think it's better if you read the files yourself. I know it will be hard to believe but when you think about it, the science could easily explain Helen Benson's alleged suicide, the assassinations at the Capitol Building, and possibly why Professor Guthrie also seemingly took his own life."

Alan glared into Jake's eyes ominously then turned to face the voice activated computer's LED monitor again. Jake commanded the system to bring up the file titled, 'Minutes of Meeting - Project Hallucineers Budget, Staffing and Strategy' and Alan read mesmerized.

The file was a complete transcript of the meeting and described in great detail how Professor Linus Gelling had posed a question to the board, "Can a hallucination be contrived and controlled to become so real as to supplant reality?"

This question and the science involved, later led to the hypothesis from which the professor began to develop the actual technology. The answer of course, would prove far more complex than the question; requiring an amazing combination of advanced pharmaceutical engineering, cutting edge computer programming, nanotechnology, dendrimer technology, and a specially designed delivery system, to produce a working model that could successfully manipulate conscious awareness.

During the meeting, the Head of Finance at Blue Sky Biotech had a rather different question, "With respect Professor Gelling, how would such a technology provide the appropriate 'R.O.I.'? I mean what commercial application could there possibly be for such a thing, aside from recreational use?".

"Ah yes, the ubiquitous 'Return On Investment'. Well, I shouldn't worry too much about that if I were you Mr. Farnsworth. The applications for such a technology are far more widespread and commercially viable than you may be aware. To name a few: proper control of psychiatric patients without tranquilizing agents or anti-psychotic medications, vastly improved quality of life for paraplegics, quadriplegics and other paralysis victims, relief from severe depression, reducing violent tendencies in psychotic criminals, and the list goes on - limited only by *your* imagination. Then there are the non-medical applications, such as inexpensive holidays for consumers in the comfort and safety of their own homes, use as a marital aid, speed-learning new languages, etc. - once again, only limited by *your* imagination. In fact, the sheer volume and monetary value of currently available products we could replace is staggering."

Alan glanced up at Jake in disbelief then turned back the file and imagined how Farnsworth must have squirmed in his chair as he was suddenly brought to earth and reminded why Professor Gelling was considered by many experts as the 'Einstein' of modern medicine. He must have realized how foolish it would have been to question such a visionary.

The transcript continued, with Farnsworth saying, "My apologies Professor Gelling. I certainly didn't intend to question your judgment. Obviously my imagination for such things is limited."

"Not to worry; I'm sure you're terribly good with numbers." Gelling said.

Alan thought that Farnsworth must be good with numbers to become the Head of Finance for such a company but it seemed his head was in the clouds if he thought he was any kind of match for the genius of the company's Head of Research and Development. He must have known that Linus Gelling was not only a board certified Neurologist and highly respected Neuro-surgeon, but also a renowned Endocrinologist and Professor of Clinical Pharmacology. Aside from his medical qualifications, there was also an MBA, majoring in Business from Harvard.

Alan considered how Gelling's youthful appearance belied his sixty five years of life and that he was possibly the most highly qualified person in the United States of America, with his initial medical degree earned at sixteen years of age. There was no doubt that Gelling was a genius in the truest sense of the word. Despite this fact, he seemed a relatively humble man who was apparently a beloved mentor and supervisor to many staff and students.

The minutes continued, with Gelling saying, "Now it's my turn to apologize Mr. Farnsworth. I did not intend to embarrass you but simply to make my point clear so that we can move on from doubt, to developing research plans and budgets for this project."

"Thank you Professor and I shan't interrupt again – unless it's to offer constructive input about numbers." Farnsworth said.

"Good, so we're agreed. Here is my plan, with projected staffing and funding requirements." Said Gelling and according to the minutes, he turned on the light projector and began his presentation detailing cost estimates, research protocols and techniques, and other corporate matters.

This was all just history now as research on the project dubbed 'Project Hallucineers' began with the purpose of developing the technology known as 'SSCH' or Site Specific Cyberceutical Hallucinogen. Now into its fourth year, advances came with uncanny speed in this normally slow moving, difficult and complex world.

Jake told the computer to close the minutes and to open a number of other files for Alan to read and sat back to reread them himself. According to the information, there is relatively little known about the human brain and there were estimated to be well over a hundred neurologically related chemicals, enzymes and hormones as yet unidentified by science.

Aside from Linus Gelling's titanic intellect, in order to tackle the project, he recruited the best and brightest minds in the various fields needed to produce results. They included the diverse talents of: Eric Rothstein, Dr. Helen Benson, Dr. Ellis McDonald, and Dr. Brian Sanders, who held over fifty worldwide patents for highly successful specialized delivery systems for various pharmaceutical and biotechnological therapies.

The goal was to develop a structure to contain a massive complex of computer programmed neuro-hormones which would attach, by means of a highly specialized delivery system, to the pons which surrounds the medulla oblangata, which is the lower part of the brain stem, and the cerebral peduncle. The implanted device would then release its payload to mimic a phenomenon known as Peduncular Hallucinosis, a very rare and little understood phenomenon which causes vivid and realistic hallucinations. It is thought that in Peduncular Hallucinosis, the pons secretes a specific neuro-hormone that triggers the peduncle to cause extremely realistic and vivid hallucinations in the small population of people who experience this condition. It is not known why or how this occurs but Gelling and his team had discovered how to exploit the phenomenon for medical use. The difference would be that the implanted SSCH would control the hallucination through Rothstein's software programming, instead of allowing it to run wild and random, as it would in naturally occurring Peduncular Hallucinosis. Such an advance would have been impossible before today's supercomputers, sophisticated diagnostics, and dendrimers but these scientific advancements are now happening at an exponentially faster rate than ever before.

Under Gelling's leadership, the team had made full use of their combined expertise to develop the first working model of SSCH technology. This involved an incredibly complex combination of technologies. First there was the purpose built dendrimer, developed by Ellis McDonald, to hold the hormonal matrix which would convey the hallucination programmed by Rothstein to the pons of the brain. This was an astounding formation which, when viewed through an electron microscope, resembled tens of thousands of elaborately constructed snowflakes, assembled into a single unimaginably intricate, three dimensional structure. This dendrimer was the only design capable of storing the pre-programmed neuro-hormones required to achieve the desired result. Next were the unique cyber-active neuro-hormones created in collaboration by Helen Benson and Linus Gelling. These were the first chemical compounds able to store and release computer programmed information into the human brain, as a silicon chip would to a computer, and a scientific wonder unto themselves. Finally was the deceivingly simple looking delivery mechanism from Brian Sandler. This small grey piece of equipment resembled a tiny hot glue gun or a miniaturized phaser from a science fiction movie. Designed to be held in the fingers like a pencil, it had no trigger but worked by lightly pressing it against the subject, which would cause the machine to release a tiny amount of high pressure nitrogen, sufficient to propel the individual dendrimer along a barrel, then through the dermis and muscle tissue, right into the dura mater, where it would attach to the pons. They were beyond the cutting edge of nanotechnology and despite their intellect and intimate involvement in the project, even to the developers themselves, the whole thing still seemed like science fiction.

Animal testing had proceeded well and while they were happy with progress in that area, they knew full well that human testing would be the only way to truly prove the technology. Since animals were incapable of giving comprehensive feedback or properly disseminating the required data, the level of success and realism achieved could not be accurately measured. Ethical guidelines dictated the pace at which they could move from animals to healthy human volunteers and on the day of their first true test, the anticipation was palpable.

The first human test subject was a male Caucasian university student with a healthy medical history, dubbed, 'Test Subject SSCH00001'. He was a self funded student so the money offered to take part in the trial was a strong motivator. Gelling and Benson wanted to limit the complexity and duration of the hallucination so that the results could be as clear as possible. Rothstein had programmed a relatively simple scenario, in which the subject would experience floating on their back in a swimming pool for approximately two minutes. The sights, sounds, smells and feel were an easily replicable template so only minor modifications were required between subjects to allow for race, gender, height, age, etc. Proceeding in this manner would give the team a strong baseline on which to establish testing of more elaborate hallucinations as they progressed. The benefit of such a simple scenario was that they could examine different data from individual subjects without the risk of outcomes being clouded by complexities. It was hoped that the differences in each subject's experience of the test would be purely emotional, based on the way each person perceived the sensations of the hallucination.

Test Subject SSCH00001 was seated in the custom made, reclining test seat and prepared with all the necessary scientific monitoring equipment. After all monitoring equipment had been double and triple checked, Dr. Sandler placed the individual SSCH in the loading chamber of the delivery mechanism then closed the device and stepped forward to position it near the base of the subject's skull, slightly to the right of the spinal column. He looked up at the rest of the team and Gelling gave him a nod as they waited in anticipation. With one smooth, quick movement, Sandler pressed the end of the device against the subject's skin. There was a very brief, muffled hiss and the implant was sent on its way to the brain stem. The chair was then moved to a fully reclined position and the team waited for the device to release its information.

SSCH00001 blinked his eyes rapidly and shook his head as he began to return to reality. The test seat had been returned to its upright position and the team was looking anxiously into his eyes for any signs. Their faces and the testing laboratory became clear to his eyes and after a brief hesitation, he began to smile broadly and the room erupted in noisy applause. They excitedly began unbuckling him from the seat and removing the EEG probes and other instruments from his body so they could begin the debriefing, record his experience and collate the data. Aside from the dramatically improved feedback and outcome data received, the only difference between human and animal studies had been that human subjects needed to fall asleep briefly before the hallucination would implant. Although a somewhat surprising development, this was not a perceived problem because invariably, the subjects would become sleepy very soon after the implantation.

Since that first subject, Gelling and his team had used the original floating hallucination in twenty different test subjects to establish the required baseline before moving on to more complex hallucinations, and the results were uniformly outstanding. Each subject had reported their experience as very vivid, highly realistic, and enjoyable. They all clearly recalled the coolness and texture of the water surrounding their bodies and its sound as it lapped against their ears. They recalled the warmth of the sun shining down on their faces contrasting against the coolness of the water, the sight of a few wispy clouds against the beautiful blue sky, and the smell of water in their nostrils. The only slight variation in results was in their individual emotional responses to the sensations they experienced. This was probably the most gratifying part of the trial for Gelling and Benson as they had originally been concerned that the hallucination may take over normal thought processes and dictate rather than evoke emotion. They were very relieved and excited to find that the individual test subjects experienced varied emotional responses to the programmed sensations, based on their own personal histories and thought processes. They could not have hoped for better results and immediately accelerated the pace of testing progression.

As their initial confidence in the safety and efficacy of SSCH technology continued to grow, even some individual team members had volunteered for testing. Brian Sandler had always wanted to go skydiving but his morbid fear of heights prevented him from doing so. Strapped into the test seat in the safety of the laboratory, he had experienced his fantasy in heart pounding three-dimensional realism and was completely astounded by the results. His experience was recorded and properly documented alongside those of the other test subjects. Eric Rothstein had also volunteered but knowing that Professor Gelling would not have approved it beforehand, he wouldn't disclose his hallucination until after it had been implanted and experienced. It seemed that his experiences as a 'geek' in high school had had a lasting impact on him because his hallucination consisted of an elaborate revenge scenario involving the complete humiliation of his teenaged tormentors and culminating in a labyrinthine orgy with his school's entire football cheerleading squad. Helen blushed constantly during his debrief and Professor Gelling was suitably disdainful but Rothstein was the only person currently capable of creating such exquisitely detailed programming so they ignored his childish excursion and went back to their properly structured testing.

Nine months after establishing the initial baseline of the study with those first twenty test subjects, Eric Rothstein had amassed an impressive catalogue of hallucinations ranging from basic to very involved scenarios. As the library built, he was able to combine different scenarios into more and more complex hallucinations of ever increasing duration. It had gotten to the point where some were so elaborate that they could last an entire day or longer. The sophistication of hallucinations being created and implanted was growing at an exponential rate and the team realized that the potential was virtually limitless. It wouldn't be long before SSCH technology would be capable of supplanting entire years of waking lives.

Gelling and Benson knew that they would soon be able to move on from Phase I safety trials in healthy volunteers to Phase II trials to test for efficacy in patients with diseases and disabilities. They also knew that they were operating in a grey area because the clinical trial requirements for pharmaceutical testing were very different to the less stringent and time consuming methods required for approval of medical devices. It could be argued that SSCH would fall into either or both categories so they were very conscious to maintain highly ethical standards throughout their testing protocols to avoid future complications. They aimed to lobby for approval of SSCH as a medical device but conducted the trials to meet the stricter pharmaceutical requirements and hoped the proven benefits and perfect safety record of the treatment would sway the FDA to agree with them.

Alan's head tilted upward to the ceiling and dragged his fingers through his unkempt sandy hair as his mind ran through the details over and over. If he hadn't known that the documents he'd just read were genuine, and if the science didn't fit the mysterious deaths so well, he would never have believed such a thing possible. He turned to Jake and said in an ominous tone, "This is some serious stuff!"

Jake nodded then said, "Somehow, 'serious' doesn't quite cover it. I've had time to digest it and realize the ramifications and potential of such technology – especially from a military perspective. Entire wars could literally be won and lost with 'SSCH'. I'll let you process what you've seen in your own time but for now, let's introduce you to Equilibrium."

Jake directed Alan to the stand alone computer which he used to communicate with Equilibrium. Alan listened intently as Jake showed him the color coded protocol system and explained the importance of sticking to the security protocols. A few moments later a secure link had been established and Alan saw his first communication with Equilibrium.

"What are those fluttery things at the top of the screen?" he queried.

"I know my way around computers but that technology is way beyond me. It's some kind of rotating encryption system that protects our communications from being monitored. It's virtually uncrackable so you can say anything you need to without fear of discovery. Equilibrium developed the system and even the CIA and NSA can't get through it."

"Welcome aboard detective." came the first message.

Alan looked at Jake enquiringly.

"Go ahead and answer. Just type what you want to say into the keyboard like you would with instant messaging."

Alan began to type, "Thanks – I think."

"Don't worry; you're in safe hands with Jake. I've read a great deal about you and I'm certain you can handle your end."

"It's kind of strange to have people looking into me like this."

"We had to be certain you can be trusted. Consider it a compliment - we don't trust just anyone."

"What do you want me to do?"

"Put your thinking cap on and give me a line of investigation to follow. I can find anything in the electronic world but Jake will have to get anything you need from the physical world. I await your instructions."

Alan turned to Jake, "Wait a second; I can't be in charge of this whole thing!"

"You're not 'in charge' of anything but your experience and success as an investigator make you our best chance at building a legal case against Devlin. If you aren't able to succeed within the bounds of the law, then I will become judge jury and executioner."

"You would kill Devlin in cold blood?"

"If you can't get a legitimate conviction that puts Devlin away for life or in the chair, I will terminate him as a hostile target without hesitation. This is not some prime time television drama; this man will stop at nothing to achieve his goals. He's already killed four people we know of and probably several more we don't. Do you really think he'll stop if he isn't forced to do so?"

"No, you're right. It's just difficult to get my head around this. Can you promise me you won't kill him until all other avenues are exhausted?"

"OK. But remember this detective; the longer this takes, the more chance Devlin's henchmen have to find Holly again. I know I said she's safe but even idiots get lucky sometimes – do you want to take that risk?"

"OK, OK... I'm on it."

Alan turned back to the keyboard, "We need to find a connection between the man who was at both crime scenes and Alex Devlin or Devlin Industries."

"Do you have a description?"

"Better – I have a picture."

"Send it to me."

Jake showed Alan how to load the image from his memory stick and they watched as the data was transferred over the secure site.

"I'll need some time on this. Some of the international agencies have rather clever firewalls to get past before I can access their databases. In the meantime, try to think of other leads."

Jake leaned over to type on the keyboard, "Did you get into Guthrie's email account?"

Alan looked at him questioningly.

"While we were waiting to hear from Walker, I asked Equilibrium to hack his email account to see if he'd found anything useful."

The hacker's reply came back, "Yes, that must be how they found out he was investigating the SSCH technology. He was obviously getting too close to the truth for their liking."

Alan's face dropped in the realization that the good-natured professor was killed for helping him. After a moment, he forced his hands back to the keyboard. "Did he have any family?" he typed.

"I know it's no great solace but not that I could find."

Jake interjected, "Criminals do bad shit – it's not your fault. None of this is anyone's fault but Devlin's, so let's get the bastard!"

Alan knew Jake's logic was correct but he couldn't help feeling remorse for involving Guthrie in his investigation. "He was a genuinely nice guy and completely harmless – he didn't deserve to die."

"Of course he didn't but bad things happen to good people. I may seem callous but that's life - you need to focus and move on. Don't let Devlin get away with this." Jake said, trying to steer Beach back to the task at hand.

"I'll get back to you soon." appeared on the page before the connection terminated and the screen went blank. Alan forced his feelings down and his investigative instincts began to overtake the sadness and remorse. He turned to look at Jake and said, "Can you get to the bodies of the three assassins and take their fingerprints?"

"Now you're thinking detective."

"If we're going to be working together like this, I'm pretty sure we should be on a first name basis. Call me Alan."

"OK; now you're thinking Alan. I'm on it."

"While you do that, I'll go back to the hotel and get my bag and my car."

"That's not going to happen. Devlin's men will be watching your hotel and won't hesitate to remove you from the equation. Anything you might need from your bag, you can find in my wardrobe or bathroom. You're on lockdown until I say otherwise. If you need anything else, I'll get it for you."

Resignation swept over Beach's face as he realized the truth in Jake's words. "I guess you're right but don't laugh when you see me in clothes three sizes too big for me."

"Now that, I cannot promise. See you soon. And don't worry – you're totally safe here. I completely redesigned and refinished the whole building. Nothing short of a very skilled explosives technician with a buttload of C4 can get to you in here. Might as well make yourself at home."

"What am I supposed to do while you're gone?"

"Watch a movie, have a shower or get some rest; up to you."

"I can't work that remote and I sure as heck can't sleep!"

"Just speak direct commands into the remote and it'll do as you ask. Now, if you don't mind, I'm going to get to work."

Alan felt a bit helpless and trapped but he knew he had no choice so he watched as his new partner put on a strange looking double shoulder holster setup built into a thin vest and grabbed the two Para Tactical 45 caliber handguns from their mounts. He checked the magazines then shoved the weapons into their holsters and put four spare mags into slotted pockets in the front of his vest. He then put on a loose casual jacket to cover the whole thing, closed the armory and briskly walked out the door.

Turning back to Alan, he said, "Unless you want to be locked in there, you'd better come out."

Alan jerked himself out of his chair and quickly vacated the room. Jake pulled the heavy door shut and punched the code to lock it then strode off through the gym without another word. Alan stood feeling a little lost for a moment before making his way back to the lounge area. He felt suddenly very alone and thought the best thing to do was take his mind off the situation with some television.

He tentatively picked up the entertainment system's remote control and spoke, "Turn on."

To his surprise, the large LED screen came to life and lights flickered on the various components that made up Jake's system.

"Menu." he said, smiling widely.

A comprehensive menu appeared showing a choice of functions including 'television stations' so he spoke the words into the remote and a huge menu of channels appeared.

"Local news."

A choice of news channels appeared and he chose the network affiliated with Marissa Wilson's station in Columbus. There was a reporter discussing upcoming mayoral elections and the bottom of the screen displayed a variety of headlines and breaking news. Alan watched vacantly for a time until suddenly, a news flash appeared that shocked him to the core.

"Manhunt for rogue Ohio police detective following triple homicide in Jersey City – details to follow."

Alan's face drained of blood as it dawned on him that Devlin must have used the opportunity to manipulate the press and disable him from moving around freely. Jake's instructions to stay put were now redundant and the detective knew with fatal realization that even if he could leave, he wouldn't get far. His mind worked frantically to figure a way out of this mess but there was none. As if the revelation of Project Hallucineers wasn't enough to deal with, on top of everything that had happened over the last couple of days, he was now faced with being a fugitive from the law.

Devlin obviously had enough power to make this happen and even if Alan turned himself in to the authorities, there was probably already enough manufactured evidence to convict him but he doubted that was Devlin's true motive. A man with that kind of influence and resources would probably have people inside the police who would either act on his behalf or allow access to assassins who would make sure Alan never made it to trial.

His mind spinning, Alan waited anxiously for the full report and his fears were confirmed. The city's police force was on full alert and his picture was plastered across the giant screen. He knew he was innocent but couldn't help thinking his career and his life were finished. The news would remain confined to local stations for now but soon it was bound to get back to his colleagues and bosses in Columbus. His thoughts were now so frantic that he even thought about trying to make an escape but knew that was futile. All he could do was wait anxiously until Jake returned, tell him the news and hope for a way out of this mess.

Alan was not a big drinker but suddenly felt the overwhelming desire to calm his nerves with some strong liquor. He went to the kitchen and checked the cupboards but there was nothing there. In a cupboard were some beautiful hand cut crystal Scotch glasses but there was no sign of something to fill them. He smacked his hand down hard on the counter in frustration and as the pins and needles began to tickle his palm, an idea struck him. He walked back to the remote control and spoke into it.

"Bar."

Sure enough, a quiet hum emanated from the opposite wall and a solid mahogany bar slowly emerged from its concealment. It held an impressive assortment of single malt Scotch whiskies and other expensive liquors. Alan selected a bottle of twenty five year old Bowmore Single Malt, took it back to the kitchen and poured three fingers into one of the heavy lead crystal glasses then downed it in two gulps. The smooth liquid went down easily but being unaccustomed to whisky, Alan's face contorted as it hit his esophagus and stomach. The feeling was hot and bracing and he poured again; this time four fingers and drained half of it then started sipping the fine Scotch to appreciate its full flavor and character.

He went back to the sofa, put the bottle on the table in front of him and sat leaning forward with the glass held tightly in both hands; warming its contents and sipping. Soon the glass was empty and quickly refilled with another four fingers. As he sat sipping and watching, the news flash kept replaying over and over on the big screen. Alan's head began to spin from the shock of the day's events and the large amount of powerful and unfamiliar whisky. Suddenly, a very uneasy feeling welled up in his stomach forcing him to sprint for the bathroom. The toilet came into view and as if on cue, the churning contents of his belly surged upward to explode out of his mouth in perfect time to land in the bowl from two feet away and continued to flow as his face pushed close to the porcelain. He heaved violently as his body indignantly rejected his mistreatment until the spasms finally subsided, leaving him breathless with tears streaming down his face.

The unbearable stress of the last few hours had finally won the battle and Alan's body began to shake with anger and frustration. Several minutes later, he finally pulled himself up from the toilet, ready to clean up any mess he'd made but thankfully found his aim had been true and one flush of the toilet was all that was needed. Completely drained, he instinctively stripped then stepped into the shower to try to wash away the day and stood with the water beating down on his neck for a full half hour before washing his hair and body. He turned off the shower, dried himself and found a thick bathrobe to wear then flopped on the bed and fell exhausted into a deep, shock induced sleep.

Chapter 14

P anic gripped Alan as he ran frantically down the cobbled sidewalk. Spotting a bar ahead and with a lead of only fifty yards and closing, he thought he might have a better chance of survival in a crowded saloon than alone on the street with four trained mercenaries but entering the room, his hopes were dashed. He stood breathlessly surveying the scene, which felt like a strange, irrational hallucination. In fact, it felt to Beach as though he was in a rather clichéd 'B' grade detective movie. Aside from the well past middle aged barman, there were only four people partaking of the establishment's wares. Two of those were obviously all day drinkers engaged in an overly animated drunken debate over who would win the Super Bowl next season. The third was a forty something woman with a heavily lined face and sad expression that told of broken dreams and long suffering. Sitting at the far end of the bar drinking a small beer, was a huge bear of a man who looked as though he may have been a boxer, judging by the thickened skin around his brow and eyes. It looked as though he'd also had a broken nose at some point but despite these facial features, was well presented in a designer tank top with a rather large gold chain around his neck. He also seemed, from a distance, to be quite sober.

Based on his summation of the circumstances, Alan felt the obvious place to be was between the unfortunate woman and the boxing bear with ham hock shoulders. He quickly made his way down the length of the bar and the barman said a cheery 'hello' then asked, "What'll it be pal?"

Alan breathlessly returned his greeting as calmly as he could, "Make it a cold beer please, and a round for the house."

"That's very generous of you. Drinks on the new guy!" he called out.

A raucous round of thanks came up from the two football fans and the lady managed a sad smile in appreciation. The big man beside him just nodded silently with a sideways glance. Just then the door burst open with the four mercenaries instinctively scanning the room to assess the situation. They saw no threat to their mission so they composed themselves and strolled toward where Jake was seated. The leader extended his arm to clamp a powerful hand on Alan's shoulder and the detective winced in pain.

"There's nowhere to hide Beach – if you come with us now, I'll make it quick and painless."

In desperation, Alan pulled his police issue Glock from its holster and turned violently to face the aggressors. As he spun around, the leader's hand snapped from his shoulder to his wrist above the gun and easily twisted the weapon from his grip. The bear watched bemused noticing the detective's shield on his belt.

"Hardly seems fair does it – four against one?" he croaked from behind his tiny glass of beer.

The leader turned to the huge man and opened his mouth to speak but before he could make a sound, the bear-man thrust his empty paw into the henchman's face with lightening speed. There was a loud crack as the man's orbital bone shattered and his partners in crime stood aghast as he slumped to the floor unconscious.

"Darn – now it's only three against one. That really isn't fair." he spoke again before lunging toward the three with speed and agility that belied his size.

Alan watched in awe as the three quickly succumbed to a startling variety of strikes and throws until all four were unconscious on the floor. He turned to look at the big man, who had already returned to his stool and calmly sipped his beer. The other people in the bar just applauded politely as if watching a matinee show. Alan tried to thank the man but before he could speak, the bear reached out his paw to shake and said, "Call me Jake…Jake Riley."

Just as Alan reached for the big man's hand, he felt a strange tingling and an ethereal female voice broke through to him

"Mr. Alan, Mr. Alan...Wake up!" she exclaimed anxiously.

His eyes opened a crack to see an attractive woman with Asian features looking down at him with concern.

"You have bad deam! Make big noise! You OK?" she continued.

Alan shook himself from his sleep and quickly grasped where he was but had no idea who this person was or how she knew him.

"Mr. Jake taining in gym. You get up now; sheets all wet – I wash. Make blekfast all leddy faw you."

Alan looked down and saw he was covered in a lather of sweat. He must have thrown the bathrobe off during the night and the sheets were soaking wet. His shock, the alcohol and the stress of the previous day had obviously taken their toll and his system had flushed it all out while he slept. Despite the vivid, disturbing dream, profuse sweating, and a devastating thirst, he felt strangely refreshed and clear. Seeing no choice but to comply, he quickly got up to shower unaware of his complete nakedness. The pretty young lady smiled widely until Alan suddenly realized his situation and quickly reached for the robe as she watched amused.

"Mr. Alan got nice butt!" she giggled. "Ten minute – blekfast!" and she bustled out of the bedroom.

Despite the compliment, Alan was flustered and embarrassed as he went to shower. A few minutes later, he entered the kitchen in an expensive track suit about three sizes too big and the little Asian lady scoffed loudly when she saw him approach.

"Mr. Alan need to eat if him want glow big body like Mr. Jake." she laughed.

Indignant, Alan wanted to know who this person was and what she was doing here so he strode off toward the gym almost tripping on his pant legs as he went. Nearing the doorway, he heard a strangely patterned rapid-fire thumping coming from the gym. The beats were so close together they were almost continuous but there was an odd split second staccato break in the rhythm. As he rounded the corner, the source of the loud beating patter became evident. Jake was stationed in front of what appeared to be a piece of car tire mounted at head height on a solid post bolted to the floor. There was a blur of movement above and around his head and shoulders as his arms moved in repetitive patterns directing powerful strikes with pinpoint accuracy onto a tiny spot on the tire. He walked closer and opened his mouth to speak but before he could, Jake said, "Give me thirty seconds Alan."

He continued the pattern of movements for another thirty seconds and Alan watched in silent amazement as small wisps of smoke began to curl and rise from a spot the size of a quarter on the tire. A few more seconds and Jake stopped then pressed his palm against the smoking spot as if extinguishing a small fire.

"Sorry to ignore you but I needed to finish my set."

"Set... set of what? What the heck was that you were doing?"

"A 'Redondo' - it's part of the Filipino martial art of 'Arnis' or maybe you've heard it called, "Escrima'."

"Oh yeah Escrima - of course...NOT! You seem to have me confused with someone who's travelled the world studying martial arts – oh wait, you seem to have me confused with you!"

"A bit touchy this morning, are we? Did Tik give you a start?"

"A 'start'?! An attractive Asian woman I've never met before wakes me from a deep sleep, sees me naked and tells me I've got ten minutes until 'blekfast', and you think I might have had a 'start'?! You're the master of understatement."

"Sounds like a pretty good way to wake up to me. You always complain this much?"

Alan looked long and hard at Jake's semi smile before replying, "OK, you're putting me through boot camp, aren't you."

"We prefer 'Basic Training' but you could say that - yes. It's time you came to grips with reality. Your inability to deal quickly and effectively with what's thrown in your face belies your job and life experience and frankly, it's becoming tedious. You need to be drilled in this skill so we can move forward without you throwing a hissy fit every time new shock comes your way. The U.S. Marine Corps motto, 'Adapt and Overcome' is one you should adopt from now on."

Alan fumed with anger at Jake's scolding but he quickly controlled his temper as his protector's words sank in and rang true, until his face visibly relaxed.

"There now; doesn't that feel better?" Jake smiled warmly.

"I'm sorry." Alan said genuinely. "You're right, I haven't handled things well but in my defense, my job experience is not what you seem to think. I am purely an investigator – and a good one - but my job entails finding perpetrators after the fact, not facing them during the commission of the crime. I'm not accustomed to having my life threatened by mercenaries, nor am I used to witnessing frighteningly violent martial arts displays that result in dead bodies, strange women seeing me naked, and being the subject of a city-wide police manhunt. Surely you can see my point."

"Very clearly but I also know that you need to deal with this shit and somewhere inside you, lies the heart of a warrior." Jake reached out to close Alan's eyes. "Keep them closed. Now let me ask you this: if those three mercenaries were hurting Holly right before your eyes and the odds were completely stacked against you; what would you do? Would you let them hurt her or would you fight to save her no matter what the personal cost?"

Without hesitation, Alan replied, "I'd do everything I could to save her, of course. What's your point?"

"My point is that you have courage – you just haven't been trained to properly utilize that courage and you're not used to dealing with such confrontations. Just like military basic training, the more you are faced with, the stronger you become – unless it's in your nature to fail but I don't think it is. You're no teenager straight out of high school; you have a lot of life experience and we need to show you how to draw on that experience to accelerate your learning curve dramatically. This situation is not going away any time soon and as you said, there is now a police manhunt underway to add to your troubles. Now you can choose one of two paths; the path of the hunted or the path of the hunter. Are you going to run and die on fear and instinct or are you going to take control of your situation and do what needs to be done?"

Jake's words and control showed wisdom well beyond his years and Alan couldn't help thinking what kind of a life could make such a relatively young man – a man younger than himself - so worldly wise. He was of course, completely right and Alan made up his mind then and there not to complain, shock, or shrink from danger again until he had done what he had to do.

"You don't need to speak; I can see by your expression that you have chosen wisely. Now, let's give you some basic but very effective techniques – just in case of emergency."

Alan was slightly taken aback by the prospect of Jake's suggestion but bit his lip and agreed with some forced enthusiasm.

"Don't expect too much from me though – I haven't done any kind of training since police academy and that was a long time ago."

"Don't worry; I have some simple tricks that will serve you well in a pinch but I'm nearly certain you won't need to use them. It's much more important to learn a few effective techniques thoroughly than fill your mind with complicated maneuvers that you won't be able to execute under pressure. You will need to be patient and focused because despite their simplicity, you will need to repeat them until I'm confident that they have become natural reflex actions for you."

"I'll do my best."

"OK, I'm going to show you each one only once then we'll have breakfast and I want you to visually contemplate each technique while we eat. We'll then do some target practice for half an hour and return to see what you remember of the techniques. It's important for me to see to what degree your mind remembers or distorts your initial impressions of what I show you."

"Target practice?"

"Yeah; when was the last time you were at the range?"

"We have to re-qualify every year."

"So you only practice once a year. How does the police department expect their people to maintain weapon proficiency at that rate."

"I guess they think that's enough for a detective. I haven't had to draw my weapon on the job in ten years."

"Well it certainly showed in the alley yesterday, didn't it."

"I guess you're right." Alan replied sheepishly. "But where are we going to shoot?"

Jake just smiled and said, "First things first...stand facing me." He then proceeded to demonstrate four basic but effective techniques in slow motion for the bewildered detective then broke off and said, "OK, let's not keep Tik waiting - Laotians can have quite a temper."

"I wondered what her accent was. How did she end up in Jersey City all the way from Laos?" Alan asked, following Jake out of the gym.

"Tik's entire family was murdered for their land many years ago so her hatred of the regime and her local knowledge made her an excellent company asset. Unfortunately, her cover was blown during a complicated mission that went bad and when I was ordered to abort the mission and leave her behind, I refused. They couldn't really argue because I funded her safe extraction myself and went through the proper channels to get her refugee status so they turned a blind eye. She has been my cook and maid ever since."

Alan grabbed Jake's shoulder to stop him so they were out of Tik's earshot and asked, "She doesn't want to do something more with her life than cooking and cleaning?"

Jake laughed, "You obviously don't understand Laotian culture Alan. She risked her life every day for a long time to avenge the death of her family but that time in her life is over and she can't go back, so now she lives to fulfill what she sees as her obligation to serve me for saving her."

"So she's like some kind of indentured servant or slave?"

"Do you really think I would treat someone that way? I let her do what she does out of respect for her culture but she lives rent free in a comfortable modern apartment upstairs, I pay her a decent salary and she is a significant beneficiary of my will. She doesn't know about the will and I prefer it stays that way - if she were to find out, she might think there is more to our relationship than there is - and I'm not the marrying kind."

Alan watched Jake walk toward the kitchen with even more admiration than he held for him previously. He broke off his thoughts and quickly moved forward to catch up but the bottom of one of his pant legs snagged on the toes of his other foot and he tumbled forward awkwardly. Uproarious laughter sounded from the kitchen as Tik held her flat stomach and covered her mouth with the other hand. Jake turned to see the object of her amusement and just shook his head. Alan regathered himself and slunk to the kitchen to join them.

"Tik, can you please go and buy Alan a track suit and some street clothes that will fit him properly." Jake said, handing her a billfold.

"Tik make Mr. Alan look sexy or seclet?"

"Secret would be best, please. We don't want him standing out from the crowd – besides; sexy would take more than clothes."

"Thanks a lot!" Alan said.

"Mr. Alan sexy enough. Mr. Jake not play nice!" With that, the pretty little woman scurried off through the bedroom and out of the complex.

"Seems she's adopted you Beach." Jake smiled.

"How does she come and go from your…uh…apartment, do you call it?"

"Apartment, complex, call it what you like; I call it home. There is a secondary security protocol programmed into the system. As long as I have already accessed the main system - which means I'm here – her handprint can also activate the door. I took the liberty of adding your right palm print to the same system while you were asleep but be aware that if I'm not here, it won't work. The same applies to getting out of the complex."

"Thanks – I think? Anyway, did you manage to get fingerprints from the guys in the alley?"

"I was able to access the bodies at the morgue but their fingerprints had all been removed either by acid or abrasion. It's quite common among some mercenaries. Sometimes they even make it permanent by having skin grafted from another part of their body onto their finger tips. Obviously, this is done to avoid identification in case they ever have to do a job without gloves."

"Damn - so it's another dead end!"

"Not necessarily; I was going to take some blood but was interrupted by the sound of high priced lawyers arguing with the Coroner about releasing the bodies so I quickly took some souvenirs." Jake matter-of-factly pulled a sealed jar from the fridge containing three pinky fingers. "I doubt they'll help though – any links between these guys and Devlin will be well covered."

Alan reeled back at the sight of the fingers but quickly composed himself, realizing that Jake was still giving him shock treatment and he didn't want to fail any more tests. "I guess they won't be needing them any more - how do we get the DNA samples?"

Jake smiled broadly. "Aah, grasshopper...you're picking it up quickly now, aren't you. Does the phrase, 'I have a friend' sound too cliché?"

"I would expect nothing less." Alan managed a half smile while still grimly imagining Jake removing appendages from the hapless mercenaries.

"I have to take these to my friend in a couple of hours so eat up and let's get to target practice."

The pair ate Tik's delicious breakfast and Alan couldn't help commenting, "I can see why you want her around – man can she cook! What is this stuff? Wait – no, don't tell me...I probably don't want to know."

"Good – I don't really know myself but it certainly is tasty."

They put their empty plates beside the sink and Alan followed Jake back to the gym. As they walked, Alan noticed for the first time, that Jake had a very slight limp and couldn't help asking, "What happened to your leg?"

"Straight to the point aren't you." Jake retorted.

"I guess it's the detective in me."

"No problem. I was shot three times and had to have my knee replaced. The whole joint is titanium now. The knee replacement itself doesn't cause the limp; the device is actually stronger than the natural knee but there was significant damage to the bones above and below so my right leg is very slightly shorter than the left now."

"Does it cause you any problems?"

"Just one – it cost me my position in the military. It's about ninety percent as good as new but that's not good enough for the Special Forces."

"I'm sorry."

"No big deal. It was time to move on anyway. Now I'm my own boss." he said wryly.

Jake took Alan to the far end of the gym and pressed a button mounted in a box on the wall. A thick, insulated panel big enough for a man to fit through, opened to reveal a single lane shooting range, twenty five yards long, two yards wide, and eight feet high. The walls, ceiling and floor were covered in heavy duty sound insulation and the end wall was piled to the top with sandbags. An automated pulley system held a standard military practice target in front of a solid countertop for resting rifles. Alan was amazed but decided to play it cool, "Not much good for rifle practice."

"That depends on the kind of rifle you're using." Jake smiled knowingly. "I took the liberty of cleaning your Glock and I'll use the Para Tacticals." he smiled, directing Alan to a gun case on the right hand wall.

Jake pulled the sound-proof door closed behind them and Alan's ears suddenly felt like he was in a pressurized chamber. The complete lack of any sound other than his own breathing was disconcerting and he wiggled his fingers in his ears trying to equalize.

"Don't worry about your ears, they'll get used to it shortly. Jake handed Alan a pair of silicone earplugs and shoved two into his own ears before they each donned a pair of yellow lens shooting glasses and Jake gestured for Alan to go first.

The detective armed his Glock, released the safety catch and raised the weapon to aim at the target twenty yards away. He carefully squeezed the trigger and released one shot then another then rapidly fired three more shots and lowered his weapon. Jake pressed the return button and a small electric motor whirred as it brought the target back to the counter.

"Solid shooting Alan – I guess we don't need to work on your aim as much as your weapon security skills. Put a few more shots into it to be certain and we'll move on."

Jake sent the target back out and Alan fired five more rounds, earning another welcome pat on the back. Despite never having used his firearm on duty, he knew he was a good marksman and was happy for Jake's recognition. Jake turned to open the door but Alan stopped him to ask, "Do you mind if I observe the master?"

"Not at all - just be warned that the Para is a .45 so it's going to make a bigger bang than your 9mm – keep your earplugs in."

Alan nodded and pushed his plugs in deeper then stood back as Jake sent the same target back out, cocked his twin Tactical 45s and fired five rounds from each weapon in rapid, alternating succession. The sound was thunderous and Alan felt the vibrations through his chest from where he stood. Jake turned and removed his earplugs then smiled and asked, "Satisfied?"

"I might be when I see the target."

"Oh, I'm sorry – you can't see it from here?" Jake smiled mischievously.

"Just push the button please –let's see what you've got."

Jake obliged and watched Alan's face as the target came into view. The detective's eyes bulged from their sockets as he surveyed the target. His own 9mm holes all lay close to the center of the target's head but Jake's .45s made a perfect circle the size of a nickel that couldn't have been more centered if he'd used a compass and ruler. Alan caught himself with his mouth agape and slammed it shut before giving Jake a sly grin.

"How do I know all shots from both guns went through that one hole?" he asked cheekily.

"I guess you'll just have to trust me." Jake winked then turned and walked out of the firing range.

Alan shook his head mockingly but knew full well what he'd just witnessed. If he was ever in a firefight, he wanted Jake Riley on his side – of that, he was certain.

Jake returned the weapons to their place in the armory and they met back in the training area to begin Alan's lessons. The next few hours were a blur of demonstrating, executing, critiquing, practicing, and repeating the four basic but effective Chinese Chin Na techniques. Jake told Alan that these techniques would see him through most situations and he wanted him to focus on the form and function of each one over and over in his mind until they became second nature.

"I know perfection is a lot to ask in such a short time but they are simple moves and you're an intelligent man. Just do whatever you have to do to get them completely straight in your mind. I'll test you from time to time when you don't expect it and I want to see expert level responses."

Alan found the techniques surprisingly simple and effective and was strangely enthusiastic about them. "I thought this would be difficult but now I'm not so sure. They feel comfortable and I'm pretty confident with…"

Before Alan could finish his sentence, Jake thrust his right hand out to grasp Alan's larynx. Alan was caught off guard and it took a few seconds for him to implement one of the techniques Jake had shown him to counter throat grabs and front facing strangles. He did eventually execute the move well but Jake looked at him scornfully.

"Never get overconfident my friend. It's not just about knowing the technique; it's about your reaction time. The second you see it coming, you must respond appropriately before your assailant can firmly establish his position. These four techniques must become second nature. If I'd been serious, you'd be dead now."

Alan looked down in shame, "I guess I just got carried away. The technique feels good but I guess I need work on my response time."

"I'm just trying to keep it real. This was the first time I tested you without warning and now we know where you need work so this test will be repeated often and unexpectedly to drill your reaction time. You'll get the hang of it soon enough – and I am impressed with how quickly you've learned the techniques. Just remember that if you ever need to use them in real life, you need to mean it. In other words, don't hesitate and always follow through – you must execute them as though your life depends on it; because it just might. When it comes right down to it though, your gun is your best weapon if it's available."

The two continued to talk and reexamine the techniques and their applications for a time until Jake got a text message from Equilibrium asking for a secure internet conference. Alan followed Jake into the armory room and they signed on using the blue protocol as instructed.

"I'm afraid I've got bad news - I found your weird little man. He was with the South African National Intelligence Service."

"Was?" Jake typed.

"He was killed during an operation twelve years ago."

"Are you sure it's our guy?"

"His face is an exact match for the picture you sent me. I guess he didn't like government service and faked his own death so he could move into the private sector."

Alan's frustration bunched his stomach into a tight ball and before he could control his emotions, he blurted, "Great, just great! He was our only lead. Now what the hell are we going to do?! I'm going to jail for something I didn't do and Devlin's getting away scot-free!"

Jake glared at Alan like a teacher at a misbehaving student. Alan immediately knew his meaning and hung his head. "I'm sorry but they're always two steps ahead of us and I'm getting really sick of it."

"So stop belly-aching and do something about it. Get ahead of the game."

"I'm glad you think it's a game Jake. This is my life we're talking about here."

"All the more reason to quit feeling sorry for yourself and get on point. Take a few deep breaths and get your shit together. The last two days should have taught you nothing if not that this kind of behavior is counterproductive. Adapt and overcome Detective, adapt and overcome."

Alan knew Jake was right but he couldn't see any clear direction. He knew he was feeling sorry for himself but couldn't seem to snap out of it until suddenly, Lieutenant Walker's words came back to him. "You've been in worse spots before and come through. Just stick with it and I'm sure you'll come up with something." Walker's faith in Alan had always been a source of strength for him and he focused hard on those words now to recharge his batteries. Jake watched him intently as he stood in entranced silence for a moment until his eyes opened to display a steely resolve.

"We need to get into Rothstein's computer." he said firmly.

Jake clenched his jaw then smiled broadly, "Now you're talking detective."

Chapter 15

Jake and Alan had spent the rest of the day developing a viable plan to access Blue Sky's well secured headquarters outside Columbus. Equilibrium's help had been enlisted to provide a way to access the data from Rothstein's computer system because it was not on line within Blue Sky's mainframe and therefore not accessible from outside the laboratory. The hacker had promised that a courier would deliver a small package containing a very sophisticated device to Jake's hangar at Teterboro airport in the morning. If they managed to get past the facility's tight security, all they needed to do was plug the device into a USB port on Rothstein's terminal and Equilibrium would then be able to access the data remotely.

Not long after contacting Equilibrium, they received a secure email with full blueprints of the building, details of its security systems and the guard roster from the human resources department. There was even a technical drawing and outline of the badge that all security staff had to carry. Alan showed Jake the route he had taken to the lab on the blueprints and Jake noted each security device he had passed on the technical drawings. Jake looked up each device's capabilities in the security data and noted the circumvention methods required. Deep in thought, he then asked Alan, "Do the security guards wear uniforms?"

"Just a navy blue blazer and business pants. The badge seems to be the only distinguishing feature, aside from their conspicuous size and suspicious glances."

"OK, I'm going to have to enlist some outside help. I need one of those badges and I know just the guy to make an exact replica. I'm going to drop the fingers off to my friend, meet my counterfeiter, and buy a navy blazer.

Alan suddenly started chuckling.

"Something funny?"

"It just sounds so absurd – did you hear what you just said? Drop off the fingers, see my counterfeiter…it all just seems so surreal."

"I suppose it would sound pretty odd to an outsider but I think we're beyond that. For one thing, you're the prime suspect in three killings that I committed."

Still chuckling, Alan said, "I'm fully aware of our precarious situation. I guess I'm getting used to it though - now I can see humor in the absurdity instead of just an endless dark tunnel."

Jake gave Alan a concerned look. "I'm not sure if that's a good thing or a bad thing. I just hope you're not losing it."

"Strangely enough, I'm actually quite fine - just glad we're moving forward now."

"Alright well, try to get some sleep – I'll need to do the same when I get back. Tik will fix you something to eat and set the sofa-bed up for you."

"I will soon but first I've got to make a phone call to organize a distraction for us at Blue Sky."

"See you bright and early for the flight to Bolton Field."

Jake strode off toward the bedroom and Alan walked back to the gym in the comfortable new track suit that Tik had bought for him. He sat down on the bench at the weight training station, took a deep breath and dialed Marissa Wilson's number.

The next morning, waking from another strange and vivid dream, it took Alan a moment to reorient as Tik's grinning face hovered over him from behind the sofa-bed. This was his second night in an unfamiliar bed, in an unfamiliar place and he was groggy from his fitful, dream filled sleep.

"Mr. Jake want me wake you up. Blekfast leddy now. I make stlong coffee for Mr. Alan wake up."

Despite his morning fog, Alan couldn't help smiling through gluey eyes at Tik's amusing accent. Jake had explained to him that while the Lao language did have a written equivalent of the 'R' consonant, it was only used to spell words from other languages such as Thai. The closest consonant sound to an 'R' that Tik could manage was an 'L' which caused the mispronunciation of many English words that Alan found rather endearing.

"What funny?" Tik enquired playfully.

"Nothing Tik. It's just nice to wake up to your smiling face and the smell of your wonderful cooking."

Tik gave Alan a wise grin. "Mr. Alan think on feet even when he sit on ass."

They both laughed as Alan realized she was onto him and knew full well that native English speakers found her pronunciation somewhat off-putting. Alan pointed a finger at her and shook his head. "You're very clever."

"Yes, Tik velly clever. Make spy for CIA in Lao you know."

Alan laughed even louder. "Yes, I know - sneaky girl."

"Yes, sneaky - Tik velly sneaky lady. You get up now – Mr. Jake leddy soon."

Alan roused himself and walked to the kitchen for some coffee. Jake soon emerged from the bedroom dressed in business pants with a shirt and tie carrying a navy blazer over his shoulder.

"Well, you already had the size and intimidating looks, now you're suited up for the job too."

"So it passes muster?"

"If I didn't know you, I would definitely think you were a guard at Blue Sky. Did you get the badge?"

Jake handed Alan a perfect copy of the badge that doubled as identification and access card for Blue Sky security staff. Once the counterfeiter had finished his task, Jake had taken the card to an electronics expert who specialized in access systems, to have it programmed according to specifications listed by the biotech company's security department. Jake would now have access to all areas of the building except for Linus Gelling's SSCH lab.

"How will you get into Rothstein's computer room?"

Jake produced a small rectangular black box with an LED panel and a multi-cable connector protruding from one end with a swipe card attached.

"This is a one-of-a-kind. The same guy that programmed the security card designed it with Equilibrium's help for another job a few months ago. It's the most advanced electronic security hacking device you can get. Swipe the card once, the device extracts the code from their system and programs it into the card then swipe it again and the door opens. There are some systems it can't access but they are only employed by government agencies in a few top secret facilities and, of course, here."

"Impressive – and scary."

Jake smiled and sat down to eat. Tik had made something she called Khao Tom Moo, a delicious Thai soup of rice, fried garlic and herb stock, chunks of ground seasoned pork, chopped spring onions and dried chillies. Alan didn't speak until he'd scoffed down his entire bowl.

"That was delicious Tik – thank you."

"No ploblem, Tik like cooking – Mr. Alan like eating."

Jake finished his bowl, turned and reached out to take Alan's chin in his hand and turned his head side to side, examining his face carefully.

"What on earth are you doing?" asked Alan.

"I'm checking your bone structure to decide on the best disguise for you. You're a wanted man in Jersey and we can't take the chance that the taxi driver or airport security won't recognize you like this. Grab a shower but don't shave, I've got just the thing and your stubble will help. Tik has laid out your clothes on my bed."

Alan did as he was told and soon returned to the kitchen in some khaki drill pants, a collared shirt and pale cotton jacket. Tik had done her job well and he looked unremarkable in his guise. Jake took him to the armory, pulled out an aluminum case and opened it. The sides splayed open like a fishing tackle box to reveal rows of small bottles, a variety of brushes and powders, clumps of human hair, strips of silicone and other unidentifiable items.

"Let's get to work."

A little trepidatious, Alan sat in a chair and sighed, "Do your worst."

Jake pulled several items from the kit and worked steadily for half an hour until he was satisfied the detective's face would not be recognized.

"That ought to do it." he said, placing a New York Yankees cap on Alan's head and handing him a mirror.

Beach looked for his reflection but instead saw a stranger. Jake had made it appear as though his brow was thicker and hairier, his cheek bones were higher, the bridge of his nose was slightly raised, there was a mid-length moustache and beard attached to his morning stubble and his whole complexion was slightly ruddy. "Wow - now that's eerie!"

"Just avoid rubbing or scratching anything. It's stuck on well but not as well as the real thing. You ready to go? The plane is fuelled and waiting."

"Lead the way."

The pair walked past the kitchen and they said goodbye to Tik. On the way through his bedroom, Jake grabbed a carry bag that held a wad of cash, a change of clothes and some other items, and pushed the card reader device into it. They made their way through the hidden exit in the bathroom and down the spiral staircase where Jake put his palm on the door reader.

"What about Tik? Won't she be locked in without you here?"

"Yes, it's her major cleaning day and she'll hold the fort in case we need anything while we're gone. Don't worry; your new friend will be fine."

They walked out to the street and Jake hailed a taxi to take them to the airport. The short ride was silent as Jake sat with his eyes closed going over the plan in his head. Alan thought about Holly and how he missed her but Jake had told him he couldn't speak to her until the danger was past or their location could be discovered. Sensing Alan's desperation, Jake dialed Walker on his encrypted phone while he explained, "I don't want to risk the possibility that his phone is now being monitored so the discussion will be cryptic and you won't be able to speak to them."

"OK, as long as I know they're safe."

Jake waited a moment before the former Ranger Instructor answered, "Hello?"

"Good morning sir." Jake began. "This is Peter Siddall from Pacific Bell – how are you today?"

Walker cursed under his breath, "Damned telemarketers!" then spoke normally, "Fine thanks but please take me off your list - I'm quite happy with my existing cell phone company."

"I understand sir but I'll get in trouble with my boss if I don't try. Can I just explain our latest offer please? It includes extras and we can also extend it to your family and friends."

"Tell your boss that you did your best but we are all more than satisfied with our current plan and I'm sure we have more extras than you could ever offer. Goodbye."

Jake turned to Alan with a smile. "No need to worry; things are well in hand. They're somewhere safe and as I suspected, he's enlisted some very potent allies. Can we move on now?"

"Thanks Jake. Now I'll be able to focus."

They went through the airport security gate where the guard politely greeted Jake and barely glanced at Alan. The disguise was flawless and he waved them through without question. As the taxi pulled up at Jake's hangar, Jimmy's smiling face greeted them.

"Hi Jake; you're off early this morning."

"The early bird catches the worm Jimmy. This is the passenger I told you about. Karl Osborn, this is Jimmy."

Jimmy extended his hand for Alan to shake. "Nice to meet you Mr. Osborn – you're in safe hands with Jake. Good luck with your deal in Columbus."

Jake had devised a cover for their early morning flight so Alan was prepared and thanked Jimmy. "Hopefully the vendor will be ready to accept our offer today. See you soon Jimmy."

The pair climbed into the King Air and buckled themselves in. Jake did his preflight checks and radioed the tower for clearance then taxied to the runway, throttled up and let the sleek craft surge forward for takeoff. Alan had never been in such a luxurious and powerful private aircraft before and watched engrossed as Jake deftly handled the big twin engine machine.

"Don't you have to have a copilot?" he asked through the headset.

"Not unless it's a commercial flight with passengers. I've got full commercial ratings for this aircraft so I can fly her solo. If the FAA ever changes the rules, I might have to downgrade to a single engine but fingers crossed they don't – I really love this plane."

"I can see why! She's got some serious power and the cabin is something else."

"I had a friend's company do the fit-out. There are a few hidden surprises back there as well."

"I won't ask."

"Then I won't tell."

The two chatted about Alan's job, the effect his decision to report his former partner's crimes had on him, and finally about losing his wife and finding Holly. The time passed quickly and soon they were on descent into Bolton Field. Their approach was approved and the runway ready for their arrival so Jake easily brought the plane in for a smooth landing and they were soon in a taxi headed for the outskirts Columbus. The cab took them to a small car rental company where a generic sedan was waiting for them to pick up. From there, Jake drove them through the city and onto the highway to Blue Sky Biotech. Twenty minutes later, they were in the main car park and they went through the plan one last time.

"No matter what you see or hear, stay in the car."

"What if you don't come back?"

Jake smiled then turned toward the driveway entrance in time to see a TV news truck arriving.

"Your friend is punctual. See you in fifteen minutes."

Before Alan could say another word, Jake was out of the car and striding toward the building's front entrance. He arrived seconds before the news crew pulled up in front of the door and the truck's passengers spilled onto the drive. They worked with military precision; the cameraman pulling the camera from its padded box, a sound technician mounting his boom microphone onto its pole and a producer holding a clipboard in front of him, directing operations as Marissa Wilson stepped in front of the door. The driver, who doubled as a live link technician, sat inside and electronically extended then turned the directional transmission dish on top of the truck to adjust for the best signal. The cameraman framed on Marissa's face as the producer cued her and as she began to speak, the two Blue Sky lobby guards were already out the door demanding to know what was going on.

Their attention fully focused on Marissa, the guards didn't notice Jake slip behind them and enter the lobby to make his way quickly to the staff access door. As the staff and visitors noisily gathered to watch the spectacle outside, Jake swiped his counterfeit ID card and said a silent 'thank you' to his electronics expert as the door slid open. Without looking back, he followed Alan's route toward Gelling's SSCH lab, making certain his face was hidden from the ceiling mounted cameras as he went. He was soon outside the lab door where he pulled a smoke grenade from his jacket and pulled the pin. White smoke billowed from four vent holes at the top of the device and Jake directed the flow toward the nearest smoke detector until a loud squealing alarm pierced the air. He threw the device down the hall in the direction from which he came so that anyone leaving the lab would be directed to the emergency exit at the end of the hall. Once through that door, they would only be able to reenter the building through the main entrance so Jake would be alone with his task.

A small high tech face mask covering his nose and mouth, Jake then moved into the smoke and waited a few seconds until Gelling, Sanders, and McDonald emerged from the lab. Rothstein wasn't with them but there was no time to waste so Jake pushed the mask back into his pocket, held a handkerchief to his face and quickly moved toward the men.

"The smoke is too thick this way, take the emergency exit!" he shouted over the alarm.

The three panicked scientists quickly followed his instruction as Jake slipped into the lab before the door could close. He stood for a second, worried that Rothstein was still somewhere in the lab but couldn't afford to waste any time so he strode toward the programmer's room, pulled out the specially designed electronic circumvention device and swiped its card across Rothstein's reader. He waited two seconds then swiped it again and the magnetic lock clunked open. Jake pushed the door open and walked past banks of servers, memory and processors to Rothstein's work station. He ducked under the bench, found an empty USB port well hidden behind the terminal's cooling box and plugged Equilibrium's device into it then got up to leave.

Just as he was about to open the door and leave, Jake heard the clunk of the magnetic lock and realized that Rothstein hadn't left the lab and was ignoring the alarm to return to his room. He assumed the famous programmer was more concerned about the possibility of his illicit work being discovered by his coworkers than he was about fire. Jake's lightning reflexes propelled him stealthily behind the door where he made himself as flat as possible in the hope that the door didn't swing widely enough to be stopped by his body and give him away. Rothstein pushed the door and rushed past quickly so Jake was able to catch it with his hand then swing himself around and out in one swift movement unnoticed by the obsessed programmer.

Jake strode toward the outer laboratory door checking behind him for Rothstein as he went. He pulled out the device again and swiped the card across the reader once then twice and nothing happened. Years of experience and training prevented any panic as he held the black box up to examine it. His maneuver in Rothstein's room had dislodged the multi-cable connection from the machine so he pushed it back in and held it with one hand as he swiped the card again. Waiting the prescribed two seconds, he swiped it one more time and the door emitted a welcome sound. Jake pulled it open then disappeared down the hall toward the lobby, picking up his smoke canister as he went.

A woman was slightly hunched over and coughing in the hall so he took her by the arm and led her to the staff door then into Blue Sky's lobby. People were still crowding their way out and the cacophony of voices combined with the high pitched alarm were easily enough cover for Jake to slip out and get back to the car undetected. He removed his blazer and threw it into the back as he jumped into the driver's seat.

Alan looked at him with a relieved grin, "You said fifteen minutes."

"Well it went quicker than expected. I hope your friend won't be too angry with you about your false news tip."

"She'll get over it once I give her the full exclusive story but I hope we don't need any more favors from her before then."

"We're heading straight to the airport and back to Jersey so I don't think it should be a problem. But first, a quick text to tell Equilibrium the device is in place."

Eric Rothstein was just about to shut down his system and leave the lab when the fire alarm stopped. He looked around nervously before running to the outer lab door and swiping his card to check the hallway. The smoke had mostly subsided so he turned and went back his room. A suspicious man, he opened his latest project for Rygaard and checked to ensure it hadn't been disturbed while he was in the bathroom. Satisfied the unfinished hallucination was still secure; he felt it was safe to get back to work and finish the project in time to meet the deadline and collect his reward.

His fingers darted over the keyboard writing the complex code required to make the scenario as realistic as possible when he suddenly stopped, his face frozen, as he watched the sophisticated CPU meter on the bottom of his screen. Rothstein had built the entire state of the art system with his own hands and his intimate knowledge of its inner workings exposed a very subtle increase in background CPU usage. He quickly shut down all user processes and sat watching the needle on his custom made meter like a hawk watching a field mouse. The needle betrayed a minuscule amount of power usage that would be completely undetectable by any commercially available CPU meter so Rothstein got up to check that all background systems were turned off before returning to observe the tiny fluctuations again. His face contorted in anger as he realized the only possible explanation was that someone had infiltrated his system with a very sophisticated and well hidden invader.

He began a frantic electronic search of all ports and processes but could find nothing. Exasperated, he jumped up from his chair and began physically searching the memory banks, processors and servers but still nothing. Scratching his head, he looked at his terminal and it dawned on him. While he was building the system, he had added several utility ports to his local cooling tower in case he ever wanted to transfer samples directly to a hard drive via USB and they had remained unused. He got on his hands and knees to crawl behind the tower and tilted his head around the corner until he saw it. Years of experience and knowledge came to play and he calmly crawled back out leaving the device untouched. He knew that there was only one way to find out who was behind the attack and that was to carry on as though nothing was wrong and set up a trace program to follow the device's pathway back to its owner. In order to draw as little power as it did, the device was obviously extremely advanced and he didn't know if Rygaard was monitoring his progress or something more dangerous was being perpetrated but he knew how to find out and that's exactly what he would do.

Chapter 16

The trip back to Jersey City was uneventful and the pair arrived back at Jake's base to the smell of Tik's cooking. They hadn't eaten since their Khao Tom Moo that morning and Alan's nostrils twitched with the exotic fragrances emanating from the kitchen.

"That smells great Tik! What is it?"

"Laab Gai with Khao Neeow and Khao Poon." Tik said proudly as she lifted the bowls of food onto the bench.

"Should I ask?" Alan grinned at Jake.

"Spicy minced chicken and herb salad with sticky rice and Lao style Laksa soup. These are some of her best dishes."

"You're spoiling me Tik – I'm not used to eating this well at home."

"You not have wife make you good food?"

"I lost my wife years ago."

"Tik understand – velly solly for Mr. Alan."

As she spoke, Alan noticed that his statement hadn't evoked quite the same depth of sadness it used to. He wondered at the change and realized that Holly was beginning to displace some of his long held sorrow. He had thought he would never be free of the haunting feelings of his beloved wife's loss and experience again, the blooming sensation of new love but there it was after so many years of loneliness. An irresistible desire to call Holly and tell her how he felt suddenly surged through him but he knew it wasn't possible now and struggled to push the feeling down.

Jake watched his mental battle and said, "Be patient Alan. Keep your priorities in order."

"I know, I know but a guy can wish; can't he?"

"I'm sure Tik's cooking will take your mind off it for a while – let's eat."

The men sat and savored the sumptuous, exotic dishes as Tik went on with her cleaning and housekeeping. The place was spotless but it seemed she was able to find fault with enough to keep her busy.

"I wonder how Equilibrium is doing with Rothstein's code." Alan said before shoveling another spoonful of the Laab into his mouth.

"If there was anything to know, we would know. Be patient; that kind of code will be extremely complex and even for Equilibrium, this will take time. When we've finished eating, we'll go and review your Chin Na techniques and if we don't hear anything in an hour, I'll initiate contact."

Alan nodded agreement as he relished the culinary delights in front of him. "I'm really not used to such spicy food. My mouth is burning but I just can't stop eating."

"It is very addictive. Tik buys fresh herbs and spices every day at the Asian market and the combination of freshness, complexity, and skill make her food irresistible. If you and Holly don't work out, you could get very fat very quickly as Mr. Tik." he said chuckling.

Alan shot him a glare and Jake, still snickering said, "Save it for the gym Alan."

The men finished their meals and went to the gym to review the lessons. Alan complained that it was too soon after eating but Jake insisted they would not be exerting enough energy to cause any problems. The techniques, when performed correctly, required very little physical effort; it was simply a matter of repetition to ensure the movements were branded into his brain so he wouldn't need to think when using them. They continued for an hour until Jake was satisfied his student was well on his way to developing reflexive expertise in the four techniques.

"OK, that's good Alan – you're getting them down very well. Let's go and check on Equilibrium's progress."

They went to the armory room and Jake sent an encrypted text. A moment later, the reply came back, "Two minutes; orange protocol."

Jake looked up the orange protocol and stood ready to connect with the enigmatic computer genius. Precisely two minutes after the reply, he clicked the mouse and the familiar flickering digits appeared at the top of the screen.

Jake typed, "Sorry to push but is there any progress?"

Characters appeared on the screen in real time, "Data transfer very slow to avoid detection. Only transferred his current project since it is largely on RAM instead of hard disc memory. Other files downloading but will take time."

"Anything relevant in the current project?"

"Hold onto your hats. The scenario is patchy because it's incomplete and my systems are still rendering the code into visuals but it looks very much like this hallucination scenario is designed for the Commander in Chief."

"The President of the United States?!" Alan asked incredulously.

Jake typed the question and the hacker's reply was, "The one and only."

"How can you be sure?"

"I'm not but the visuals are showing parts of the White House that very few people have access to."

"Could be a Secret Service agent?"

"I thought the same until I came across visuals of a hand signing specific documents with the seal of the Office of the President on them."

"My God – Devlin's going after the President!" Alan gasped.

"More to the point, it sounds like he's going to manipulate the President into signing documents. The question is: what is on those documents?"

Jake quickly typed, "Can you make out document content?"

"It hasn't rendered yet – just the seal and the hand signing."

Jake rubbed his chin thoughtfully. "Devlin is already close to the President through his façade of philanthropic ventures and heavy campaign contributions. His industries are big lobbyists so I don't understand what else he could hope to achieve with this."

"Maybe he's trying to overcome more barriers to his expansion plans?" Alan suggested.

"Maybe but based on how Devlin has been hiding the full extent of his market dominance and corporate structures, why would he need to overcome barriers when he's simply been circumventing them?"

"I guess we have to wait until Rothstein programs the code for the document contents?"

Jake typed again, "Focus on the written content. Any updates at all – even a few words, let us know immediately."

"Way ahead of you."

Jake turned to Alan and spoke, "We need to reexamine all of Matt Lewis' research and try to find possible reasons for this. Devlin must have an overall plan that's driving him to this course."

He ordered his voice activated system to bring up the files and the two men went through them page by page, taking notes as they went and mapping the tendrils that linked different ventures on a whiteboard. Hours passed as they continued examining every detail of the documents until Jake received a text from Equilibrium, "Two minutes – protocol grey."

They connected and watched as characters appeared on the screen, "Still very patchy but some very disturbing renderings now clear – they have to do with executive authority during military conflict. It looks to me like they're going to manipulate the president to allow for tactical nuclear strikes in the Middle East and North Korea."

Alan's jaw dropped as he turned to Jake in horror. "How is that even possible?!"

Jake's jaw muscles flexed rhythmically as he processed the information. "He can't be certain this will work – unless he's got other plans in motion simultaneously – he knows that such a thing would require Congressional approval among other official processes."

"Exactly – so how does he think this is going to get him anywhere?"

"I don't know but I do know that this guy is very devious and capable, and there is nothing he won't do. We don't need to know any more than this – we have to stop him. Legitimate options are closing to us at every turn; we need to do this my way."

Alan's gut churned at the revelations before them and his morality struggled with the ramifications of Jake's statement. He desperately wanted to follow the rules but could see that Jake was right about one thing. They needed to fight fire with fire and the rules were hamstringing them but he still couldn't bring himself to agree to Jake's methods.

"If you kill Devlin, we are just as bad as him and that defeats the purpose of justice."

"I disagree. If there are no legitimate means to destroy our enemy and stop this madness, then we must do whatever it takes. I know this is difficult for you but it's a simple decision for me. What's more important: your morality or the security of this nation?"

Alan looked thoughtfully into Jake's eyes. "I know the decision is black and white for you but there may be a better way."

Jake studied Alan's face. The detective formed a knowing half smile and Jake listened intently as he began to lay out his idea until suddenly the communication page with Equilibrium began to display more characters, "Jake – I think I have a problem."

"What is it?"

They waited for a reply but nothing came. Jake typed again, "What's wrong?"

Almost a minute passed before a reply came, "Remember all those years ago when you tried to find me? It looks like you're going to get your wish."

"What do you mean?"

"Someone is breaching my perimeter. My security system shows multiple intrusion points. I have measures in place but they won't last forever and it's not like I can call 911. You're my only chance Jake."

Jake's face drained of blood. He had been unable to locate Equilibrium with all the CIA's resources behind him, yet he was now being told that someone had done the seemingly impossible.

"How can that be? Do you know who they are?"

"I don't know who they are. I can only assume Rothstein's system was designed to detect the minutest of CPU usage and he found my device then traced the feed back to me. It would take someone of his caliber to follow the path as it's covered by a fluctuating source code - but I was overconfident that my invention would go unnoticed so to save time; I only used a standard trace prevention technique. I should have coded it through the trace-proof system we use for communication. A foolish mistake and now it looks like I'm going to pay for it."

"Can't you get out? Escape plan? Weapons?"

"My facility is so well secured that there is only one emergency exit but as you know, any escape route offers vulnerabilities. They have already discovered my one way out and neutralized it – now I'm trapped and I don't know how long it will take them to get to me. I have one handgun – not enough to fend off multiple intruders. I need you – here's the address."

Jake stood in silence continuing to watch the screen until the very location that he'd so fervently sought years before, was now voluntarily given by his former quarry. He felt a degree of disillusionment as the legendarily elusive hacker typed an address near the Apple Warehouse District of New York on the screen. It was almost as though a respected mentor had failed him. His mind drew a comparison to the emotions evoked by his brother's death and how it was caused by the poor judgment of his superiors. Suddenly, a thought crossed his mind and he had to be certain it wasn't a trap.

"How do I know this is really you?"

"Is Beach with you?

"Yes – why?"

"Don't let him see the screen."

Alan looked at Jake and nodded. He walked around to stand behind the terminal and watched Jake's brow furrow into a deep frown as he read what Equilibrium typed. The message obviously convinced Jake because he looked up from the screen and said tersely, "It's not a trap. I have to go – now!"

"What about my plan?" Alan asked.

"I heard enough to agree to it and I haven't got time to argue anyway. You go ahead and set it up. I have to try to save Equilibrium – I owe him that much."

Alan watched as Jake quickly pulled on a thin gold tinged vest and covered it with a black turtle neck shirt then donned a double-sided harness, checked and loaded his two Heckler & Koch MP7A1 submachine guns and slid them into the holsters. He grabbed six spare clips and pushed them into the nylon webbing pockets of his harness then clamped a Special Forces dagger onto his belt and shoved a Microtech Automatic knife into his pants pocket. Finally, he mounted an ankle holster on his left leg and slid a Ruger LCP Coyote compact semiautomatic into it. Jake looked up to see Alan staring at him in amazement. He gave the detective a quick nod and started for the door.

"How do I get out of here while you're gone?" Alan stopped him.

"You don't. Use this disposable phone to make your call." He tossed the phone to Alan then continued, "If I'm not back tonight, the mission is a bust and the only hope you'll have is Walker. But don't call him unless you're sure I'm not coming back."

The finality in Jake's voice concerned the detective. He knew that if Jake didn't return it was because the odds were too overwhelmingly against him and if they could defeat Jake, he would have no chance against them whatsoever. He decided it was best not to think of the alternative and said, "I'll see you tonight."

Jake gave him a half smile and disappeared through the door.

Alan watched him leave then picked up the disposable phone and dialed.

"Blue Sky Biotech – how may I direct your call?"

"Professor Linus Gelling please."

Chapter 17

The late evening air ripped past Jake's helmet as he guided his customized BMW R1200 R through the streets of New York on his way to Brooklyn. With instant throttle response, and superb braking and handling, the beast easily answered all demands as Jake broke every road rule on his way to the Brooklyn Naval Yard area. Before leaving his base, he had programmed the address into the dash mounted GPS system and slid a counterfeit license plate into the purpose-built holder. His normal plate was registered under a different name, to a different address but in case the police witnessed his blistering ride and gave chase, he might need to reach around and remove the fake then take a different route. There was no possibility a squad car could even come close to keeping up so the police radio system was the only thing that concerned him and he would not allow his mission to be foiled.

It was less than half a mile to the Holland Tunnel where he flew past cars so fast that one driver thought she'd seen an apparition and another slightly paranoid individual presumed it was some kind of military experiment. Jake kept the machine pointed at Chinatown and was soon blasting through traffic around St. John's Park on his way to Canal Street. Seconds after passing Church Street, a police siren blared to life behind him and after spotting the pursuers in his mirror, he automatically calculated a maneuver to elude the lone unit. Still a couple of hundred yards in front of them, he threw the bike into a sharp right at Lafayette then turned left going the wrong way into White Street. Dodging oncoming vehicles, he prepared for a sharp left into Centre Street then a quick right into Walker to reemerge onto Canal. Heading to Manhattan Bridge for the sprint across to Flushing Avenue and onto the Apple Warehouse District near the naval yard, he knew the men in the squad car couldn't have seen his license plate and didn't bother changing out the fake one. The severely outgunned squad car pulled over on Lafayette several hundred yards back and the driver said to his partner in resignation, "If he wants it that bad, he can have it." His partner; still amazed at the speed of the bike through New York traffic, just nodded agreement.

Jake was soon near his destination so he pulled the Beemer over fifty yards before the address Equilibrium had sent. He dismounted, kicked out the stand, and pressed the remote alarm button on its key so that the only way it could be stolen was by lifting the five hundred pound beast onto the back of a truck. He checked and cocked his Heckler & Koch automatics then strode toward what resembled an old warehouse.

The large structure was made of red brick and surrounded by a ten foot fence plastered with signs declaring the building unsafe and warning trespassers to keep out for their own safety. It looked, for all intents and purposes, like a stalled development project waiting for funding and demolition approval. To Jake's trained eye, it was ideal for a secret base of operations. He immediately picked out several high definition security cameras well hidden amongst the damaged eaves, broken lamps and disused electrical connections. The former operative knew someone of Equilibrium's caliber would have set the place up with secured underground wiring, communication lines and an emergency power generation system. He knew the building was much more than met the eye but not yet sure of the structure and layout, he needed to do some reconnaissance before marching in blindly, guns blazing.

He moved stealthily along the perimeter, quickly gathering and assessing intel to prepare for his breach. Approaching the Southeast corner, he suddenly stopped and crouched. A man in black fatigues was sitting on his haunches peering inward through an opening in the fence. He was armed with an M4 machine gun and holding a small pair of binoculars to his eyes. Jake pulled his Special Forces dagger from its sheath and moved like a giant cat toward the enemy. Taking a leap of faith in the veracity of his associate's situation, he violently pulled the man's head backward while sliding the blade cleanly across his left carotid artery and around smoothly onto the right. With his head tilted back and

Jake's hand firmly over his mouth, the hapless watchman was unconscious and well on his way from this world within a few short seconds.

Jake pulled the body behind him with one arm as he entered through the same hole the man was guarding and lay him down between the fence and an old dumpster then continued toward the brick structure. He kept low as his eyes darted about searching for any sign of detection but the intruders had no reason to expect his assault so their focus was purely inward, toward their prey. Seemingly, their only precaution against outside interference had been the single sentry who'd already met his fate, leaving the former Delta Force Specialist able to move unhindered to the outer wall of the building.

Arriving at the wall, Jake found a steel door which had been drilled and breached. He flipped out a small, custom made, periscopic mirror from the side of his Heckler & Koch and moved the muzzle into the door frame to get a glimpse of the interior. Seeing no immediate threat through the mirror, he eased his head in until his left eye peered into the dimly lit warehouse for a more thorough assessment then used the mirror to check each side and entered the doorway. There were hushed voices and footsteps in the distance, deep within the facility so he hugged the perimeter and followed their sound. The warehouse presented a maze of hallways and Jake knew immediately that Equilibrium had set the structure up this way to confuse intruders. The walls and doorways were made to look historically authentic but Jake knew the old building's original purpose could never have been served by such a setup. It was more like assaulting a ship than an open warehouse and close quarter assaults like this were where Jake's skills and training came to the fore. Years of real life practice dictated his steps as he ducked to check blind corners and whisked through doorways toward his quarry. Jake didn't yet know the odds against him but he was certain that the element of surprise was on his side and even more certain that his skills in this arena were among the highest in the world.

Rounding one of many corners, another doorway came into view and Jake's hair bristled as he heard a low voice speaking in a heavy Eastern European accent on the other side. He pushed his gun into its holster and unsheathed his dagger again, not wanting to make enough noise to warn any other intruders unless he had to. By the sound of the muffled conversation, there were only two men through the doorway but he wasn't certain of their positions so he proceeded with his preferred strategy for such a scenario. His mirror useless in this situation, he moved to an angle where he could see almost half the view of the other side and knew that the men were both positioned to the right side of the door. He picked up a loose stone from the floor and tossed it down the hallway on the other side and immediately followed it through. The intruders' reaction times were quick but they were not clever enough and they both turned simultaneously toward the sound of the stone hitting the ground instead of seeking the actual source. The split second their gazes turned to the stone's point of impact, Jake's knife flashed through the semi darkness and drove downward into the first man's neck behind the collarbone, turning to an angle of forty five degrees to enter the trachea below his voice box then immediately retracted, ready to satisfy its appetite once more. A grotesque hiss issued forth from the man's wound and mouth simultaneously and the second man started to turn as Jake's arm moved upward and around behind the first guard then continued in a smooth arc directly to the second guard's throat, where it sliced neatly through his left carotid then circled around to pierce directly into his larynx. It wasn't the quickest or cleanest way to kill but given the situation, Jake needed to ensure neither man could call out before they died so it was the most effective technique to prevent that possibility.

Jake looked down at the men on the floor, both desperately grasping at their own necks, their eyes bulging in horror as they beheld their nemesis in disbelief. They would expire soon but Jake couldn't risk that they might squeeze off a warning shot before they passed so his hungry blade returned for more and quickly sliced through both men's femoral arteries as he pulled their guns away from them. The ugly gurgling from the first intruder subsided quickly and Jake moved on down the hall, following other sounds.

He continued toward his goal, soft soled military boots and stealthy movement concealing his advance, until the sound became clearer after rounding another corner. A doorway came into view and he approached cautiously, his dagger in one hand and a Heckler & Koch in the other. There were multiple voices through the doorway so Jake sheathed his dagger and pulled out the other H&K assault weapon. He readied himself for the expected scene, checked the doorway as far as he dared then burst through silently into a cavernous area with a single concrete structure in the centre of the room. There were four intruders dressed in black assault gear at a solid steel door. One man was facing outward as the other three worked on opening the door. One of the men focusing on the door had a portable welding torch and was cutting the thick steel around the door's handle while the other two prepared an explosive charge. The one guarding the scene spotted Jake's looming figure and started to raise his weapon when a single shot rang out from Jake's gun, piercing the man's throat. The other three were completely exposed with their weapons lying on the floor as they worked. Jake pulled the trigger to the end of its range on one weapon causing a rapid fire burst to spray across the three intruders then he dropped to his haunches, put one gun on the ground to use the other sniper style, and quickly picked off the exposed parts of their bodies above and below their bullet proof vests. The echo of Jake's gunfire rang through the chamber as he quickly retrieved his other weapon, pointed both muzzles in front of him and searched the area for more assailants. There was silence and he could see no others so he changed the clip on one weapon and made his way to the steel door to check the bodies. Satisfied he was now alone; he put his ear to the door then suddenly jumped back and to the side, training both guns on the opening. There was an audible clunk then a strange whirring sound and the door loosened from its position. Jake strained to see through the widening crack as his fingers sat ready to squeeze their triggers. The door slowly opened to reveal a silhouette.

"Jake, it's me – don't shoot."

Jake's mind temporarily hesitated as it processed the scene. He knew what he'd heard but couldn't believe it. He edged slowly toward the door, guns still trained on the opening until the light evened out and the source of his confusion became clear. His years of blind association with Equilibrium had covered the truth and now before him stood not a man but a beautiful raven haired woman with piercing emerald green eyes. Jake's arms dropped to his side as he continued toward her, completely disarmed by the shock and her beauty. Her teary eyes gazed into his and her lips began to form a thank you when a single crack pierced the air and a round struck Jake's back with a heavy thud. His body was propelled forward by the force of the bullet and he slumped forward into Equilibrium's arms as she screamed, "No!"

She couldn't hold him and fell backward under Jake's weight. She pulled her leg out from beneath him and reached for his arm, trying to drag him into the safety of the concrete structure but he was too heavy and she wept as she struggled in vain, calling out his name and yanking his arm with all her strength. The source of the single shot now loomed from the darkness and Equilibrium watched in fear as the bear of a man became clearer in the light of her bunker. He was huge; well over six feet tall with a barrel chest, thick bulky arms and a long ugly scar from one corner of his mouth to his ear. His eyes spoke of cold hearted and evil deeds as his mouth formed a menacing grin.

"Playtime." he hissed, his eyes locked on hers as he neared Jake's motionless feet.

Equilibrium immediately knew his intent and whimpered as she pulled herself backward in desperation but it was no use. A small handgun and the heavy steel door had been her only protection until Jake arrived and now none of them could help her. She had left her handgun deeper within the protected safe room and knew it could not be reached before he got to her but she had to try. Turning away from Jake's body, she scrambled to gain her feet as the enormous man quickly stepped over Jake to claim his prize. Just as she got her feet beneath her, there was a loud thump and a groan from behind. She turned to see the big man's face grimaced in pain and arching his body to hold his hand over his right kidney. To her amazement and relief, Jake was standing behind the giant throwing a bizarre formation of rapid-fire strikes into his head and neck. Doubled over now, the bear dropped his gun and instinctively swung a massive arm outward, connecting with Jake's stomach. Air exploded from Jake's mouth as the wind was knocked out of him but he was relentless. He reached for his dagger and thrust it toward the big man but a colossal balled fist struck down heavily, knocking the dagger from his grip. Jake lunged back a step to draw the Microtech automatic knife from his pocket and the blade sprang forth ready for action. He straightened his muscular frame to centre himself against the big man's coming onslaught and watched as the right hand thrust toward him. In one lightning fast movement, Jake caught the fist in his left hand and with his right, traced the blade upward across the incoming wrist then circled it down through the crook of the elbow and turned back upward like a tree snake climbing a branch. Pulling the arm toward him with his left hand, Jake then guided the knife onward through its slithering, slicing journey until it slid under the armpit and withdrew in a circle then surged across the left carotid artery. Jake let go of the fist, took a half step backward and to the side as his arm looped downward, plunging the blade into the man's bulky thigh then turning in a tight semicircle, leaving a four inch slab of meat hanging from the gaping wound. The giant roared in pain as blood surged forth from his wounds and Jake bent over to grab his Ruger from its ankle holster. He stood and pushed the small weapon upward into the man's chest, thumping four rounds into his lungs and shoving him away with the other hand. Jake's mammoth adversary slumped to his knees, blood gurgling from his mouth until the Ruger barked again, driving a single shot into the center of his forehead.

Without looking at Equilibrium, Jake turned back to where he'd fallen in the doorway and retrieved his SMGs. Holding the weapons in front of him, his eyes once more searched the outer room for assailants before he finally holstered the guns, returned his gaze to the object of his mission. He went to speak but wasn't sure what to say. The shock of finding a woman, after all these years assuming Equilibrium was a man, still consumed his thoughts until finally, she broke the silence.

"I thought you were dead! I can't see a bullet-proof vest – how can it be?

"Later." Jake said. "We need to get out of here. What's your exit strategy?"

"I've already covered it – all my data has been transferred via secure link to a storage server at another location and I've destroyed my terminal, memory banks, and all equipment here –

except for my laptop. There's a button under that panel behind you, beside the door. All we have to do is press that three times as we leave and a sprinkler system will spray everything inside with high octane gasoline then it will be automatically ignited. We shut the door and the fire will be contained to the safe room so it won't damage the rest of the warehouse."

"Is there a paper trail to tie you to the building?"

"Nothing the police or FBI could follow."

"So…the bodies?"

"No need to move them. As long as you left nothing incriminating behind, there is no way they'll ever be able to explain it."

"I'm impressed – Let's move!"

"I'll just grab my laptop."

Jake waited until she reappeared then walked through the door, guns at the ready, while Equilibrium pulled the panel open and pressed the red button three times then pulled the door closed just as gasoline began hissing out of pipes near the ceiling. They quickly made their way through the outer room and into the maze of hallways as a small ignition system activated in a corner of the bunker and the room burst into flames. There was enough oxygen in the safe room to ensure that everything was damaged enough to be useless in any investigation then the flames began to subside as the pair reached the outer fence and exited the compound where Jake had entered.

"You've left quite a trail of destruction Jake." she said, looking at Jake's first victim.

"I didn't have time to take prisoners."

"I'm not complaining – it's just that I've never seen your work up close before. I've always observed remotely so it never seemed truly real until now."

Jake looked at her and lowered his head. "I'm sorry you had to see all of that."

"I'm a pragmatic girl – better them than me. Besides, I know you a lot better than you may think and there is a big difference between the soldier and the man."

She smiled warmly and Jake was strangely relieved. He had never tried to apologize for his actions in battle before and was glad there was no need to do so now.

"We'd better keep moving. It's quiet now but we won't be alone for long."

They moved quickly toward the BMW and Jake pressed his key to unlock the silver beast. They straddled the seat and took back streets to avoid attention. She clung tightly around his waist as they wound through the streets of Little Italy and Soho then into the Holland Tunnel and on to Jake's building in Jersey City. Approaching the driveway, he pressed the remote to open the outer door, rode through then stopped to place his palm against the reader and the big steel door began to open. He urged the bike forward and parked it in the center of the garage.

Jake dismounted, removed his helmet and turned to stare at her. She could see the disbelief in his eyes and broke the silence, "I hope I haven't disappointed you."

The statement struck Jake as absurd in its conflicting effect. There was a small and irrational feeling of let down but that was purely a matter of pride – at the same time he was entranced by her exotic beauty. His mind quickly darted back and forth through time, trying to recall any specific instance when she may have intentionally misled him to think she was a man but could recall no such ruse. The level of mutual respect and trust they had shared through the years seemed to take on a completely different meaning now and he looked deep into her eyes as he spoke, "I'm not disappointed – and it wouldn't be your fault if I was. I was a fool to assume you could only be a man. Forgive my unintentionally sexist attitude."

"Not at all – I relied on it for years! If you had suspected for a moment that I was a woman, you may have caught me years ago - and you came very close to doing just that. My communications with you were always worded in a masculine way until tonight. I'm surprised the penny didn't drop when I practically begged you for help."

"Men are not beyond begging when the need arises."

"True but I really stepped out of character. I knew you were my only salvation so there was no longer any point trying to hide it."

"Apparently I was too one-eyed to notice."

"I hope I haven't upset you."

Jake chuckled, "How could I be upset by such beauty."

She blushed and looked at the floor as Jake tried to salvage, "I'm sorry – I didn't mean to…well…I mean…I have a great deal of respect for you."

She drew close to Jake and suddenly, for the first time in years, he was self conscious of his ugly facial scar and shied away as she reached up to touch his face. Her hand gently coaxed him back until their eyes met then she laid her index finger across his lips and soothed, "As do I for you." Gazing deeply into his eyes, she then reached up and softly traced her finger down his scar intending to show him that it didn't bother her. The seasoned killing machine trembled almost imperceptibly at her touch and, sensing his discomfort, she glanced over at the spiral staircase and quickly changed the subject, asking, "Are you going to invite me in?"

Still slightly flustered with himself, he recovered, "Yes, of course - after you."

She started toward the staircase and Jake followed, silently admonishing himself for his momentary lapse in self-control. The shock of finding his long time collaborator a woman – and a beautiful one at that – had pushed him into new territory and he hadn't reacted with his usual calm and control. He now forced himself to come to terms with the situation and deal with it professionally.

They got to the top of the stairs and Jake slid past her to open the hidden door, revealing his bathroom.

"Nice." she said. "Very good taste."

"It's home." Jake tried a more nonchalant tone.

He led the way through the bedroom and into the cavernous kitchen, dining, and living area where Tik and Alan were quietly chatting at the table. Tik spotted them first, jumping to her feet and Alan turned to see what had startled her. A wave of relief rolled over him and he smiled broadly at his new friend. Then he saw the dark haired beauty following and his mouth opened in disbelief. Staring intently as they walked toward him, sudden realization struck and an even broader smile grew on his face. He stood to greet them and extended his hand to Equilibrium. "Amazing…simply amazing!"

She looked at the detective with a raised eyebrow and said, "Should I take that as a compliment?"

"Absolutely! I certainly don't mean to objectify but I didn't expect a gifted computer genius to come in such a beautiful package. I suppose you get sick of the label but there's no denying that you are a very attractive woman."

She smiled warmly, "Thank you. I really don't meet many people face to face but it's nice to hear it put that way."

"Well, someone had to address the elephant in the room. I don't imagine Mr. Special Forces here would have done so yet." he teased then laughed as Jake shot him a piercing glare.

"I think he was a little shocked at first but you have to remember how much history we have and I never gave him the slightest inkling of my gender."

Jake looked relieved that she was defending him and added, "That's true but it just goes to show how wrong assumptions can be."

Tik had been silent but now piped up, "Where you manners?! Lady must be hungly."

"Actually, I'm starving." the hacker smiled at Tik. "I heard about your legendary cooking skills while you were still operational in Laos."

"Jake tell me you help me get out and make document for immiglation. Tik thank you." She said smiling warmly.

"It was my pleasure Tik. The CIA was wrong to desert you in your time of need and Jake was adamant we get you out. He didn't tell me how pretty you are though."

Tik looked down, embarrassed then scurried off to prepare a plate of food for their guest as Alan pulled out a chair for Equilibrium and she sat. The men followed suit and Alan squirmed slightly in his chair before speaking. "No offense but is there a name we can call you other than Equilibrium? It seems a bit awkward and inappropriate now we're face to face."

"I suppose it is a bit cumbersome. Call me Angie."

"Well, I don't know if it's your real name or not but it's a very pretty one." Alan smiled.

Jake turned in his chair to get up for some water and winced as he rose. Angie saw the pain in his face and suddenly remembered. "Your back! I wondered how it was possible you survived that shot when I can't see a bullet-proof vest."

Jake pulled his turtleneck off to reveal the thin, gold tinged vest Alan had watched him put on before he left.

"I was going to ask you what that thing is. I've never seen anything like it." he said.

Jake replied, "It's experimental technology. The gold woven fabric is made from threads combining the silk of the Golden Orb Weaving Spider and a rare metal alloy. Its tensile strength is vastly greater than Kevlar. It covers a thin layer of titanium alloy, and together, they make an effective, lightweight but very expensive bullet-proof vest. It's so thin that it's virtually undetectable unless you know what to look for."

He pulled the vest over his head and turned around to reveal a dark bruise about four inches in diameter, almost black at the center. Without a word, Angie went to the freezer to get some ice and wrapped it in a kitchen towel then pressed it against Jake's back. "Now I feel bad for hating spiders." she smiled.

"Tik brought Angie's food to the table and they talked about old missions together for a while until the subject turned serious and Jake brought them back to reality. "What about your plan Alan – did Gelling go for it?"

"I'm not sure yet - we might be sunk. He didn't respond well when I first explained everything to him but he seemed a little more accepting when I told him that Devlin was responsible for Helen Benson's death. He needed some time to think - I've got to call him back in half an hour for his answer."

"I guess it's a lot to ask a geek like that." Jake reasoned.

"It's a long shot for sure but it's our only chance."

Alan quickly explained his plan to Angie and they discussed details. They went to the armory to examine Matt Lewis' documents and the specific threads that led Alan to develop his rather precarious plan. Angie had some suggestions and they fine tuned tactics as much as possible until Angie declared that she needed a shower. She turned to kiss Alan on the cheek and said, "I'm very happy that Holly is safe. You deserve some happiness in your life."

Then she turned to Jake. Her green eyes sparkled in the light as she pulled him toward her and kissed him softly on the lips then said, "Keep him safe Jake."

Jake nodded, "I will." and she left the room.

Somewhat flustered at Angie's unexpected kiss, Jake turned to meet Alan's cheeky grin. He shook it off and said, "Is it time for that call?"

Alan picked up the burner phone, dialed the private cell number Gelling had given him and waited. His eyes darted up to Jake's as a faint smile grew on his face. He listened intently without a word until Gelling finished speaking and the phone went dead.

"We're on!"

"He said 'yes'?!"

"I'm as surprised as you but he's in."

Without another word, Jake went to the workbench and started preparing equipment for the next day. The two men worked methodically for almost an hour, testing and retesting equipment and going over every detail of the plan with a fine tooth comb. When Jake was satisfied they had done everything possible, they went back to the kitchen. Alan asked Tik where Angie was and she shrugged her shoulders, saying, "Lady like long shower."

Jake said, "Maybe she's fallen asleep. I'll go check on her."

He walked to the bedroom to find her sprawled on the bed, fast asleep. The stress of the day's events had obviously taken their toll so he didn't want to wake her but couldn't help gazing at her beauty for a moment before going back to the kitchen.

"She's out like a light." he told them. "Who knows how long it's been since she slept. I guess I'll be bunking in with you tonight Alan."

Chapter 18

Alan awoke from a fitful sleep. He had become very used to sleeping alone and after all his years of solitude, it had been difficult enough to sleep properly in the same bed as Holly, let alone a six foot one military grade killing machine like Jake. An unfamiliar aroma filled his nostrils and he turned to see that Jake had thankfully risen before him so that particular awkwardness had been successfully avoided. He rose to see the big man busily at work in the kitchen and went over to see what he was up to.

"Tik didn't come today?"

"No. It's very strange for her – she would normally have one of her exotic delights waiting on the table for me by now."

"Maybe she wants to give Angie some space. Perhaps she thinks there isn't room for two women in your life." Alan smiled broadly.

Jake shot him a glare.

Alan chuckled and continued, "I'm just saying…"

"You talk too much."

"Oh come on big fella; don't be shy." Alan teased. "Now who's the 'Grasshopper'?"

"Don't test me." Jake said sternly.

Alan was enjoying the turning of the tables but thought better of provoking such a man. He thought it wiser to change the subject and said, "Smells good – what is it?"

"S.O.S."

"S.O.S? That sounds ominous."

"It's an old time military breakfast. It stands for 'Shit On a Shingle'."

"Now that really sounds ominous!"

"You're obviously not familiar with Marine talk. Many years ago, a cook made this breakfast and served it to a Gunnery Sergeant. Being a Gunny, he called it as he saw it and the name stuck but it's known as S.O.S. for short. It's just creamed beef on toast with scrambled eggs on top and a side of bacon. Trust me; it tastes a lot better than it looks."

He dropped a plateful of the slop on the countertop and Alan tentatively took a mouthful. Within two seconds, his apprehension disappeared and his eyes widened in appreciation. "Wow, this is really tasty!"

"The secret's in the sauce. If you don't get it right, it not only looks like shit on a shingle but tastes like it too." he chuckled. "Eat up – we've got a big day ahead."

The two ate their breakfast in silence until Jake suddenly stopped chewing and looked up mesmerized. Alan followed his gaze to see Angie approaching dressed in nothing but one of Jake's business shirts. Its size made a perfect dress that showed just enough of her shapely, athletic legs to stimulate the imagination. Her raven hair was tousled from sleep and her deep jade green eyes sparkled against her porcelain complexion.

Jake was speechless and Alan followed suit as she approached them. She finally broke the silence, "What's a girl got to do to get a cup of coffee around here?" She said sleepily; seemingly unaware of the effect her appearance was having on the two men.

Jake managed to close his mouth and turned to start making her a coffee. As he twisted the handle into place and his senses returned, he called out, "Espresso? Cappuccino? Latte?"

"Nothing fancy – just plain black coffee please." she said plunking herself down on a stool. "I slept like a rock. That's some bed you've got there Jake. I'm sorry to have displaced you but I couldn't keep my eyes open."

Jake had to wrestle with all the thoughts in his head as he imagined her body wrapped in his sheets. He shook himself loose to say, "Mi casa es su casa." then silently admonished himself for saying something so corny and out of character. The machine finished its loud sputtering and Jake turned to hand her the steaming cup. She took it gratefully in both hands and sipped carefully at the hot liquid then looked at Jake and sighed, "That is so good. I'm terrible without my morning coffee."

Alan and Jake looked at each other in disbelief. Her natural beauty was startling and her obviously unabashed manner and lack of pretense clearly showed that she was oblivious to her appearance and accustomed to living alone. She began to emerge from her morning fog and soon the three were chatting like old friends. Her easy unpretentious style put both men at ease and conversation came easily. They continued for a while until she decided to go for a shower. They watched in silence as she disappeared into Jake's bedroom and Alan said, "Looks like we've both found love my friend."

Jake looked down, his face slightly reddened.

"You're crazy if you don't make the most of this opportunity." Alan said in a big brotherly tone.

Jake was not going to discuss his feelings and changed the subject. "Isn't it time we got moving?"

Alan checked his watch and sighed as he nodded agreement then the two got ready to leave. Angie reemerged from Jake's room dressed in her previous night's clothing and Jake offered to have Tik go and buy her some replacements. She gratefully accepted and Jake phoned Tik then gave Angie his WiFi password so she could continue rendering images from Rothstein's computer. Soon Angie was wishing the men luck as they collected their equipment and prepared to leave. Once again, she approached Jake and gave him a brief but tender kiss on the lips. Alan shot him and 'I told you so' look and they headed down to the garage to embark on their risky mission.

The two sat in silence as Jake drove them through Jersey City toward the I-95 for the forty five mile trip to a semi-rural area outside Princeton, where Gelling had told Alan to meet him. Alex Devlin kept a small estate in the area, to be near his company headquarters when he wasn't staying at his penthouse in New York City. Gelling told Alan that he had arranged to meet Devlin there on the pretense of discussing a possible problem with his research. That had been enough to ensure Devlin made himself immediately available to meet the professor alone, in the privacy of his provincial New Jersey retreat.

As they glided down the highway, Alan kept glancing over at Jake, knowing the euphoria he must have felt at finally finding the elusive Equilibrium and the promise of things to come with the beautiful Angie. Jake focused straight ahead but could feel Alan's eyes darting to and away from him. Suddenly, he turned to the detective and in a calm, controlled voice said, "Stop that please."

Alan replied, "It would be very easy to become distracted right now."

Jake glared at him and said sternly, "You just worry about your end. I could do this with my eyes closed."

Twin turbochargers whined as he surged his powerful Audi S8 forward to overtake another vehicle. They continued in silence, and as the distance closed to the gas station where Alan was to meet Gelling, he began going through the plan again in his mind. It was risky at best and he needed to be completely prepared for his part but stay flexible enough to deal with possible contingencies. Jake had coached him through each detail and he was relatively confident he could pull it off but he was still dubious about whether Gelling would follow through with his end of the bargain or not.

The turnoff to the gas station appeared about two miles after they passed Pigeon Swamp and Jake guided the car onto the off ramp, into the station and behind the main building. He gave Alan a serious look and asked, "Are you ready?"

"As ready as I'll ever be."

"Be clear Alan; if something goes wrong, you give me the word and I'll come in guns blazing. Put your earpiece in for a communications check."

Alan placed the tiny device at the opening of his ear canal and pressed it in as Jake had shown him in the armory. Jake turned on the base station and the scrambled UHF signal came to life. They used cutting edge technology and with its hidden transmission signal the device could only be detected through close visual inspection. The powerful signal had a range of almost a mile and through the button microphone on Alan's shirt, Jake would hear everything Alan did. The system immediately passed the communications check so Jake extended his hand to Alan and said, "Good luck and good hunting."

The mission was not even underway yet but Alan felt a small surge of adrenalin flow through his body, causing the hairs on the back of his neck to bristle as the reality of the situation hit home. He steeled himself, gave Jake a nod and turned to walk around the building into the gas station's store. As he rounded the corner his eyes surreptitiously searched the pump stations and car park for Gelling's face but it was nowhere to be found. He began to worry that the professor had changed in his mind – after all, it was a huge step for such a man. Alan continued on until he reached the doorway and entered the store. Being conscious not to stand out, he maintained a relaxed posture and focused on appearing as unremarkable as possible. His eyes continued to search for the professor until he saw a lone figure at the rear of the store, near the drinks refrigerators and made his way toward it. As he approached, the man turned toward him and a wave of relief came over the detective. He was glad the professor had come through but then felt a wave of anxiety, knowing the plan would soon be fully in motion and there could be no turning back.

"Hello Linus; I'm glad you came."

The professor, obviously nervous, answered, "I owe it to Helen Benson and her family. I did some digging of my own and found some very disturbing, fully rendered hallucination scenarios on Eric Rothstein's computer. There is only one person who could have ordered such things. Devlin must pay for his crimes."

"I'm glad you have seen the truth for yourself. I know it's a lot to accept and I appreciate your help." Alan said sincerely.

Gelling's eyes watered slightly as he said, "Devlin can rot in hell for all I care. I will always have to live with the fact that it was my invention that killed Helen. It was intended to help people and I was blind to its sinister potential until now. You must think me quite naïve."

"Not naïve professor – idealistic and driven, yes but you were only doing what you thought was right. You can't blame yourself for Devlin's deeds."

Gelling pulled some keys from his pocket and handed them to Alan. "You drive detective - I need to focus and load the device."

Alan followed Gelling out of the store to his rented car parked a few paces away from the entrance. Gelling walked to the passenger side and Alan pressed the key's remote unlock button. The pair got into the car and drove out of the gas station toward Princeton. As Gelling gave Alan directions to the estate, he pulled a small aluminum case slightly bigger than a cigarette pack from his jacket pocket. He opened the case to reveal the small pistol-shaped SSCH delivery device and loaded a tiny, round capsule into its chamber then closed the device and pressed a button on the side. The machine made a quiet click as it pierced the outer capsule to release the pre-programmed SSCH, and it was ready. Alan had seen a blurred image of the device on security footage from the elevator at Helen's building but was surprised at just how small it was in real life. He turned back to the road and continued toward their destination. The road was sided by verdant grass shoulders and neatly trimmed hedges. The area was obviously well moneyed and it was apparent not only in the sparsely distributed estates themselves but in the quality of road maintenance and landscaping. Gelling said, "This is it, just ahead on the right. Pull up to the gate and enter the security code."

Alan did as instructed. The twelve foot tall gate was cast iron; large and ornate but obviously built to withstand most intrusions. It was framed by two stout and heavy pillars with security cameras mounted on top and the whole property was surrounded by a solid ten foot wall. The security pad was located at the driver's side to allow access without leaving the car. Gelling told him the pass code and Alan rolled down his window then pressed the corresponding digits. There was a loud clunk then a quiet electronic hum as the gate slowly swung open. The detective bristled as the lens of one security camera focused on them and panned to follow as they entered.

"Don't be concerned, it's fully robotic – he probably isn't even looking." Gelling said, intercepting Alan's thoughts.

"What about security staff?" Alan asked.

"Devlin doesn't trust his thugs with such sensitive matters as Project Hallucineers so I'm sure he will have sent them away for our meeting. He is expecting me at precisely this time so our path will be clear."

Alan shrugged and drove through the gate toward the main house. Chunky grey gravel crunched beneath the tires as their car slowly made its way up the long driveway leading to a large circular close in front of the house. Detached from the house stood a four car garage and diagonally behind that, a large swimming pool separated the main house from a two bedroom guesthouse.

"He won't allow the maid in the house while he's here so she stays in the guesthouse until he leaves – we should have complete privacy. We just need to make sure he's not near his gun cabinet when he realizes what's going on. We may have to physically subdue him until he goes to sleep."

"How long does that take?" Alan asked nervously.

"It depends on the individual but anywhere from five to twenty minutes, depending on their stress levels at the time."

"That's a long time to have to subdue someone!"

"We can use your handcuffs if necessary."

Alan was slightly disconcerted at Gelling's level of awareness in the circumstances. Obviously his genius extended well past the fields of science and business. He parked the car in front of the large Georgian style building and they walked to the heavy oak double front doors together. Gelling pressed the button on the intercom at the door and Devlin responded, "Linus?"

Gelling answered, "Yes, it's me." The door buzzed open and the professor turned to Alan before they entered, whispering, "When he confronts you, keep his attention for as long as you can while I get behind him."

"I'll do my best but don't waste any time."

Alan drew his Glock and followed Gelling in and down a wide hallway toward the cavernous living area. Alex Devlin was seated at a huge antique desk with his back toward them, typing at a computer terminal. Without turning, he spoke, "Come in Linus; I'll just be a minute."

As they approached, Alan began to assess the room in his peripheral vision until he suddenly froze in his footsteps as the muzzle of a gun pressed into the small of his back. The assailant's approach had been undetectable and Alan instantly knew the futility in trying to overcome such an obviously well trained mercenary from such a position. The blood drained from his face as he raised his hands in surrender.

Gelling reached out a trembling hand to take Alan's gun. Devlin continued typing calmly and said, "Welcome to the lion's den Mr. Beach." Then he got up from his desk, turned to face them and continued, "I'll take it from here Linus. I know this was very difficult for you but I can assure you it is absolutely necessary for the security of Project Hallucineers. Take the car and go back to Blue Sky. I'll be in touch tomorrow."

Gelling, shaking nervously, asked, "What will you do with him?"

Devlin shot the professor a stern glare and repeated, "I'll be in touch tomorrow. Now go!"

Gelling looked apologetically at Alan and said, "I'm sorry detective but my work is too important." Before handing the Glock to Devlin's thug and turning to leave.

Devlin ordered Beach to slowly take out his handcuffs. Alan did as he was told and Devlin told him to sit on a large sofa behind a massive cast iron coffee table with a glass top. "Cuff your hands through the ironwork of the table and don't try anything or this man will not hesitate to shoot you."

Again, Alan obeyed.

"Now lean forward."

As Alan complied, Devlin drew an SSCH device from his pocket and pushed it against the back of the detective's neck. The instrument emitted a quiet click and Alan winced slightly then jerked back with a horrified look on his face.

Devlin lowered his weapon and relaxed, turning to look out through the huge sliding glass doors overlooking his property.

"What have you done to me?!" Alan asked; his voice full of dread.

"All in good time Detective but first I want to have a little chat. Stay calm; I don't want you falling asleep just yet. As long as you keep your pulse down, you'll remain awake for up to twenty minutes - long enough to satisfy your curiosity. "

Alan's face took on the look of a beaten man. Devlin gave him a sympathetic smile and continued, "I must say that I'm impressed by your tenacity and dedication. I even admire your idealism and sense of justice..." then his smile changed to a menacing glare. "...but your bleeding heart attitude disgusts me.

On balance, I think you deserve an explanation and I deserve the pleasure of watching the look on your face as you discover the truth."

Devlin grinned with satisfaction at his captive's obvious fear as Alan shrunk in his seat. "You have caused me a great deal of inconvenience. I find it quite surprising that one insignificant policeman could be such a fly in the ointment."

Defiant, Alan said sarcastically, "Glad I could help."

"Your witticisms don't amuse me detective. Are you sure you want to waste your final minutes on futile gestures of defiance?"

Alan looked up at the tall, slender man and saw single-minded evil in his deeply set brown eyes. His sheer presence was intimidating and Alan could clearly see why he was such a feared and respected business mogul. His hair was a distinguished salt and pepper, silver at the temples, and his long face had high cheek bones and a strong jaw line surrounding thin, angry lips. Still defiant, Alan said, "It's your dime. How the hell did you convince a guy like Professor Gelling to participate in premeditated murder?"

Devlin's cruel mouth creased to form an evil grin. "Are you really so naïve? Linus is nothing more than my pet genius – he has no idea that I used his invention to kill. If he knew the truth about Helen Benson and the others, he would be horrified, and I may well have had to silence him too. No; Rothstein is my only inside man at Blue Sky and the only one I need since he controls the content of the hallucination scenarios. Gelling is all about the science and saving people – rather misguided altruism – but I have to respect his scientific prowess."

Devlin continued, feigning lament. "Dr. Benson's death was the result of an unfortunate assumption on the part of my Head of Security, Kurt Rygaard. Regrettably, I was not informed that she had inadvertently seen the hallucination scenario we designed to implant into Damien Fraser's brain to get rid of Congressman Taylor and Matt Lewis. If I had known, we could easily have convinced the good doctor that it was simply one of Rothstein's video games and she would still be alive – quite lamentable. If she hadn't been so efficient in her work, Kurt's error in judgment may have jeopardized my plans. "Don't worry, he has been suitably reprimanded." He smiled coldly.

As soon as I was informed of Linus' hallucineering theory, I could see its true potential and all I had to do was play on Rothstein's greed to get what I wanted. A small price to pay in the scheme of things. You see, Devlin Industries represents only a portion of my true wealth and power - the rest is carefully hidden from public scrutiny. It has taken almost thirty years of single minded dedication but now my influence is well beyond measurement by current global standards."

"If you're so powerful, why do you need technology to influence the President?"

"Now you're getting to the issue detective, you're a bit of a plodder but I knew you would get there eventually. I find our politically correct systems and procedures rather tiresome. This is the most powerful nation in the world but our government is so busy tiptoeing around everyone else's sensibilities that we look more like simpering cowards than the greatest superpower the world has ever known - and I own a significant portion of this nation so its future is of great concern to me. To answer your question detective, simply put, I am orchestrating the approval to use tactical nuclear weapons to put an end to the stupidity once and for all."

Alan looked at him incredulously. "You know you're insane, don't you?"

Devlin laughed aloud. "Is it insanity or genius detective? They say the two are closely related but I don't expect someone of your inferior intelligence to properly understand or agree with what I'm saying. You're just like all the other sheep that do what they're told and scamper when they're frightened. It takes true courage and discipline to challenge the status quo, to face danger and adversity head on, and do what needs to be done."

Alan shook his head, smiling as if dealing with an unruly child. "Quite insane."

"If your goal is to infuriate me, you're wasting your final minutes of life." Devlin said calmly. "You will soon fall asleep then awaken to feelings of overwhelming despair in the knowledge that you will be convicted of murdering the three men I sent to kill you, and lose everything you ever had in life. The whole thing will be too much for you to bear and you will put your service weapon in your mouth and pull the trigger. There is nothing you can do to change that. The SSCH is summoning sleep hormones as we speak and the hallucination Rothstein designed will soon take over your conscious mind."

Dread fell over Alan's face as he watched Devlin's evil grin and laughing eyes.

"So, now I've got your attention. Shall I continue?"

Alan nodded in resignation.

"I thought so. Now tell me detective, can you honestly say that you've never wished we would just drop a bomb on those ignorant, greedy, violent oil rich nations of the Middle East and be done with it? Aren't you tired of America being held to ransom by third world royalty and psychotic dictators?"

"So you think we should allow a greedy, insane, self serving, behind the scenes dictator like you to run the show instead?"

"You're welcome to your opinions Mr. Beach but I'm the one with the power so the decisions lie with me. I for one will no longer allow our precious resources to be wasted on futile games of international politics. I for one refuse to allow insignificant banana republics to continually outvote us at the United Nations when we dutifully give the same countries tens of billions of dollars in charity each year as our budget plunges ever deeper into the red. It's time the ungrateful realized their folly in underestimating our resolve. It's time we put America first and stopped pussyfooting around with these vacuous fools. What have they ever contributed to the civilized world but misery and suffering?"

"You're talking about wiping out millions of innocent people! Can't you see how wrong that is?" Alan stressed.

"There is no innocence in those countries." Devlin retorted. "Do you really think that the men, women and children of these countries, who have grown up generation after generation, numbed to violence, and taught to despise us and our ideals of liberty, are innocents? You must be sadly misinformed. I can assure you that there are children as young as six years old in these countries, who would happily kill you just because you're American. They are taught to hate us from birth by corrupt religious fanatics who bend the teachings of their holy book to suit themselves. Nuclear obliteration is the only way to rid ourselves of this menace and as a personal bonus, I will become even richer; since I own most of the facilities that are capable of manufacturing the weapons."

"You can't really think you're going to get away with this Devlin!"

"Oh, I'm quite certain I will." Devlin pointed to a security camera mounted on the ceiling and continued, "Do you see that camera Detective? When you fall asleep, it will begin recording and when you awake and kill yourself, it will be indisputable evidence. When you're gone, Alex Devlin, the well known billionaire philanthropist and successful corporate executive, will call the police and they will quickly close your case and that of the three dead men in Jersey City.

Your friends and family will mourn your loss with a bitter taste in their mouths and I will use Gelling's invention like a puppeteer to manipulate global and domestic policy. Within two years, I will have ridden this country of simpering fools like you. I will cleanse the nation of the corrupting influences of false religions, welfare dependents, cowards, and criminals. America will soon rise past its former glories to fresh heights in my new world order."

Alan shook his head disdainfully but decided it was futile to antagonize the obviously power mad Devlin further so instead he asked, "Why did you need to kill Congressman Taylor and Matt Lewis?"

"I could not afford to have that clever little weasel nosing around in my affairs and the congressman was the only remaining powerbroker in Washington who could have upset my plans. They had to go."

"But how did you know Lewis had damaging information on Devlin Industries and that he was meeting with Taylor about it?"

Devlin smiled malevolently, "Senator Davies has been under my control for over five years and he called to warn me of Lewis' plans immediately after he told him."

"So Davies is on your payroll?"

"No, Davies is too ethical for bribery but too useful to kill. Good old-fashioned blackmail was what I used on the venerable senator. I arranged for a very attractive young woman to entice him into a well hidden affair some years ago. One moment of weakness and he's mine forever."

Alan yawned widely and Devlin smiled. "You're getting sleepy. It seems we are coming to the end of our discussion detective." Then he called out toward the kitchen door, "Please, do join us Mr. Riley - and don't try anything foolish. I'm sure you've realized by now that what my friend lacks in stature, he more than makes up for in cunning."

Startled, Alan looked up to see Jake being led in at gunpoint by the strange little man wearing an overcoat and hat. His heart fell in dismay to see the seemingly infallible Jake Riley at the mercy of this odd little assassin. His shock quickly turned to concern for his friend and he asked, "What are you going to do to him?"

The little man, keeping a safe distance, had moved around his considerably larger captive to his right side. He smiled cruelly and in his thick South African accent said, "Where I come from, this is how we control unruly prisoners."

He lowered his aim to Jake's knee and squeezed the trigger. Jake let out a loud involuntary grunt and fell heavily to the floor, holding his wound as blood oozed through his fingers.

Alan was horrified by the despicable act and the assassin's cold cruelty. His beady eyes darted to Alan and he said, "Now I can relax and enjoy the show and if your stupid friend here can stop his sniveling, he can watch too."

Alan was now yawning uncontrollably and Devlin, smiling smugly said, "It won't be long now. Very soon, sleep will overcome you and the hallucination will implant. Don't worry; once the killing code in your brain has done its job, we'll give your disappointing friend a fitting farewell. Goodnight Mr. Beach."

Alan's head slumped forward. Devlin went over and pinched the detective's ear hard to be certain he was asleep then unlocked the handcuffs and replaced the Glock 9mm into its holster at Alan's side. He contemptuously patted Beach on the back of the head then turned to walk back to his desk and out of the camera's view. As he sat down, he clicked the remote to start recording but when he looked back at Beach, the blood drained from his face. Devlin's gaze was locked; watching in stunned silence as Alan calmly raised his Glock to point it not at himself but directly at Devlin. The billionaire's jaw dropped in shock and he tried to speak but nothing would come out. Beach smiled and in a mocking tone said, "Surprise."

The South African assassin started to raise his gun toward Alan but before he could get a bead on him, Jake loomed up from behind and smashed the heel of his hand into the side of the small man's head, shattering the temporal bone and rupturing the temporal artery. The little man slumped to the ground with blood quickly filling his brain cavity. Before the assassin could die from excess intracranial pressure, Jake grabbed his Para .45 and pumped one of the heavy slugs into Rygaard's knee. As the man shrieked in pain, Jake said, "One good turn…" and a few seconds later the South African was dead.

"What…how…" was all Devlin could manage as Alan walked toward him to take his pistol from the desk.

Jake pointed his Para .45 at his titanium knee. "Titanium beats lead every time." he said.

With Jake covering Devlin, Alan returned his Glock to its holster then reached up to the front of his neck and began peeling a layer of perfectly matched skin color latex away from his throat. He continued to pull the material all the way around the back of his neck until it finally let go with a comical 'fwap'.

"You were right Jake, that spider web stuff did the job. What was it…Golden Woven something?" He asked while carefully examining the tightly woven, gold tinged material inside its latex outer coating.

"Golden Orb Weaver." Jake said matter-of-factly.

"Wow, that implant thing must be really small – I can't see it anywhere." he continued calmly. "Oh well, I guess they'll find it at the police lab."

"Yeah, I guess they will Alan." added Jake, as Devlin grimaced in disbelief.

"And I bet they're going to love this high definition recording of Devlin's victory speech!" Alan said smiling as he held up his digital recorder.

"I'd put money on it!" Jake laughed.

Devlin's face turned bright red with anger and he suddenly lunged at Alan, grabbing for the detective's throat. Reflexively, Alan swung his left hand inward toward the back of his attacker's right hand, clamping his fingers around the meat of the thumb. His right hand rose simultaneously to hook his thumb underneath Devlin's hand as his fingers gripped the middle of the palm. Continuing the single smooth, circular motion, Beach twisted the business mogul's hand counter-clockwise and past the shoulder, forcing him to his knee then onto his back. Alan held the hand tightly in place, jamming his knee into Devlin's ribs then he knelt on his prostrate body and looked up at Jake for approval.

"Ten out of ten grasshopper...ten out of ten." Jake said proudly. "Now, do you mind if we get a bandage for my knee?"

Chapter 19

A lan leaned back with a sigh of satisfaction with Holly draped across his lap on the sofa. He stroked her soft brown hair then sadness briefly crossed his face as he traced his finger gently over the scar on her shoulder and surveyed the moving crates piled neatly in various spots around the room until Holly suddenly sat bolt upright, exclaiming, "It's on Alan!"

She reached for the remote to turn up the volume and they both watched intently as the special news bulletin began.

*****

"This is Marissa Wilson with our continuing exclusive coverage of the Devlin Industries conspiracy case. It's been almost a month since I first broke this astounding story and I'm now standing outside the federal courthouse where the multibillionaire owner of Devlin Industries, Alex Devlin, and Eric Rothstein, the well known computer gaming tycoon are facing multiple murder charges, and several counts of criminal conspiracy, as well as sedition and potentially; treason. The role of Professor Linus Gelling, Head of Research and Development at Blue Sky Biotech, in the case is sealed by the court. The prosecutors so far, will not discuss the reasons for sealing Gelling's involvement but a secret source has told this reporter he may have turned state's evidence against the conspirators in exchange for leniency. Neither the Department of Justice nor corporate executives from the Devlin group or Blue Sky Biotech are available for comment.

The evidence has mounted quickly and the US Attorney's office has committed a team of the country's top prosecutors to see this case to a speedy conclusion. A verdict is expected to be forthcoming within the next few days.

I will keep the public informed of any updates as they come to hand. This is Marissa Wilson reporting from Washington."

*****

Holly turned to Alan wide-eyed, "Wow…looks like she really owes you now!"

"Yes, that should keep her off my back for a while. And there should be no hesitation if I ever need a favor from her again. The network has moved her to Washington on a permanent basis and her status is virtually untouchable. Apparently they've even given her an executive producer title."

"Well, I'm not sure if that's a good thing or a bad thing – is she still going to be trying to get in your pants?" she teased.

A cheeky smile creased Alan's face, "Well, she's only human after all."

Holly grabbed a cushion and swung it playfully into Alan's face. "You tease!"

He chuckled good-naturedly and wrapped his arms around her. "Don't worry darling, I only have eyes for you." Then he stared deeply into her eyes as sadness fell over him and he said, "I'm so sorry for what happened to you. I don't know what I would…"

Holly placed her finger over his lips and said, "Shhh…It wasn't your fault. Besides, I'm more than capable of dealing with it – I'd better be or I won't make a very good psychologist, will I. Now that we're safe, I can look at the whole thing from a different perspective. This may sound strange but it was actually rather exciting – and I finally got to meet your boss!" she smiled playfully. "Don't worry Alan, I'm fine; honestly."

They kissed deeply until Holly pulled away and pouted, "I'm going to miss you though."

"It's only a few weeks Doctor Stuart. Now that you've finished your dissertation, you can move to New York and set up house for us. I'll follow right after graduation."

"Do you really have to go through the whole training course?"

"It's the FBI honey; I don't think they're going to let anyone cut corners at the academy."

"Well, I thought that Jake's friend would have been able to help you out."

"I think he's already done more than enough. To get into the FBI Academy at my age and without having to go through regular channels is a big deal."

"Considering what you did, they should make you Honorary Director of the whole bureau!"

"I'm sure I'll be getting some leg-ups once I'm an agent. The president certainly was very expressive of his gratitude but this is the real world and any recruit who wants to be an agent needs to be properly trained and pass all the required tests."

She sighed then looked away, "I know…I'm just going to miss you."

"I'll miss you too but it's not like I'll be locked away in some kind of boot camp. I mean you can come for weekends and holidays. The training will be over before you know it and we'll be together for good."

"I like the sound of that Special Agent Beach!"

"Whoa, don't jump the gun. It's only Agent Trainee Beach for the next five months."

"With your experience and success as a detective, you'll be Special Agent Beach soon enough."

"Maybe you're right but if it wasn't for Jake, I never even would have applied."

"Speaking of Jake, when are we going to see him and his beautiful new lady again? I'd like to thank the man who saved my future husband's life again."

"Who knows? Angie's very secretive about her location – she could be anywhere really. Obviously Jake knows where she is but I guess they're probably onto some new case by now. With Jake, you never know – he's one very motivated and disciplined man.

Anyway, are you ready for dinner with Captain Walker and his clan?"

"I just need to put some lipstick on and I'm ready. It seems funny to call him Captain Walker after becoming so close to him and his family while you were off saving the world."

"I wouldn't say saving the world – more like catching a madman. Anyway, Tom deserved the promotion and having one of his detectives involved in the biggest case this country has seen in years didn't hurt his chances. I'm really happy for him but at the same time, quite amazed that he was able to keep your rescue off the books. I still have trouble seeing him as a highly trained killer. He's such a family man!"

"Well, you didn't see him in action like I did. Trust me; be glad he's on our side."

As the couple got ready to leave Holly's apartment; halfway across the country, near Groom Lake, Nevada, a helicopter approached the side of a massive rocky escarpment. Professor Linus Gelling watched out the window as the military chopper neared its destination. It was his third trip back since he was seconded to the top secret base a month earlier and he was always amazed by the fact that there was no road or track leading to their destination. In fact, even from the air, there was no trace whatsoever; no indication of what lay under that huge, red, rocky escarpment. He wondered how they managed to bring in so many supplies and so much technical equipment without leaving the slightest trace. He didn't dare to imagine the amount of earth moving and construction equipment it must have taken to build the massive bunker in the first place.

The Twin Huey utility chopper touched down twenty yards from the edge of a large outcrop and waited just long enough for Gelling and his two guards to exit before the pilot wound up the rotor, adjusted the pitch and lifted the powerful beast into the sky, heading back to the secret air base it came from.

The three men walked in silence to the foot of a rocky wall and one of the guards put his hand on a natural looking six inch square rock, which silently drew inward and to one side to reveal a high tech biometric security system with enhanced retinal scanning technology. He entered a code into the keypad then moved his face in for the system to scan his eye. The other guard did the same, followed by Gelling, and the huge rock wall emitted a deep groan as it began to pivot on a twenty five inch diameter case hardened steel spigot. A few seconds later, a gap wide enough for a supply truck opened up for them to walk through. The door was elevated two inches above ground level to avoid leaving any trace of its movement across the desert floor, while still allowing trucks to drive into the facility's loading bay.

As they entered, the massive door began to close behind them and two MP's approached to pat all three men down and check their identification. Once satisfied, they waved Gelling and his guards on to the metal detector and body scanning station, and from there, they continued toward the elevators. A guard pressed the call button and they boarded as the elevator doors swished open. He then selected underground floor number seven and the car flowed smoothly downward to its destination.

The doors opened to a wide hallway and the men turned left then walked about seventy paces past various electronically sealed, steel doors with coded numbers above them. Gelling wondered how many of these rooms there were in this place but whenever he asked, the response was silence. They finally reached the number Gelling had come to know as home. One of the guards leaned in for a retinal scan and Gelling followed. The magnetic lock clunked open and the guard pushed the door open for Gelling to enter then let it close automatically.

Alone again, Gelling reflected on his new life. His room was certainly comfortable and well appointed with every accessory he could ask for. It had tall ceilings, a gourmet kitchen, a very comfortable lounge area with a modern entertainment system, and his sleeping quarters were like a five star hotel. He really couldn't complain, but the fact that he was basically a prisoner in this secret facility was a feeling with which he was still coming to terms.

Still; his work had always come first and his laboratory was comprehensively fitted with the most up to date equipment of its kind in the world. He had excellent support staff and the freedom to work unhindered – as long as he met the milestones his military hosts set for him. In the outside world, he had lived for his work. He'd sacrificed any kind of personal life many years before so if he thought pragmatically, this was really no different to his former life as a free man – at least he hadn't been sent to some maximum security federal prison, like Devlin had. No, he really couldn't complain. The government needed him and it was nice to be needed. His work was just as important to them as it was to him so he should be happy – but he still felt strangely unsettled and couldn't quite put his finger on why.

He made himself a cup of tea and was sipping it while reading the newspaper, when the lock on his heavy door clunked open and a guard appeared. "Colonel Watson would like to see you in his office professor." the man said.

Gelling put his cup in the sink and followed the guard out the door and back to the elevators. They went to underground floor number five and the soldier led him down the hall to Watson's office. Gelling had met the colonel many times before to update him on his work so such visits were not unusual but this time was different. As he entered the office, Gelling saw the back of someone seated, facing the colonel at his desk. Their meetings had always been one on one up until now so he didn't know what to expect.

"Come in Professor." Watson called out. "There's someone I'd like you to meet. Actually, I think you two are already acquainted."

The person stood, and as she turned, Gelling recognized her stern face. They had met at an international conference a few years ago and he'd found her work most intriguing. Dr. Olga Voronin was a renowned expert in her very specialized field of sensory signal interpretation. She was known to have discovered several previously unknown neural pathways associated with how the brain receives and interprets sensory inputs from all five senses.

"Dr. Voronin; it's a pleasure to see you again. But I don't understand – how can you be here?!" he asked.

In her heavy Russian accent, Olga greeted Gelling, "Eet's good to see you again too professor."

"Dr. Veronin has become, shall we say, disenchanted with her masters in Russia. They cut her budget dramatically because they felt that her research was stalling and would not produce any useable technology. Combine that with third world living standards and she thought it was time to approach us. Once we knew the extent of her research, the potential of combining her discoveries with your project became very obvious. The CIA helped her to defect and here she is."

Gelling's brilliant mind immediately tried to process the possibilities but he couldn't clearly identify any real benefit from combining Olga's research with Project Hallucineers. "I'm sorry colonel but I can't see the applications."

"That's because you think like a scientist and not a strategist professor. You designed SSCH technology to help people with psychiatric disorders. It was Devlin who corrupted it for his own use. You're looking for general human benefits where we're more concerned with the military and economic health of our great nation on a geopolitical scale."

"I'm afraid I still don't follow."

"I'm really not sure I do either colonel." Olga said.

"This is exactly why the military should be in charge of such ventures. We can see not only the big picture but identify opportunities where others would see nothing. You two are going to have a wedding."

"Vot?!" Olga demanded.

"Not that kind of wedding doctor. You are going to marry your technologies to develop the most potent and adaptable tactical weapon ever conceived – aside from nukes. With this technology, even armies the size of China's will be no challenge for our forces."

"How can our research on the human brain possibly make an advanced weapon such as this?" Gelling asked.

"The possibilities are staggering if you put your mind to it. Imagine a foot soldier that can see like a hawk, smell like a bloodhound, hear like a rabbit, and feel no pain. Then imagine that same soldier programmed with SSCH to achieve his mission without fear or remorse, yet still have the ability to adapt to changing circumstances. We already have powerful anabolic technology to dramatically boost physical strength and endurance so when we combine all these elements, each one of our soldiers will be worth ten of any other army's. And that's just the beginning – imagine a fighter pilot supercharged with the same technology...and the list goes on. We've always had nuclear superiority but with this, we'll be unbeatable in conventional warfare too."

Gelling's mind raced as he realized that the colonel was right – all this was theoretically possible. "But how can we do this to our troops. These are free human beings with lives of their own, and families, and rights. The anabolic treatments cause serious long term health problems. And that doesn't even address the ethical concerns."

Watson smiled knowingly. "Follow me."

The colonel walked out of his office, Veronin and Gelling following closely as they looked at each other, shocked by the revelation. Flanked by two guards, they went to underground level eight, almost directly below Gelling's laboratory. They entered an anteroom with a viewing window, made from super high strength hurricane glass, overlooking a laboratory. There were four burly military guards armed only with high tensile batons, handcuffed to each wrist so they couldn't be disarmed. In the center of the room was a reclining lab chair with heavy restraints mounted to eight different points around it.

"Society is cluttered with useless human refuse. These people add nothing to society and are a major financial burden as well. I'm talking about murderers, psychopaths, rapists; you name it. Why should we, as a society, keep them safe and warm with three squares a day in their bellies, when there's no hope they will ever reform or make any useful contribution. Your combined technologies are going to change all that."

Watson signaled one of the guards inside and he opened a door at the far end of the room. A man heavily strapped to a tilted mobile table began to enter the doorway. Just as he was pushed fully into the room, Watson said, "Doctor, Professor; I would like you to meet your first test subject. This is Bryan Adler."

Printed in Great Britain
by Amazon.co.uk, Ltd.,
Marston Gate.